Elizabeth Taylor

THE
SLEEPING
BEAUTY

With a New Introduction by
Susannah Clapp

Virago

TO
OLIVER AND EVELYN
With Love

Published by VIRAGO PRESS Limited 1982
41 William IV Street, London WC2N 4DB

Reprinted 1983

First published in Great Britain by Peter Davies Ltd 1953

British Library Cataloguing in Publication Data
Taylor, Elizabeth, 1912-1975
    Sleeping Beauty — (Virago modern classics)
    I. Title
    823'.914 [F]   PR6039.A928
    ISBN 0-86068-262-5

Printed in Finland by Werner Söderström Oy,
a member of Finnprint

was born Elizabeth Coles in Reading, Berkshire, in 1912. The daughter of an insurance inspector, she was educated at the Abbey School, Reading, and after leaving school worked as a governess and, later, in a library. At the age of twenty-four she married John William Kendall Taylor, a businessman, with whom she had two children.

Elizabeth Taylor wrote her first novel, *At Mrs Lippincote's* (1945), during the war while her husband was in the Royal Air Force. This was followed by *Palladian* (1946), *A View of the Harbour* (1947), *A Wreath of Roses* (1949), *A Game of Hide-and-Seek* (1951), *The Sleeping Beauty* (1953), *Angel* (1957), *In a Summer Season* (1961), *The Soul of Kindness* (1964), *The Wedding Group* (1968), *Mrs Palfrey at the Claremont* (1971) and *Blaming*, published posthumously in 1976. She has also published four volumes of short stories: *Hester Lilly and Other Stories* (1954), *The Blush and Other Stories* (1958), *A Dedicated Man and Other Stories* (1965) and *The Devastating Boys* (1972). Elizabeth Taylor has written a book for children, *Mossy Trotter* (1967); her short stories have been published in the *New Yorker, Harper's Bazaar, Harper's* magazine, *Vogue* and the *Saturday Evening Post,* and she is included in *Penguin Modern Stories 6*.

Elizabeth Taylor lived much of her married life in the village of Penn in Buckinghamshire. She died in 1975.

Critically Elizabeth Taylor is one of the most acclaimed British novelists of this century; of her works, Virago publish *The Sleeping Beauty, Mrs Palfrey at the Claremont, In a Summer Season* and *The Soul of Kindness. Angel* will be published in 1984; others are to follow.

INTRODUCTION

'WE never read books written by men, do we? Just library books all the time... We ought to go in for psychology, or something like it.' Evalie and Isabella in *The Sleeping Beauty,* worrying about their calories and lack of strenuous menopausal activity, talk of a kind of literature which has dogged Elizabeth Taylor's reputation. Her books are pleasing to read, and much taken from libraries; they are undogmatic, unpretentious, clear and kind. But they are also more than this: quick-eyed and wonderfully funny investigations into the loves and loneliness of people's lives.

Her own life was more domestic than literary. 'I write slowly and without enjoyment,' she explained in an interview, 'and think it all out when I am doing the ironing.' She was born Elizabeth Coles in 1912, the daughter of a Reading insurance agent. At the Abbey School, Reading, she wrote plays–'with a dozen changes of scenery and huge casts. Terribly dramatic with about three lines in each scene' – failed maths, and began to collect rejection slips for her novels. After working for a time as a governess–an experience which she put to gothic use in an early novel–she married John William Kendall Taylor, the director of a sweet factory; her first published novel, *At Mrs Lippincote's,* appeared when she was 34. She was elegant, reserved, anti-religious and a Labour voter. Elizabeth Jane Howard remembers her with affection, seated in a big chair in her Buckinghamshire home, writing her novels in beautiful longhand, breaking off whenever one of her two children wanted attention. When she died, of cancer, in 1975 *The Times* obituarist, speaking with unnecessarily faint praise of her 'reticent dialogue' and 'unassuming wit', pronounced that 'the true asperities of modern life seemed to elude her'.

Elizabeth Taylor wrote about people who are comfortably off and who feel uncomfortable. Each of her novels shows a distinct and particular world: in *A View of the Harbour* she examined the varieties of life in a small seaside town; in *The Wedding Group* she satirised the pretentious ethnicity of an artistic community; in *Mrs Palfrey at the Claremont* she chronicled a solitary old age. Yet what she returned to time and again, what makes these diverse novels recognisably hers is a careful and unreverent documentation of middle-class life.

In *The Wedding Group* a placidly disgruntled female journalist looks around a pub and complains: 'The reason, they say, that women novelists can't write about men, is because they don't know what they're like when they're alone together, what they talk about and so on. But I can't think *why* they don't know. I seem to hear them booming away all the time.' Men are always booming away in the background of Elizabeth Taylor's novels: about second-hand cars and betting, furtively about sex, brashly about drinking. She shows the kinds of ease pub life affords – the chumminess which demands comradeship from an acquaintance – and the behaviour on both sides of the bar: 'Mrs Brimmer drew her blouse away from her creased chest, glanced down mysteriously, blowing gently between her breasts, then fanned herself. "I hear Charlie's gone," she said.' She also shows the close but often uneasy associations of domestic life: 'Oh, for

vi

someone warm and gossipy!' exclaims one of the young women in *A Wreath of Roses*. 'The cups of tea we could dawdle over at the kitchen-table; and the talk of disease and funerals.' The kind of daily woman she has in mind is often, as seen by Elizabeth Taylor, less tenderly loyal than her employer cares to believe: likely to be found, fuelled with malicious speculation, chopping parsley 'with not just *kitchen* venom'. Residential southern England – with its monkey-puzzle trees and banks of rhododendrons, its small hot railway stations and riverside lawns – provides a landscape which can nourish, but which can also appear a soggy parochial mess:

> The herbaceous borders edging the drive were full of stakes and withering Michaelmas daisies. A few greyish-brown sparrows hopped about on the wet lawn, and raked among the clutter of damp leaves underneath the trees... The horror and sadness of the late afternoon were immeasurable, but it was part of living in the country, Mrs Secretan thought.

Elizabeth Taylor credited the middle classes with a larger capacity for joy and pain than they are usually allowed. Her novels show lives of respectable regularity not untouched by the extraordinary and fierce. In *A Wreath of Roses* she came near to producing a thriller, one which the *Evening Standard* was able to commend as a book that 'quivers with nerves, moods, impressionability'. Several of her novels are alive with sexual feeling, most notably in *In a Summer Season* where quarrels and reconciliations between the central characters are commented on by a maiden aunt: '"He must have taken the bull by the horns last night,' Ethel wrote rather confusedly to Gertrude.' Nevertheless,

vii

because she documented a particular section of society, and one whose public behaviour was generally conventional, perhaps because she did this so accurately, her books are open to accusations of narrowness. Her admirers felt she could be charged with lack of ambition; her detractors thought her smug. Most critics praised her craftsmanship rather than her imagination.

The danger of lapsing into cosiness was one that Elizabeth Taylor attended to on more than one occasion – most notably in *A Wreath of Roses*. The character of Frances – a painter whose cultivation of a bourgeois anti-Bohemian life is such that she would 'rather be praised for her crab-apple jelly than her painting' – may be thought to have something in common with her creator. Frances, who has given a lot of pleasure by painting small scenes well, rebukes herself in old age: 'I committed a grave sin against the suffering of the world by ignoring it, by tempting others with charm and nostalgia until they ignored it too.' She turns away from her pictures of fruit and flowers and sunlit rooms, and in her new paintings shows 'the white bones of the earth and dark figures scurrying against a violet sky'. Frances's concern for the world outside her own is seen as genuine and admirable, but it is not clear that her newer, more violent paintings are successful. The arguments of an old admirer of her former work are given full weight. His way of looking at things had been changed by an early modest picture: 'that old picture of Liz sitting on the sofa, seen through the rain-washed window, turned life a little under his very eyes.' His argument – that the small fragments of life that she shows yield a larger sense of life – is in time with the manner of Elizabeth Taylor's novels: she is a novelist of scenes rather than themes, of small confrontations rather than large plots – and a novelist whose sensibility is not limited by that of her characters.

It is no accident that the clean little seaside town in *The Sleeping Beauty* is called Seething. This clue to what life is like for most of the town's inhabitants could, in the general placidity of the story-telling, pass unregarded – in a way that Stella Gibbons's Howling couldn't. For much of the time the narrative is busy with the daily details of fifties urban life. In Seething, nursemaids are rebuked for sauciness; young men, raw from National Service, loll in milk bars; tennis shoes dry on window sills; women adjust their pearls. In the nearby market town, 'coaching-inns and old-fashioned drapers surround the squares'. Yet in this novel a young girl awakens a household at night with her screams; a beautiful woman walks the cliffs in a trance-like state, a respectable man commits bigamy; two women have been left widows by violent deaths.

Towns from which people retire, towns from which men commute to mysterious lives in the city, present a particular style of female society. Marooned in the Turkish baths, where the sound of middle age being massaged is a 'terrible ovation', Evalie says to Isabella: 'We look discarded, sitting here…As if we were waiting for a train which never comes.' The remark carries desolation for women who have spent many afternoons in the past waiting for the sound of the car on the gravel, for the sight of a stream of traffic that means the husband-filled London train is in. The comfort of feminine exchanges depends on men's being in the background. One of Elizabeth Taylor's funniest, though sketchiest, short stories features a group of wives who meet for coffee, banded together by the enjoyable bitching that can take place when one of them leaves, and united also by the pleasurable confidence that all are womb-owners. A thrill of horror runs round the group when, after a discussion of the pains of childbirth, one woman – a vegetarian outsider – announces: '"I thought neuralgia was worse..." At first they were too surprised to speak. After all, *men* could have neuralgia.' Malice and discomfiture aren't the whole story, however: female jaunts are relished. Camilla, in *A Wreath of Roses,* provides a wistful picture of a childhood among men: 'A dark Victorian house, muffled rooms, too many books. My brothers walking up and down *discussing* ... It was all exclusively male. No one talked about hats.' No one in Elizabeth Taylor's novels is despised for talking about hats: an interest in how things look – even one's own body – is seen as part of attending to the world. Isabella's 'entirely feminine' days in London – spent with meringues and hairdressers and 'delightful tracking-down of gloves to match a blouse' – are sympathetically detailed. So is the loneliness of a widowhood which has as much to do with losing a social position as with losing a husband. Isabella's life gently prefigures the loneliness of Mrs Palfrey – at, but not of, the Claremont: a life which Elizabeth Taylor described with crispness in a letter to *The Times.*

> The dreadful lack of purpose and function, the aimless sitting around waiting for the next meal or, if one would be dramatic, to die. Entertainment, however pleasant and desirable, is no substitute for a daily purpose... If only homes could be run as an ordinary home is – each member having a job that contributes to the running of the community.

The irony of Isabella and Evalie's position is that, though they have no real purpose in their community, they are what could be called its pillars. Isabella has sat on many platforms, 'holding bouquets and smilingly looking down at her little feet'; Evalie organises the Moral Welfare bazaar. These women exhibit some of the less pleasing behaviour in the novel. Isabella crushes Betty the nursemaid, partly out of maternal possessiveness, partly from a sense of upholding respectability; she also betrays Vinny's secret. Evalie compounds the betrayal, out of malice but also from a belief that a crime is being condoned. Both by the limitations of their feelings illustrate the truth of Camilla's cry in *A Wreath of Roses:* 'People who have personal codes do such dreadful things.'

The havoc wreaked by the highly principled is a recurring preoccupation in Elizabeth Taylor's novels. She is acute in her tracings of self-righteousness, seeing the blighting effects of the 'rural charity – so much more pleasant to give than to receive'; in the portrait of a vicar swilling rhubarb wine she disposes of sanctimoniousness in two sentences: 'He could afford to seem over-occupied with little worldly pleasures. He seemed to display this minor trait in such a way that it indicated more clearly the great spiritual side of his nature lying in the shadow.' But her most idiosyncratic portraits are not of prigs but of soft-hearted well-wishers. She identified a particular limitation of imagination – that of people whose outstanding quality is compassion. In *The Sleeping Beauty* Vinny cherishes an over-easy sympathy. He is Emily's saviour and, because of this, the hero of the novel, but he is within a smile of being a cad: a more subtly drawn cad than most, for it is his best qualities – pity and curiosity – which lead to the most harm. His dreadful competence at human relationships, particularly those which involve a sense of people injured, incomplete, in need of succour, is not a ploy: 'His letters to the bereaved never expressed inadequacy on his part: they seemed simply to be the reason for his existence.' But the naive romanticism which envisages others as the arena in which his own sensibility can delicately and caringly play doesn't include the idea that their response may be to demand something in return. He leads Isabella to dream of a proposal of marriage (preferably one that is annually renewed); he realises too late that 'although we cannot often help loving, we can sometimes help being loved'.

Failures of imagination matter more in this – as in most of Elizabeth Taylor's novels – than lapsing from a moral code: committing bigamy is not the worst thing that Vinny does. Elizabeth Taylor never hectors: her commentary on her characters takes the form of quiet, often funny revelation. Characters are, of course, allowed their own jokes: 'You know where you are with her,' says Emily of Mrs Tumulty. 'Yes, but you don't want to *be* there,' Vinny replies. More often, however, humour comes unwittingly from a speaker: it is never a question of quickly slapping someone down, but a means of expanding and explaining. Her humour can point to the gap between what people say and what they are, without glibly pronouncing them hypocritical: '"I did not know how to hold up my head." As she spoke, she held it very high, her usual posture.' It can with equal ease acknowledge a redundancy of speech: 'After a while, feeling that he had offered nothing about himself, he said: "I'm in the Army." She glanced gravely at his uniform, not smiling.' Throughout her novels, common phrases and clichés are toppled by a deadly literal-mindedness: 'people in the town say he drank. As if everyone doesn't.' In all of them, people's private ordering of their worlds is shown in its dogmatic oddity: not ridiculous but arbitrary. 'Surely prostitutes don't cry?' Isabella thinks. 'Harlots, still less.'

In an interview with Geoffrey Nicholson, shortly after the publication of *The Wedding Group*, Elizabeth Taylor explained: 'I always feel that in many ways I ought to have been a painter – and I can't even draw a rabbit... Even describing a room I see it just as if I'd painted it.' She is generous in granting her characters a similar vision, and in allowing them to see and sense more than they can say. Laurence, grumpy, guilty and awkward, is stirred by 'the lovely violet light over the town, flowing down the streets'. Vinny's feelings for Emily are suddenly focused when, confronted with her in beguiling disarray, all dressing-gown and flowing hair, he watches, 'as if it were the most surprising and exotic revelation, her pink heels lifting from her slippers as she climbed the stairs'. Catching delight – and showing that delight is a matter of such moments – is one of Elizabeth Taylor's greatest gifts. *The Sleeping Beauty,* which is her most romantic novel, is one of her saddest in showing how close delightful melancholy is to despair:

It looked a sad, unwelcome garden with its yellowing leaves. Rotten fruit lay in the grass. A mist was breathed upwards from clumps of rusty leaves and the mauve flowers. Remote, pervasive, so Englishly moody, with its muted colours and still air and medlar-scent, it appeared expectant, ready to match itself to an intruder, to be in tune with the nostalgic or the romantic; with magic for lovers; and echoes for the forlorn. Rose had nothing: was nothing.

Moments of vision are not allowed to degenerate into mere displays of sensibility in Elizabeth Taylor's novels: they are a way of expanding character – what people brood about is as real a part of what they are as what they do. This is particularly true in *The Sleeping Beauty,* a novel in which dreams come true, and one that is full not of romantic figures but of romancers. People tell themselves stories to shape their lives, yet their experience of life is piecemeal: it is easier to see purpose and tendency in retrospect. In *Contemporary Novelists* Elizabeth Taylor is quoted as saying: 'I write in scenes, rather than in narrative, which I find boring. I am pleased if the *look* of a page is interesting, broken by paragraphs or dialogue, not just one dense slab of print.' Her novels bear the marks of this preference: minor reversals may be persuasively turned; larger resolutions are frequently perfunctory – inconvenient husbands are suddenly dispatched in car crashes, confirmed bachelors yield with improbable speed to rather feeble girls.

There is nothing clammy or precious in her presentation of life as a series of random, vivid moments: she investigates people's sense of themselves with her sense of humour. There is nothing cosy either. Most people's lives are laid waste not by one fell blow, but by a daily piling-up of small losses or small lies. Two characters can lay claim to the title of *The Sleeping Beauty:* one gains happiness; the other is the sleeping beauty whom kisses will never awaken.

Susannah Clapp, London 1982

Chapter 1

"THERE's Vinny going in with the wreaths," Isabella had once said.

Now that her own time to be consoled had come, she was glad of him. The wreaths she had mentioned were a figure of speech—her way of associating Vinny with condolences and gloom; for disaster could always bring him to a scene. He went with sympathy professional in its skill; yet adept, exquisite. More personal than the professionals whom he excelled—doctors, priests, undertakers—he fired his reliability with talent and imagination. His letters to the bereaved never expressed inadequacy on his part: they seemed simply to be the reason for his existence. Flippant people—Isabella was one—felt that his presence was a foreboding, or a dismal signal, like drawn blinds: but behind the closed doors where sorrow was, he sustained and comforted.

Seeing him standing in the parlour, looking stouter, greyer than she had remembered, she felt remorse at never having treated him seriously, and she went quickly to him; first took his hands and then put her head against his shoulder to hide the distortion of her face.

One thing Vinny never said was "Don't cry". He waited patiently for her to finish, standing quite still, his glance directed about the room which he had not seen for ten years. Without moving, he could not take in more than an edge of the bay-window and none of the sea beyond; but seaside light is always noticeable and on this early Spring evening the room was washed with it.

"Forgive me!" Isabella wept. "I have not cried before—I was too sad."

A large part of Vinny's usefulness was the coaxing forth of such tears as are better shed. He stroked her untidy hair, until after a while she steadied, gathered herself together, dabbed her eyes, disengaged herself and gave the usual rueful smile.

"You are so good to come."

While she tried to patch up her poor face, he walked over to the window and then felt tactless at going too soon to look at the sea, which had so recently claimed Isabella's husband and had nearly claimed her son at the same time.

The window gave immediately on to the sea-front. The terrace of little houses were close to the jetty and the road ran behind them. The lavender paving-stones were patchily wet. The low sun broke into the puddles in a great dazzle. All steamed and shimmered. A row of iron chairs stood by the sea-wall.

Out on the sands, two children ran at the water's edge, trailing seaweed, bending for shells. Behind them came an elderly lady with a large umbrella, which was shut up but not furled. It stabbed the sands like an arrow, sometimes knocking aside pebbles or spearing pieces of seaweed for the children. They moved along like a frieze against the brown sea, with the grey beach to themselves.

"The Tillotson children," Isabella said, coming to stand beside Vinny. "And Nannie," she added.

"Who are the Tillotson children?" Vinny asked, putting his arm through hers.

"They had whooping-cough," Isabella said vaguely. "I was thinking, Vinny, that 'inevitable' can mean nice things, too. It had never occurred to me before."

"What has been inevitable?"

"Why, you! I waited for you to come. I thought 'Vinny at least will come.' Although we never heard from you all these years, only the card at Christmas."

"I was busy. You didn't need me. I thought of you often, and imagined you three here for your holidays, and Laurence growing up."

"I was simply convinced you would one day walk in. One is left so much on one's own. People are shy of the bereaved. They don't quite know what to *be*. And they feel that they must not flock down, like vultures. . . ." Vinny frowned. . . . "They say: 'Other people are nearer to her, it is not our place to presume or intrude.' And because they all say that, in the end no one comes— from nicety, of course; not cruelty. Or are they just too embarrassed and waiting for death to blow over? Time heals everything, especially embarrassment. But perhaps you think I am bitter?" she asked, with a little pride in her voice.

"You, Isabella! Oh, my darling, no one less, ever."

"You are so fatherly," she said coldly. Yet his laughter had made the room more normal. No one had dared to laugh before.

"There they go, up the steps!"

The children had crossed the sands and begun to ascend some rustic-work, zigzagging steps up the cliff. Sometimes Nannie urged them on, shooing at them with her umbrella as if they were geese. They plodded upwards in their wellington boots. One threw down her seaweed in despair and seemed to be coughing.

3

"Where do they go?" Vinny asked.

"Up to Rose Kelsey's guest-house."

At the top of the cliff, but mostly hidden in trees, he could see a gabled Victorian house of tremendous ugliness, ivy over its dark walls and one upstairs window glinting evilly in the sunset.

"How is Laurence?" Vinny asked, reminded by the sight of the children that the last time he had stayed with Isabella her son had been a boy, out on the sands all day. Vinny had built castles for him and dug channels to let in the tide, the soapy water like ginger-beer.

"I can't help worrying. There is the question of what one calls his *future*. In fact, how to scrape together two halfpennies for himself when he has finished his military service." She tried hard not to feel aggrieved with her husband for leaving her before they had settled anything.

"It might be a chance for me to help. Where is he now?"

"He is upstairs in his room, sulking. What am I saying? *Studying*, I mean. Studying."

"What is he studying?"

"Well, reading then. I always say 'reading' when people are lolling in a chair, or lying on the sofa, or in a train. But studying when they sit up to a table."

"What does he read?"

"Books and papers and magazines." She turned her cuff back secretly to glance at her watch, thinking of the meal in the oven. "And library books," she added.

"Pretty comprehensive."

"Yes. It was such an ordeal for him. He seemed quite stunned. Unimaginably horrifying: and so brave of him, trying to save Harry like that. It was hopeless. He barely saved himself."

4

"I know. I read of it," Vinny said, glancing at her.

"He seemed ill for days, chilled and dazed and exhausted, poor boy . . . and talking in his sleep, though nothing one could hear; and being so very difficult. Antagonistic."

The children were at the top now: they disappeared behind some macrocarpa trees. The sunset had struck a different window of the house, and fell differently into the little parlour, which had a selfconscious, but charming, marine atmosphere—sea-green wallpaper, and furniture inlaid with mother-o'-pearl; on the chimneypiece, ships in bottles and spiked and curly pink shells. The pictures were of steamers, and paddle-boats painted on glass and having a darkly thunderous quality. By the window was the telescope on its stand. Isabella had often turned it on Harry's yacht as he set off from the jetty, swinging round at first uncertainly, then settling to the water and at last disappearing round the cliff. She had probably watched it on the last day, Vinny thought, when Harry and Laurence were late returning. She had always been particularly anxious when Laurence had gone, too. He wondered how she could bear to keep the telescope there: then he realised that, sometimes, to take action over a thing can make it seem more real.

"I may appear inevitable," he suddenly said, "but no more than that—not, for instance, punctual. I wanted to come earlier, but could only write. *Now* is really too late. All I can do are practical things . . . what to arrange for Laurence, for instance."

"You came just right," Isabella said. "When one is too shocked, one cannot . . ." She put her rolled-up handkerchief to her mouth, and then went on: "After when one begins to feel the emptiness . . . and being so unpopular, because grieved . . . and then practical things I never could do . . . nor had to . . . not now, really . . . there wasn't even a funeral, you see."

"No," said Vinny reverently. He tried not to imagine Harry's body dragged to and fro on the sea's floor, with no tide ever sweeping him to rest.

"Oh, we ought to have some sherry," Isabella said, remembering. She had grown careless about such things, and often, when she was alone, did not bother.

When she opened the door, a dismal smell of cooking flew in. Vinny could envisage some dreary, woman's meal—cauliflower-cheese, he thought—placed in the oven by the daily-help who had admitted him—a frantic-looking woman, who stood by the door, skewering in hatpins, to show she was just off.

There was dust on the stopper of the decanter Isabella brought in. She handed him his glass triumphantly, as if she had brought off a conjuring-trick.

"I will call Laurie," she said. "You can have a drink together while I make up your bed."

"But I shall not stay here," Vinny protested. "I mean to take a stroll into the town and find a room at The Victoria."

"The Victoria! Out of season! It is half shut up, and no staff, and you would be much better off here, and are so *wanted*."

For a minute or two, they played their game of doubt and reassurance. He threw to her protestations and got back over-riding assertions, as he expected. In the end, she went away to prepare his room, and to fetch Laurence. At the door, she asked: "*How* long can you stay?"

"Over the weekend, I *could* . . . but are you sure . . ." but before he could begin again, she disappeared.

He turned once more, instinctively, to the window. The pinky sky had faded into a muffled blue, the beginning of darkness. A shred of moon had appeared, and the windows of the house on the cliff were blank and shadowed, as if lids had closed on them. On the wide curve of the sands, two figures walked; no longer the Tillotson children skipping along, but a woman walking gravely, abstractedly, at the sea's edge, followed by a young girl who, like the children, bent sometimes to pick up a shell. When she stopped, the gap between the two figures became greater, for the woman herself did not pause. She walked on at the same pace, her head erect, as if she noticed nothing at all, or else always the same thing ahead of her. Her arms were folded, her hands thrust up the wide sleeves of her dark coat. They made a most beautiful picture, Vinny thought; mysterious, romantic. He could not imagine any words passing between them: they were too together— seemed too much in accord—for any but the most broken phrases, the most disjointed sounds. Perhaps mother and daughter, he decided. The girl's long pale hair blew away from her shoulders, but then (when she stooped for a shell) fell across her face and, with a gesture, immature, impatient, she brushed it back. It was too dark for him to see the woman's face, but he was certain, from her walk, that it was beautiful. She went on slowly and dreamily along the shore. Beautiful women do not need to hurry. Then she turned and paused, looking back: the girl came nearer to her, and together they crossed the sands and began to climb the rustic steps, the private way up to the house above,

7

where now a light or two was switched on in upstairs rooms. He watched them going up the steps in single file, the girl first now. At the top, the wind blowing stronger, the blonde hair flew about and the woman took it in both her hands and smoothed it away from the girl's face. When she had done this, she bent her head down as if she was kissing the girl's brow.

Vinny could see all this. He watched it intently, with fascination. When they had gone from view, he turned back to the room, and found it dark now, and very small.

*　　*　　*

Laurence, hearing his mother coming upstairs, opened the evening-paper at a different page and was discovered by her studying as usual, sitting up at the table; his elbows on either side of The Londoner's Diary; his fists against his cheeks. When he did not look up, she sighed.

"Don't work too hard, darling, or try your eyes."

He turned his chin to rest on his fist now and at last glanced at her. The red pressure-mark on his face made him look feverish, but soon faded.

When Isabella snapped on the light, the white boarded walls shone brilliantly. The room looked extremely neat, except for all the papers littering the table.

"Vincent Tumulty is here," Isabella said. "I don't suppose that you remember him. He spent a summer holiday with us here when you were a child."

Not committing himself to any such memory, Laurence asked: "What is he here for?"

Isabella just parted her hands helplessly, appealingly, at this heartless remark. The sight of her glazed and puffy eyes angered him. He looked away again. "What a *name*, anyhow!" he said.

"We can put him up for a couple of nights." She spoke in this grudging way, implying inconvenience, to hide her real pleasure. At least Laurence was with her in desiring a third person. The two of them had become such a wounded pair—in everyone's eyes, and their own. One more would help to break the agonising fusion. Lately, when she had handed him a cup of tea, or made any other simple, trivial gesture, it had seemed to have a horrifying significance. "You are all I have now," seemed to hang in the air. He hourly dreaded the words themselves, and if Vinny could stave off the phrase for a day or two he could not be more welcome.

"If you would come down and have a drink while I make up the bed . . ."

He stood up, his hands still clumsily fidgeting with the papers on the table. He was tall, and because he wore his old school suit—the grey double-breasted flannel, which had shrunk at the cleaner's—his wrists shot out too far from the sleeves and too much sock showed between turn-up and shoe.

He seemed reluctant to leave his papers until his mother was well away, and fidgeted about waiting for her to go. Her very appearance sometimes enraged him, although it was that of a rather nice woman. She was deeply interested in clothes, but in an academic, objective way. She was always reading fashion-papers and criticising her friends' efforts, yet dressed mostly in pale twin-sets and seated skirts. Her silver-blonde hair was turning to real silver without any change to her pink-and-white attractions. Her fat arms and shoulders gave her a top-heavy appearance, especially as her feet

9

were tiny—such little girl's feet, in fact, that her high-heeled shoes made her look precocious. She was kind and simple and it would have been nice for her if Laurence had sometimes teased her, or said "Cheer up, mum," or something a little more homely than his present manner of fending off and backing away.

He followed her downstairs. Vinny turned from the window to greet them. He had drunk very little of his sherry, which was not pleasant. He came forward to shake hands, with the grave and slightly suspicious air of a psychiatrist. Laurence felt the authority, the calm fatherliness; firm, yet casual; detached, yet compassionate. The brown eyes looked directly at him, but veiled his impressions. The handshake was cordial. "You are welcome to follow me to the ends of the earth", Vinny seemed to be assuring people when he was introduced.

Laurence tried to pull his shirt-cuffs down before taking the sherry. Going straight from school into the Army had meant that he had very few grown-up clothes. Nothing fitted.

"Aren't you having a drink, Isabella?" Vinny asked.

"No, darling, thank you. I feel rather thirsty," she said vaguely. "Well then, if you will excuse me, I will just . . . oh, *Vinny* you know, Laurence, used to build sand-castles for you. I remember that so clearly."

She could not have left them feeling more daunted than after this remark, and both smiled apologetically— Laurence, for his mother; and Vinny, for the sand-castles.

Laurence sipped his sherry desperately, as if it were his bedtime glass of hot milk, and gazed at it intently rather than glance anywhere else.

"A beautiful spot," Vinny began, with a backwards gesture towards the window.

"Yes, very."

"I have never seen it out-of-season before."

"Oh, no?"

"No. It hardly seems the same place."

"Awfully quiet," Laurence suggested.

"The sands so deserted, and no children . . . there were some earlier on, but they seemed only to accentuate the emptiness."

"Would you like some more sherry?"

"I still have some." Vinny lifted his glass as proof. "That house on the cliff is a guest-house, is it? Or some sort of private hotel? I never know the difference. I don't remember it in the old days."

"Perhaps it wasn't there. It used to be a private house, but I think the woman got hard up. Rose someone-or-other. My mother would know," he said restlessly. "I'm not here much now."

"How do you like the Army?"

"Oh, very well, thank you," Laurence added, after a pause. In truth, he desperately longed for his leave to be over. Army life had its own frightfulness; but not the emotional burdens of being at home.

"The steps up the cliff, I suppose, are a private way up to the house," Vinny asked.

"Yes."

Laurence felt again that the man was like a psychiatrist, asking questions which really were not those questions at all, but deeper ones. The manner was so artfully veiled.

"I saw those children going up there." Vinny half-turned back to the uncurtained window, although it was now dark outside. "And then just now a woman and a young girl . . ."

To this, Laurence felt he really could not be expected to reply. He poured himself some more sherry, after giving a sidelong look at Vinny's glass.

"Would she be the owner of the house, this woman with the girl?" Vinny shamelessly persisted. He felt that he did not care what Laurence thought, as long as he could find out without asking Isabella.

"It's her sister who has the daughter, I think. I believe she's not quite all there, that girl . . . not right in the head, you know. . . ." He looked for the first time boldly at Vinny, as if to say: "Now let me alone. There are bigger fish in the sea than you dreamed of." He could not rid himself of the suspicion that Vinny was probing his mind, and testing his reactions. For this reason, he felt a great desire to come up with some enormity, to give him something to digest. But this manner seemed to bounce back to him, hitting Vinny with scarcely any effect. "I may be wrong," he muttered. "I don't know them . . . she *looks* jolly odd . . . funny eyes . . . and I heard rumours. Mother would know," he concluded.

Yet, although Isabella came in then, he said no more, sensing that Vinny did not want the conversation to go on. Isabella drew the curtains across the windows with a flourish; then, thrusting a hand down the neck of her jumper, seemed to be dragging shoulder-straps into place. She gave a tug at her girdle through her skirt, pulled her pearl necklace round, so that it was graded right, with the largest pearl in the centre-front, and having settled herself, said: "How nice and cosy!

12

If you like to show Vinny his room, Laurence, supper will be ready."

*　　　*　　　*

During the supper and afterwards sitting by the fire while Isabella cracked cob-nuts into her lap and scattered the rug with shells, Laurence listened to the story of the past and hoped that the conversation would stay there rather than turn to the future, the thought of which filled him with dismay and a sense of inferiority. He could not think what he should do when his military-service was over. His father had only vaguely spoken of 'pulling a few strings' and 'having a chat with so-and-so some time'. "Now he's left me high and dry," Laurence thought bitterly; but it was not a nice metaphor to have chosen and he swung his thoughts clear of it at once.

Vinny and his mother, he learnt, had first met one another at the very beginning of the war, at what Isabella called 'the blood-donating', to which she had gone 'for a lark', 'to see what it was like', and Vinny, Laurence guessed, because of the general trend of putting people under an obligation to him, even people he would never know, even to the tune of a bottleful of his blood.

They had sat next to one another in a queue, holding the same coloured cards. "We have only the most ordinary kind of blood," Isabella had whispered to Vinny—for she would always talk to strangers. "The most *useful* kind," Vinny had said reproachfully. "The more of us there are, the more there must be who need it." When it was their turn, they lay down on beds next to one another in what was as a rule a school class-room. Lying there waiting, they were conscious of the oddest intimacy. The situation had seemed ludicrous, they now decided. A young doctor was pacing up and down, like an animal in a cage, distracted with boredom. He barely said 'good-evening' as he stabbed them in the arm, fixed the tubes, and paced away. All down the room, figures lay on beds, whispering to the nurses or staring up at the ceiling as the blood drained away from them; orderly; quiet; very English. The English cup of tea was being prepared in a corner. Vinny had finished first and was led away to recuperate on another bed. Immediately Isabella's feeling of a 'lark' faded. Without him, she grew anxious. She confessed to him now that he had taken steadiness from her when he moved away. She had wondered if perhaps she had no more blood in her and would die. Her arm had grown numbed.

"Oh, stop!" Laurence said suddenly. "You make me feel faint."

"He can't abide the sight of blood," Isabella said proudly, smiling as she cracked away at the nuts.

Vinny held his hand out for one.

"Ah, they were the good old days," Isabella went on. "When I did get over to lie beside you, you leant over and tucked the blanket in for me. So kind."

"It all sounds ambiguous and absurd," Laurence complained.

But the ambiguity was the great fun of it. She was laughing quite merrily now; although Vinny, like some gloomy Nannie, forecast to himself more tears before bedtime.

"It was so lulling," Isabella said. "The peaceful whisperings; the chink of crockery, so muted; the tiptoeing about."

14

"I always think of you when I go now," Vinny said.

"I never went again. I thought the novelty would have worn off."

"Mother!" said Laurence in his scandalised voice.

"You drove me home, Vinny. Do you remember that flat we had in Westminster—it was boarded up last time I saw it. A bomb next door. You and Harry found you were at school together."

"Didn't—father—give his blood, too?" Laurence asked off-handedly.

"Oh, no, darling. He was much too busy for that sort of thing," Isabella said reprovingly.

Harry, in fact, had been a Member of Parliament. Isabella had often sat on platforms holding bouquets and smilingly looking down at her little feet: not making speeches ever, because, like most chatterboxes, she became tongue-tied if requested to say a few words.

Because of Harry's public position, his death had been reported on the front pages of newspapers, with his photograph, commendations of Laurence's attempt to save his father's life, and, lastly, a note about the by-election resulting from the tragedy, with the figure of Harry's previous majority.

Isabella, reminded of all this, suddenly said: "I am afraid he will lose to Labour," then put her hand over her mouth in an appalled way.

Laurence, his face pale with embarrassment, stood up and walked across to a fruit bowl and began frantically to eat an apple.

"Oh, dear," Isabella said weakly, "what am I saying? I cannot seem to realise what has happened. For a while everything seems ordinary, then—not."

Vinny moved over and sat on the arm of the chair.

15

Her tears fell into her lapful of nutshells. She leant easily against his shoulder. It was as if she had done herself up in a parcel, addressed to him, left on his doorstep; from now on, his responsibility.

Laurence, neither comforted nor comforting, tore enormous pieces out of his apple and stood as far away from them as he could, chewing furiously and frowning.

Chapter 2

IN VINNY'S experience of women, their tears were of a great sameness, and fits of weeping went in twos. First, came the exhausting catharsis; followed by weakness— a sense of irresponsibility, as if all were washed away, even decorum; a little shaky gaiety. Reacting from this, and in remorse, steady tears would flow for a while —the clearing-up shower. The early tears were of despair, rebellion, outrage; the later ones signified a grieved settling again to the world; after them, convalescence could be hoped for. This Vinny now hoped for for Isabella, and his plan was to keep her busy all day long with little things.

The next morning was bright and gusty and the Tillotson children were on the sands early, flying their kite. Vinny watched the scarlet wedge of it tottering and dropping, the wind tugging and relinquishing it, then suddenly taking it up, lifting, bearing it away. . . . He felt elevated too.

"Oh, you look extraordinarily happy!" Isabella said, coming into the room with some of his ties which she had been pressing.

"I felt I *was* that little girl," he said, nodding towards the beach. "When the wind really takes it—that's exciting—the kick of it, like feeling a salmon at the end of the line."

"How strange! I thought salmon were caught with spears. See, Vinny, what having a wife would mean to you—your ties would always look like this. . . ."

17

He turned to her, glanced at the ties, his head on one side. His excited look faded.

"I shall never marry," he said. 'And, oh!' she thought, 'the gravity of it, the headmasterliness!' Then she remembered her own new situation and thought that in future she must not try to chide bachelors into marriage, as she had once liked to do when protected by her own husband. From now on, a man might think she was trying to marry him herself.

"Well, there are the ties," she said awkwardly, and hung them over the back of a chair as if averting further intimacy.

"Now let us go out for coffee," Vinny said, "and change your library book, buy a cake for Sunday tea and have a drink at The Victoria. Then I shall be sure I am at the seaside for the weekend."

"I don't know about Laurence."

"Dearest, *leave* Laurence. Don't interfere with his studies. *Leave* him."

"Yes . . . well, then, yes, I will."

"Put on a wonderful lot of make-up and hurry."

The morning did her good. Vinny, over coffee, and while she shopped, watched her recuperating. In the café, the residents, who never went there in the season, exchanged glances. The gilt basket-chairs creaked as women turned discreetly to look at Vinny, taking him in as they seemed to be checking their watches with the clock, or signalling to the waitress.

In the little town, the wind sprang at them at the corners of streets, it came up from the sea and was bandied about between the shop-fronts in no particular direction, swirling dust before it on the pavements. Isabella turned up her collar and bent her head. The veins on her cheeks were a violet confusion; her eyes watered. But Vinny insisted on looking in all the shop-windows, standing gravely bowed over displays of coral necklaces; handkerchiefs embroidered 'A Present From Seething', boring thick pottery. He bought two coloured postcards showing the esplanade with bathing-huts, flowerbeds let into the asphalt, and wind-gnawed shrubs. He chose them with care, turning the revolving stand with great absorption. For Sunday's tea he bought a walnut-cake, for Saturday's tea a bag of prawns. He made Isabella enter into the shopping with much serious discussion. Once, an acquaintance stopped to speak to her, and he sauntered on and stood a little way up the street with his hands behind his back. Isabella, hurrying towards him, wore once more her defeated look. He had to begin all over again, and damned her friends.

But in spite of such little setbacks her morale steadily mounted and he took immense pride in it. Their drinks at The Victoria helped. He made his way towards the bar through the Saturday morning crush and hubbub. Glancing back as he waited, he saw Isabella stretch out to take a discarded newspaper from the next table. She smiled at him and began to study the headlines. When she looked again, he seemed to be examining a potted fern on the bar, and she took a hasty glimpse at the back page. He returned, carrying their drinks steadily; and lazily, languidly, she cast the newspaper aside, dis-engaged her attention from it, leant forward to pick up her drink and, when she smiled, seemed like a young girl being taken out for the first time. 'I am all yours,' her smile seemed to proclaim, 'in return for the drink, all my thoughts shall be bent on you. Simply *bent*.' He knew the smile was something heedless and automatic, conjured-up from long ago, to conceal guilt. After a second or two, she found her bearings again and composed her features. Before he went for another drink, she mentioned the Ladies, and, edging herself through the crowd impatiently, even desperately, ran all the way to the foyer to telephone her bookmaker.

She had not come back when Vinny brought the drinks to the table. While he waited, he took out his picture-postcards and scribbled messages on them, to his mother, and to his wife.

*　　　*　　　*

After tea, Vinny went down for a walk on the shore, alone. The tide was out and the wet sand sucked at his shoes and rose to fill each footprint. When the lights along the esplanade came on, it seemed all at once much darker. He went towards the cliff, where seaweed heaped the rocks, its coarse bladdery succulence hiding encrustations of limpets, smelling evil, dripping into pools.

His footprints now held in the sand and he looked back to see the neat shape of his shoes following him. At that moment, as he glanced back, a woman going swiftly along the sands, her head bent under the hood of her coat, her hands thrust up her wide sleeves, was brought up sharply by his pausing there; *felt* before *saw* him, jerked up her head and, as he turned, stumbled into his arms. He felt her own arms folded across her breast, for she could not disentangle them to thrust him away. Stepping back, to steady her he touched her shoulder for an instant. His apology was hesitant. He forced his lips to move as he looked down at her face, which was white in the shadow of her hood and of a perfect, even beauty; mask-like and, in the gathering dusk, terrifying.

Her bare hand drew the hood closer to her cheeks and her sleeve fell back to show her thin wrist and forearm. He felt her shoulder move impatiently as if to shake off his hand, then she hurried forward, across the sands to the cliff-steps—the steps he had watched her climb the evening before. Her straightness, the hands in her sleeves, he recognised at once. What he had not been able to imagine had been the strange quality of her beauty, its faultlessness and blank terror.

He walked back under the cliff. The sea was so far out in the bay and the air so silent that he felt wary; he had an impression of her standing quite still on the steps watching him. Although he tried hard not to look, after a while he turned his head. She was going slowly up the steps and had almost reached the top. Her hood hung from her shoulders now and he could see her dark hair. He turned right round and stood still, hoping that the cliff's shadow obscured him, that he would become —to her, if she glanced down—one with the rocks. At the very top of the steps she paused and he drew back until he touched cold seaweed. The wind lifted her hair away from her face and he could see her pale hand against her coat. He could not visualise again the earlier moment when he had touched her and spoken to her; but he remembered that she had not answered him or added an apology to his.

Pacing the sands more and more slowly, because unwilling to return to Isabella, he tried to go back over that experience; but failed. He could only feel the shock of, the inexplicable recoil from, her beauty—as if a moth had brushed his cheek and terror had driven him to beat it off; a terror ridiculous, instinctive and humiliating.

Nearing fifty, Vinny felt more than ever the sweet disappointments only a romantic knows, whose very desires invite frustration; who loves twilight rather than midday, the echo more than the voice, the moon more than the sun, and women better than men; adoring all scarcely-revealed things; insinuations, whispers; eyes veiled, landscapes veiled; the imperfectly remembered and the half-anticipated. Past and future to him were the realities; the present dull, meaningless, only significant if, as now, going back along the sands, he could say to himself: 'Later on, I shall remember.' To link his favourite tenses in such a phrase was to him the exhalation of romance, and the fact that such phrases had preceded all his disappointments, heralded all the counterfeit and treachery he had worked or suffered, could not detract from its magic. He disdained to learn from so drab a teacher as Experience.

When he reached Isabella's little house by the pier, he saw Laurence come to the parlour window to draw the curtains. Although, with the light of the room behind him, he could not have seen Vinny out in the dark, his gesture seemed insolent, and the drawn curtains an affront.

*　　　*　　　*

Laurence continued to be exclusive for the rest of the evening, so that his act of drawing the curtains became symbolic to Vinny, who seldom in his life had been up against just such an unrelaxed dislike in a person. Other people, thinking: 'We cannot all take to one another,' would turn from or return the antagonism; but Vinny did not: he grieved. It was his business to be loved—a mission created afresh with everyone he met—and he was always conscious of another's coldness. Uneasily, he would be aware. He could not work his magic.

That anyone so in need of comfort as Laurence was should reject him was especially putting-out. He seemed like a traveller dying in the snow from cold and exhaustion, yet turning pettishly from the St Bernard dog, saying: "I do not care for brandy." Vinny tried to dislike him and he found much—Laurence's resolute adolescence, his indifference to his mother, his laziness, his greediness over sherry and the butter ration—upon which to hang his distaste; but in the end only pity hung there, and his own rejected sympathy.

*   *   *

It was the last evening of Laurence's leave. After tea on Sunday he must return to Aldershot. Vinny, who had often driven through the place, thought it intolerable. The whole idea depressed him and he could visualise the dismal landscape of playing-fields, with cloddish, Breughelish figures at football; the avenues of leafless chestnut-trees; hutted sites and barracks separated by roads named after forgotten generals. He felt that it was no wonder that Laurence, with, after all, so many causes, should be downcast.

While Isabella was telephoning in the hall, sitting neatly up to the small table as if she would be there a long while, Vinny tried to discuss the future with Laurence. He could tell that Isabella was talking to a woman, for she said 'my dear' a great deal: to a man she would have said 'darling'. He guessed that it was one of the long daily conversations women have, the idea of which was charming to him and not in the least bit irritating.

Laurence was cleaning a clock. Parts of it were spread over a newspaper and he was brushing them with a gull's feather dipped in oil. His grubby hands had the clumsy-looking delicacy of a schoolboy's, ill-adapted to the task, yet sure. His nails were bitten; cropped down; uneven; consistent, Vinny thought, with his secretive and nervy air.

"I was talking to Isabella," Vinny said. To say 'Isabella' was supposed to suggest equality and was more informal than 'your Mother'; he fèlt that this 'Isabella' promoted the lad and drew him into the grown-up world. "I want to help her about the other house—your home really. I expect she has discussed it with you."

"No," Laurence said.

"She thinks it best to sell it."

Laurence held up a little jagged wheel and looked at it against the light with one eye screwed up.

"I told her I would go down to Buckinghamshire with her to arrange about the furniture, to pick out what she wants to keep, before the auction sale."

He got so little response from Laurence that he began to walk about the room, and even filled a pipe, a thing he only did when driven to it by interviews of this kind.

"I expect you would like to think over what you want brought here. All your private things, naturally; but in the way of furniture for your room, I meant."

"There isn't anywhere to put any more furniture in my room."

"Well, there may be something. The ideal plan would be for you to go down there to see."

"I wouldn't get any more leave."

"No, well . . . Are you unhappy at leaving the other house?"

Laurence for a moment looked quite surprised. "I couldn't *be* there," he said. "I can't be here, either. It makes no difference now I'm in the Army."

"You won't always be in the Army."

"No, but even when I'm not, I shan't be living at home with mother." Utter consternation was on his face. He really is awfully stupid, Vinny thought.

"What *will* you do?"

"Father used to say something about going into business." He resumed his work, which he had paused in for a moment.

Looking at his bent head, Vinny said: "That sounds rather vague."

"I know."

"What are your own ideas?"

"I wouldn't mind working on a farm," Laurence mumbled.

For the first time, Vinny thought that he was getting somewhere, that he had drawn close enough to this timid ambition to throw a noose over it.

Warily, he said: "Have you always wanted to be a farmer?"

Laurence looked up. "Oh, I don't want to be a *farmer*. There's too much worry in that, and filling in forms, you know. Your job's never finished . . . really no life. I meant a . . . labourer."

The boy's seriousness warned Vinny. He said gently: "What would you live on, firstly?"

"They get six pounds a week. That would be enough for me. My needs are not great," Laurence said with dignity. "I have learnt that they aren't—at school, in the Army." He glanced at the decanter on the sideboard and added: "I don't really drink sherry, except in people's houses. I mean, I wouldn't dream of buying it. I drink mild-and-bitter and sometimes just mild. Very little of that, too. And I never smoke—or very rarely. Sometimes when I'm offered one, I take it."

"One day you'll want to get married."

"Oh, I don't know." Laurence worked very busily, breathing on a ratchet and wiping it on his handkerchief. His business was to hide the quick, sly look he had not meant to give Vinny. "After all, you never have, sir."

The 'sir' infuriated Vinny. It was a snub to his 'Isabella'.

"And," Laurence went on quickly, "farm-labourers get married, don't they?"

"What girl that you know, whom you would be likely to want to marry, would even contemplate it under such circumstances?"

"I don't know any girls. So I couldn't say."

He began to reassemble the clock calmly and methodically. In the hall, they could hear Isabella rattling on.

"If I'm hard-up for a bit of money, I can always get it," Laurence said.

"From your mother, you mean?" Vinny was trapped into icy disdain, and Laurence calmly said: "No, I am lucky with horses."

He shut up the back of the clock and turned the little key. Then he wiped his hands on his trousers.

"Better not tell mother that," he added, "she might worry, thinking I should lose my head."

'You'll never do that,' Vinny thought scornfully.

Laurence returned the clock to its place on the chimneypiece. Then he said quietly: "I know I would never be allowed to do it—farm work I mean. I should never get my way. It is only a thing I fancy and I should not have burdened you with it. I suppose I shall have to go into business and that that is why my mother is selling the house and furniture. Any advice you could give would be very useful, I am sure, as you are in business yourself."

Vinny, who was an underwriter at Lloyd's, ignored this; for he thought he could hear Isabella winding up her monologue. Very hurriedly he said: "I want you to feel that I would always do anything for you. Not only from respect for your father and mother, but from fondness for you yourself. I'll leave you my address, and you can always write—no need to worry your . . . Isabella. I should be glad to hear from you in any case, especially if you have any . . . information . . . for me." He smiled primly. "I haven't much time for studying form."

'What dreadful chumminess!' Laurence thought.

"Are you upset at having to go back tomorrow?"

"Oh, no!"

"Plenty of friends there?"

"Only men," Laurence said cautiously.

"You feel quite fit again?"

"Yes, thank you very much."

"It was a ghastly ordeal for you, but it would be unwise to try to push it to the back of your mind."

Laurence leant awkwardly against the chimneypiece in a rather pansyish pose.

"Better face it as the tragedy it was, and know that you did your best and were very brave."

"I wasn't really," Laurence said. "I didn't like to tell mother quite the truth. In actual fact, I got the wind up and left him there."

"That was Evalie Hobson," Isabella said, opening the door suddenly. "An old friend of mine . . . so amusing, Vinny. I met her at the Turkish baths."

*   *   *

Laurence went up to bed early, and Vinny and Isabella took a stroll along the esplanade—a breath of fresh air before turning in, they said; an elderly phrase which always made Laurence impatient.

They walked slowly, arm-in-arm, and paused sometimes to lean over the sea-wall. He was glad that she had turned away from the cliff and that they were going towards the centre of the town and away from the rustic-work steps and the house among the trees.

"I should like to come down again during the week," he said. "On Thursday, if you would like that, if there is anything I could do." (The by-election was on Thursday.)

"How good of you, Vinny!"

"Don't make any arrangements for me here. . . . I will take you out to luncheon . . . and perhaps you could get a room for me somewhere."

"But, of course, you will be with us."

"Not when Laurence is away."

"Darling, don't be pompous. Who's to care?"

"I care—for your sake, if you will not care for your own."

She was most touched by this and could not reply.

"What silly little shoes to come walking in," he said.

She glanced down to see which shoes they were, then

asked: "Won't your mother miss you, if you are away so much?"

"No."

"Shall we turn back now?"

The moon seemed to be racing up through the clouds, which looked too cumbrous to move. Macrocarpa trees glistened under the lamps as if wet. Isabella, seeing the lighted windows at the cliff-top, suddenly said: "Perhaps Rose Kelsey would have room for you. It would be nice and near. If you are sure that you must be so prim."

"Quite sure."

"But at our age . . . !"

"I am quite sure," he repeated.

He was so afraid lest his excitement should be communicated to her that he withdrew his arm and pretended to be going to sneeze. Halted, fumbling for his handkerchief, he felt stricken by his recollection of the woman on the sands. Only with difficulty did he take Isabella's arm again. They walked on more briskly, without a word; but in the hall, as she was unwinding her scarf, she asked:

"Why do you look like that?"

Inevitably, he said: "Like what?"

"You've stopped now. You looked . . ."

"Yes?"

"As if you were thinking of something."

He laughed, but she was not so undiscerning that she failed to detect relief in his laughter.

"Would you like some whisky?" she asked. "I quite forgot to ask you last night. Such a terrible hostess. Harry always did the drinks."

"You are the loveliest hostess, because you make people happy as well as comfortable."

29

"I don't think *I* was making you look like that."

"*This* night, I should like some whisky please."

Following him into the parlour, she persisted: "But why *this* night."

"Because I had some luck today."

"What sort of luck?"

"A little horse-racing sort of luck," he lied.

"How nice!" she said, after a pause. They drank in silence, with alternate glances at one another.

"And what was the name of the horse?" she suddenly asked, in a rallying, condescending way.

"Well, my dear Isabella, as I imagine you don't know one horse from another, you need not be bored with all that."

"Do you often do it?" she asked dully.

"Very seldom; but this was a special tip. My dear, don't look so disapproving! I am sure you sometimes have had a little flutter on the Derby."

"Never," she said truthfully. Neither she nor Evalie concerned themselves with the big races. They felt contempt for those who did; as regular churchgoers must feel contempt for the crowds who worship only at Easter and Harvest Festivals.

"I have enjoyed myself enormously," Vinny said, smiling at her vexation.

* * *

He awoke the next morning to a brilliant room and gulls making peevish noises near the window. He had wakened abruptly, bringing a remnant of dream with him, disturbing, erotic. In this dream, from the influence of which he lay still and bewildered, the woman on the sands had not broken away from him, nor recoiled from his touch. Having created a personality for her, and behaviour, and even response, this dream had in a way presented her to him; given her a voice and words to say.

'But she is not even a woman I know,' was his first thought. He wondered how he could ever make of her a stranger again; for him, their dream-intimacy had overstepped preliminary revelation, hastening them beyond solicitude for one another, even curiosity. If they were to be condemned, as dream-figures, to meet always in a void, he envisaged the uselessness of ever seeing her again. Worse than strangers, too impatient to retrace their way, heedless of all small discoveries, lovers' pleasures, they were committed to one another, by trickery of his unconscious mind.

When he could thrust aside the heaviness of sleep, he began to be ashamed, and struggled to call the dream a dream. This was difficult. In dreams, he had often before discovered the truth, or invented a condition which later became the truth. In dreams, he had fallen in love, and, waking, found his relationship with someone unexpectedly, perhaps irremediably, changed. He would see them afterwards in a different light, unable to believe that they did not hold the dream in common.

Today, during which church-bells rang, the sea crashed bleakly upon the rocks and footsteps hurried on the esplanade, he felt unreal and troubled. He needed to convalesce from sleep, as if from a severe illness.

They spent an edgy day. Isabella over-roasted the meal, was all hurry and confusion with no Mrs Dickens to help her. After tea, Laurence put on his army boots and the sour-smelling battledress, and he and Vinny went off to the station.

*   *   *

Before he went, while he was lacing up his boots and breathing heavily, Laurence said: "I hope, by the way, that this Vinny is not one day going to be a father to me."

Isabella said "Shush" and pointed towards the door. "He's in the lavatory."

"Well, I will assure you, you have nothing to worry about. He's not the marrying kind and neither, any more, am I."

When they had gone, she began to wonder why the idea had seemed so objectionable to Laurence. She felt sad and lonely in the empty house, and longed for Thursday to come.

Chapter 3

THE first symptoms of life's regaining normality began
for Isabella during Vinny's stay and, in the days which
followed, more and more of her previous existence
returned. Evalie Hobson, who had not dared to do
more than write one scared letter, now began to call
again. She and Isabella had only a superficial acquaintance, but this made it all the more precious to both of
them. Talk skimmed along, chocolates were chosen
from the box, tea drunk, sherry sipped. Scrawled notes
passed between them, handbags were rummaged
through for recipes and diet sheets. They met middle-
age together—a time when women are necessary to one
another—and all the petty but grievous insults of greying
hair, crowsfeet, and the loathed encumbrances of un-
wanted flesh, seemed less sordid when faced and fought
(though fought spasmodically and with weak wills)
gaily together. They laughed a great deal over their
experiments: one week they bent and stretched with
such fury that Evalie broke a blood vein in her eye; the
next week they drank nothing after luncheon; another
time ate only grapes all day long. They counted up
calories, bought new corsets and tried new face-creams;
cut paragraphs out of magazines for one another and
went together to the Turkish baths. They remained the
same—two rather larkish schoolgirls. This they realised
and it was the piteous part to them of growing old.
"We haven't changed enough," Isabella once said.
"We don't any longer match our looks. We've got lost

and left behind." "We ought to take up something," Evalie agreed. "Not read the books we do. For instance, we never read books written by men, do we? Just library books all the time. You see how American women go to all those lectures when they reach the change of life. It's only trying to catch up with their looks. We ought to go in for psychology, or something like it."

They went to two lectures—one on spiritualism, by which they were nervously amused; and one on social pragmatism, which disheartened them.

After a while, they turned to gambling. They did this not as at any reckless crisis in their lives, but because they needed money for their face-creams and fashion-papers. Industriously, they studied form; jockeys' names became as familiar to them as their own relations': secretly (for their husbands would have disapproved), they progressed from little flutters to a cool and steady daily appraisal of all the runners and riders; to having an account with a bookmaker instead of giving half-crowns to Evalie's gardener. They gave up morning coffee in the town and hurried to one another's houses to make their plans for the day and to lament or rejoice over the day before. This was more of a tonic to them for having to be indulged in secret. They missed one another very much when the House was sitting and Isabella was obliged to return to Buckinghamshire.

That they hid their secret was no credit to their dissembling; for, when they overheard others talking of racing, their faces became so devoid of expression as to have invited suspicion if anyone had noticed. But they were perhaps beyond the age for being noticed.

34

"Wouldn't it be dreadful if we won so much one day—on the accumulator, perhaps—that we had to *tell*!" Evalie said.

When their husbands had suggested taking them to Goodwood for a treat, they were full of excuses: they hadn't the right clothes and their feet would ache. "So much bustling about" and "a very tiring day", they said. Isabella went too far and said that horses frightened her. "We are not asking you to ride them," Harry had said. "You used always to enjoy Ascot." "Oh, that was in the old days," Isabella said. She had meant the days before she took the matter seriously. "When I was young," she added. "And loved nice clothes."

"My God!" Evalie said afterwards. "We should never have got *on* with them hanging about. And fancy having to go to the Paddock and look at the horses. And ask them to put ten shillings on something—Oliver and Harry I mean." "And perhaps see Mr Syd Woods himself chalking up the odds. I should faint," said Isabella.

Their complicity was a bond which had loosened when Harry died. Evalie stayed away; for she could not think of anything suitable to say. They missed one another. When, on the Saturday evening, Evalie had telephoned for the first time, she heard with relief Isabella's laughter, and on Monday morning she was round as usual with *The Sporting Life* hidden at the bottom of her shopping-basket.

On Thursday morning, Isabella was in the kitchen making a cake. Mrs Dickens was polishing the silver. Her sad and colourless face was reflected in the spoons, first wide, then long, when she turned them over. Isabella, with a cigarette in her mouth, mumbled at

35

Evalie, and felt in her overall-pocket for a piece of paper. "So busy this morning. I came to my conclusions directly after breakfast," she said mysteriously. "You might look it over and see what you think. Oh, damn, now the ash has dropped into the mixture. Never mind, perhaps he will think it's a seed cake."

Mrs Dickens, who guessed what they were up to, could not understand their secrecy.

"What time is he coming?" Evalie asked.

If she had been a spy, Mrs Dickens thought, she could not have slipped the paper into her glove more expertly. The only wonder was that she did not swallow it.

"Before lunch. He is staying at Rose Kelsey's as he obviously couldn't stay here again, with Laurence away."

"Oh, naturally not," Evalie said.

"At the weekend, Laurence was here all the time."

"Quite."

"He has to have the garden-room, they are so full up with Tillotsons."

"I suppose so," Evalie said.

Mrs Dickens thought their conversations oddly flat, and wondered if they were devised for her benefit. Sometimes, they even forced her to join in, and she did so resentfully, quite rightly detecting condescension in their voices. Something revivalist in their tone whenever they turned to her, antagonised her—"And what do *you* think, Mrs Dickens?" or, with wonderful tolerance, "I'm afraid Mrs Dickens won't agree with us at all." At election-times, Evalie said, benignly: "And how's Labour getting on, Mrs D.?" Isabella (who had been told not to, by Harry) said nothing. Mrs

36

Dickens was torn in two today. She had loved Harry, who, as she said at home, was the one she could get sense out of; but he was dead now and beyond being hurt and she would above all like the Liberals to get a slap in the face at the by-election. Harry's successor was a Lady Violet Liberal, although Harry himself had tended to be the Lady Megan kind. Mrs Dickens was Doctor Edith Labour, but she had been brought up Liberal, she sometimes admitted, though not Lady Violet Liberal.

She looked quickly away from the cake Isabella was putting into the oven, as if she had glimpsed something indecent. It was bound to rise up in the middle and crack into two blackened peaks. Slack mixture. Hot oven. Salute to the British Housewife, she thought malignantly. All that we heard on the wireless in the war, not mentioning the wasted ingredients.

"If you could ring up Mr Woods for me," Isabella said, when she was seeing Evalie off. "I may not get a chance with Vinny here."

"Oh, naturally, my dear. I only wish I could see him for an instant. Vinny, I mean."

"Yes, it is a pity," Isabella said firmly.

"Never mind, I do have a vivid picture of him in my mind, from all you've said."

"Such as what?"

"Oh, that kind, effeminate sort of man who is so nice to women."

"Vinny is extremely manly—very broad across the shoulders. He went half-round the world once, serving before the mast."

"My dear, you say everyone has served before the mast. Except me."

Isabella, who hoped to tidy herself before Vinny came, did not reply.

*　　　*　　　*

The garden-room was a small, dank bedroom on the ground floor. It had a glazed door opening on to a gravel path and shrubs, and oddments of furniture not needed in other parts of the house. Rose Kelsey apologised for everything and hoped, aloud, that the bed was properly aired. The room was only used in summer emergencies, she explained, and this Vinny soon proved to himself by finding some old heather in the waste-paper basket, discarded, he supposed, by last year's guests. He did not think he would be very comfortable. The carpet was worn away by so many gravelly boots coming in through the french window. An orange cover clung limply to the sagging bed. Rose said: "The children are above. I hope they won't disturb you."

Rose was the most English-looking woman he had ever seen. Her light-brown hair was taken back neatly in a bun; her carriage was straight, but stiff. She had grey eyes and a beautiful skin; large feet and lovely hands. Her clothes—as Isabella had warned him—were unconsidered; for she wore a satin blouse with her tweed suit and pale shiny stockings with brogues. Her manner was frigid, though she was not at a loss for words: in fact, she was rather brisk and under control and Vinny could not imagine her being otherwise. He had seen too many mothers like her—on railway platforms as the school-train went out, and standing on doorsteps in Harley Street with their children—to wonder how she had ever come to have a child. He now took that miracle for granted, supposing that everyone has their informal moments.

Such women are a product of English imperviousness and courage which contain both fanaticism and narrow loyalties. In foreign countries (and Rose seemed so much a soldier's wife) the lack of sensuality was a defence and at times a maddening challenge. The attribute was always jealously fostered and guarded by husbands.

"If it is raining," Rose said, "you could go up this staircase and across the landing—the bathroom is there—and then down the main stairs to the dining-room; but if it is fine, it is quicker to go round the garden way."

Seeing Vinny touching the catches of his suitcase she hurried out, through the shrubbery to the lawn, where Isabella was walking up and down in front of the house.

Vinny spread about a few of his possessions, then opened the door leading to the stairs. He found himself in a sealed-off part of the house beyond the kitchen. A tap dripped and a cistern hissed. There was a depressing smell of scrubbed deal, still wet. At the top of the stairs, which were covered with old linoleum, was a baize-padded door. He imagined his room having once been a housekeeper's sitting-room.

To get to the front of the house, without climbing the stairs, he could see that he would have to go through other rooms and that Rose had shown she was un-willing for him to do so. Even using the staircase made him feel guilty and he hoped that he met no one.

It was the dead time of the day, just before four o'clock, and the landing was full of shadows and deserted, with all its doors closed. A draught lifted a mat outside one bedroom. It looked like a poor spent animal lying

at a door and panting its last. Even the door itself shook
frantically, tugged by the wind, and he visualised the
bleak room beyond it, with curtains flying out like flags
from the opened, seaward windows.

It was the dreariest house, he thought; an inherited,
unaltered house. The only touch upon it for years had
been the shabby touch of time. Nothing lively was
added: no one had put up a new picture or tried a
different colour anywhere. 'I am too much for them,'
the house cried, and the exquisite Sheraton chest-of-
drawers on the landing had a bloom upon it, and its
oval handles were tarnished. This Vinny did not like to
see. He loved furniture; and the love, cancelling out his
recent caution, took him across the landing so that he
might run his hand over the bow-front and lift the brass
handles. He forgot Isabella on the lawn and simply
desired to spend half an hour polishing the mahogany.
He knelt down to examine the boxwood inlay and was
still on his knees when one of the landing doors suddenly
opened. It was the one behind the fretted mat.

Was he always, he wondered, to be in the wrong with
this woman—running into her in the dark; wrong in
his dreams; and seeming now, at best, a ridiculous, an
insufferably prying interloper? She gave no sign of
recognition or surprise, and when he stood up and
began to explain and apologise, glanced at him with
indifference and then bent to straighten the mat. He
thought: 'I have never heard her voice, except in my
dreams'; and when she spoke he was amazed because
it was unexpectedly light and faltering.

"Rose has other pieces you should see—a William-
and-Mary tallboy with beautiful marquetry in the
drawing-room."

He especially disliked the period; for it seemed to him un-English—an adjective he often fastidiously applied to anything too decorated.

He remembered Isabella on the lawn. "I should like to see it, another time."

She rested her hands on the banisters and leaned over, looking down into the hall. Her hair, like her sister's, was knotted back; but with what a difference, he thought: since it seemed arranged not merely for neatness but from a habit of beauty.

He wondered why the phrase 'habit of beauty' had occurred to him. Her beauty had not gone: it was, in fact, the staggering perfection he had first thought it. Her dark dress dramatised the whiteness of her skin and her flawlessness. Yet the feeling that her beauty was over persisted in him, however much the beauty itself remained before him as contradiction.

"I am here," she called, and she drew back from the banister-rail and went to the head of the stairs. Seeing her more clearly in the light which flowed up from the hall, he thought that her face contrasted strangely with her hurried way of speaking and her graceful nervous movements, and as she ran downstairs it looked expressionless, with a slack grace, like the portrait of a great beauty by a not very great painter who had caught all the listed features, but not the living stir of loveliness—the ripple, and quickening, without which beauty is . . . is terrifying, he decided.

He followed her slowly down the stairs and saw her disappearing through a door with her arm round a girl's waist. Rose's daughter, he thought, who, Laurence had said, was 'not all there'.

A grandfather clock in a corner whirred asthmatically

41

ready to strike and he started at the sound. He cast a quick glance round at the red-papered walls burgeoning with antlers and masks, barometers, warming-pans, and stepped out on to the lawn.

Rose and Isabella were going down the border examining the plants and Isabella was pointing at them with her umbrella. She looked up at Vinny with the relief of a woman who has been left too long with someone she dislikes.

"But won't you have tea?" Rose asked.

"Mrs D. will have it ready for us at home. I mustn't annoy her," Isabella said hastily. "And I made a special cake. We just thought it better to bring Vinny's things before it grew dark."

Round the macrocarpa trees came the Tillotson children, straggling and calling, and as Vinny and Isabella walked out of the gate on to the cliff-road the Tillotson baby (too young for the sands) was coming along in his pram. They could see his mittened hands waving on either side of the hood. The young nursemaid, buttoned up in her reefer coat, stared at them boldly as they passed.

*   *   *

Harry's name was in the nine o'clock news, and Isabella insisted on listening to it and insisted on crying a little in a fussy way when she did: and all her bracelets jingled as she dabbed her eyes.

Polling had not been heavy. "There, you see," she said accusingly to Vinny. "I am sure they will have lost to Labour. I am glad that Harry never lived to see this day."

Vinny was oddly unable to attend to her. For the first

42

time in his life tears were distasteful to him and he was struggling against impatience and fatigue. The arrangement and planning, enabling him to get away on a Thursday, had tired him, he reasoned with himself. He would not entertain the idea of being bored with Isabella's grief. He drove the notion away before it could cross the threshold.

"What are you thinking?" Isabella asked.

"Of you."

"Then why frown and shake your head?"

"Worry for you."

"How wonderful! If you are to worry for me, I need not. It will be a great relief. Harry always did the worrying, like carving the joint and seeing to the drinks."

'Such a silly woman when one gets to know her well,' he decided.

"Do you hate me to speak of him?" she asked.

"Hate?"

"I notice that people do hate it. They take a step back, away from me, and half-close their eyes, waiting for me to stop. Evalie always does. Yet how else can I keep him going?"

"You shall talk of him all the time, if you want to. And I will often do the same. I should warn you, though, that talk alters people."

"How can it, if we only say the truth?"

"You won't. You'll leave out, for instance, the days when you were not on speaking terms. I vividly remember one of them myself, when you spoke at one another through Laurence and me. It was painful and embarrassing for us all. And when you had an argument with him, he would suddenly lower his own voice and tell you not to shout. Very adroitly he did that—one of the tricks of his trade, I expect. 'Of the dead only good' is what really finishes them off. Death from romanticism. It is always destructive."

"But I could not go about telling people how we quarrelled. And we seldom did."

"I meant that when you and I talk I won't have some idealised Harry foisted off on me."

"No one else *cares*!"

He did not deny this, and when he did not, she went on: "I do blame God for that . . . making the pretence of caring suddenly fall in, so that we see we are really alone all the time."

"No need for God if it were otherwise," Vinny said carelessly. He was not intending to be drawn into religious discussion.

"But when it *dawns* on one!"

He took a bunch of keys from his pocket and examined them intently, one by one—a sign, which Isabella did not recognise, that he was choosing words carefully, sorting them over, as he appeared to be sorting over the keys in his hand. She did, however, notice a change in his voice when he spoke.

"Does Rose Kelsey back away, as it were, from mention of Harry?"

"But I *should* not mention Harry to Rose Kelsey."

"Why?"

Their talk was slowing up with suspicious pauses.

"I . . . faintly dislike her."

"Why?"

"I am not at ease with her."

He returned the keys to his pocket and then looked straight across at Isabella. "She is not warm-hearted?" he suggested briskly. His careless way of seeming to wind up the conversation was a trap which she fell into. No longer suspicious about the tone of his voice, no longer feeling drawn, she was now ready to talk about Rose for an hour or more.

"I really can't bear her. She dresses so badly."

"Yes, you warned me."

"The colours! Navy blue and brown her favourite combination and always a bit of pink petticoat dipping down at the back edged with coffee-coloured lace."

"Darling!"

"But I can't criticise her behaviour, because *she's* had a hard life and you know that excuses any sort of off-handedness."

"It sometimes appears so."

"When her husband died she hadn't any money, and had to take in all these paying-guests. I didn't know him, but people in the town say he drank. As if everyone doesn't. At any rate, it was his fault about Emily."

"Emily?"

"Rose's sister. If you keep taking out your keys, I shall think you are bored and want to go to bed."

"I'm not bored."

"Well, do say, darling, when you want to be off. Don't let me keep you up."

'And don't let her change the subject!' he prayed. He did not know how to bring her back to the point, without the direct questions she resisted.

"And then there is that child, Philippa. Loopy or mentally-retarded or whatever one calls it. Oh, it is enough to make anyone dress badly . . . such a great heap of trouble."

"What happened about Emily?" he asked.

"She was with Rose's husband in the car, and

45

whether he had one of his bouts or orgies going on, I don't know, but he ran the car into a wall and killed himself, and nearly killed poor Emily as well. For months she was in hospital, and when she came out, Rose began to devote her life to her and has done so ever since."

"Has she no life of her own, then?"

"None any longer. Her fiancé left her because of the accident. One reason for not liking Rose is that, when she told me that, I thought she relished the idea."

"Why should he have left her?"

"Her face was ruined, you see. I mean, the face she had. She came from hospital looking quite different— very beautiful in a way, but not in the way in which she had been beautiful before. In fact, the look of her now rather appals me."

"Yes, yes, I see."

Isabella looked up quickly in surprise.

"I saw her in the house," Vinny said. "It must have been she. . . . But for this man to break off the engagement . . . I thought that was never done . . . one never hears of anyone doing it . . . of refusing the chance for martyrdom. It's a kind of caddishness I haven't met before and I thought I had met every kind. And . . . she is nevertheless very beautiful."

"He didn't know that she was going to be. She was many months in bed with no one to see her; for she must not move or speak or cry."

He imagined her lying there, piteously preconceiving all injury she had yet to suffer, in chrysalid isolation; no longer herself: not yet emerged from nothingness.

"She has no one now but Rose and that loony child who treks about everywhere after her. Rose protects

46

her. Rose is washing away her husband's guilt. I hope it is not too macabre for you up there, but it is only for the night and I think that Emily is rarely seen, or Philly either. What unhappy lives people have—always a more dreary sort of unhappiness than one's own."

"Looks matter more than anyone could imagine," he said.

"I have always said so," Isabella agreed complacently, touching her pearls.

"I think I should go now."

"Yes, I suppose Rose won't like you to arrive too late."

"I shall see you in the morning. Then we must talk about the Auction Sale."

In the hall, he kissed her goodnight and walked away from the house in a dream.

He thought of Emily lying under the spell of her alien beauty and Rose's devotion enclosing her like a thicket of briars.

Chapter 4

How the weeks spin by, Rose thought, or spin *round*, it
sometimes seems, as if it were the same Friday coming
again and again.

Since she had become happy, the days were all alike;
dates flew off calendars as they do in films; mornings
were dealt out with scarcely any variety—a different
breakfast, a different coloured sky—and even the headlines of newspapers repeated the briefest sequence of
hate and foreboding. The passage of time was most felt
at the end of the afternoon, with the day heeling over
into oblivion—oblivion, because no day was to be
remembered when all days were the same.

She had always loved monotony and the small recurring excitements of domesticity were enough for her
—shopping triumphs; satisfactions of meals served and
eaten; the interest of keeping an alert eye on the staff.
The job was difficult enough to challenge her courage.
Often she was tired. The inconvenient old house cried
for attention, money, at every turn. She wore herself
out on inanimate things and was at peace. She had never
been at peace as a wife; never, in the old days, at peace
as Emily's sister. As girls, Emily had been the gay, the
party-going one; and Rose, lacking, as far as looks went,
only vivacity, spent too much time in the cloakroom at
dances, agonised at having to reappear and be again
rejected. If she unbent, it was only into foolishness, and
silences fell. 'Forfeits' at parties had frozen her. She
had felt her nerves growing taut with apprehension.

48

Nowadays, no one asked her to bow to the wittiest and kneel to the prettiest. No one asked her to discard her dignity. No one made love to her, or drank too much when she turned away from them. Devotion could at last be what she had always understood it to be, a matter of favourite puddings, carefully aired clothes and leaping fires in sick-rooms. The burden of her maternity—tenderness—Emily took from her. She could feel that she had done everything for Philly because Emily did not mind becoming a child again and playing foolish games; did not mind kissing, caressing; implied no condescension. Rose had a special voice for her daughter—a bright, inquiring voice, which in its effort to drive out dismay left out love. She had never left out any other thing. All that anyone could suggest had been attempted for Philly. She did not grow up. Her eyes could reflect cunning or desperation but not intelligence. 'She might have been pretty,' Rose sometimes thought. But something had not quite met, not quite budded together, so that she was not whole, could not transmit thoughts wholly, nor receive them. Little took root in such stricken soil; though sometimes ('Oh, not increasingly!' Rose often prayed) a murderous growth was glimpsed. A word, an association, would suddenly tug at this mandrake-like horror, and a scene of sharp evil would erupt, not to be warded off; for neither Rose nor Emily could deny that it was unequivocally brought about. The most haphazard phrase or suggestion might disclose her virulence. And Rose hoped that Emily would always be there at those times, to hear out the inarticulate rage, take the anger to herself and in the end draw the sobbing and contorted creature to her breast.

For the most part, Philly was contented and the days passed for her—and for Emily as well, since they were always together—in busy idleness. In Rose's sitting-room, where Rose never had time to sit, they arranged collections of shells; they combed one another's hair, and watered their pots of ferns. ('Like two Victorian mermaids,' Emily often thought.) For hours, Philly sat at the table, doing what everyone called her 'shading in'—filling in pictures in old magazines with pencil strokes and smudges, working with clumsy absorption. Emily would sit at the window and watch the sea, a piece of sewing in her hands. That Rose, from posses-siveness, kept her idle, she realised; but was too apathetic to demur. She felt locked away in herself, but ignorant of her identity, and often she awoke suddenly in the night, without any idea of who she was; thinking, firstly, that she had died. Fighting her way through veils, layers, of darkness she would reach at last the small reality of being alive and in her own bed. When she could struggle towards and grasp her name, she was always reassured, and would lie back upon her pillow in relief, though weakened and depressed.

To steady herself, she tried to remember the past—the safer past of girlhood. She would cling to the picture of herself and Rose, with their long hair over their shoulders; their old-fashioned life in their chintzy, pretty home. Telling herself the story calmed her. 'Rose always wore pink,' she would lie and remember, 'because of her name, and I wore white. Father called us "the girls". We lived in a gentle world, as gentle as the names our mother had chosen for us. The tennis-court had plantains in great patches, and a sagging net which we were always running to measure with our

50

racquets. There were river-picnics: our dripping arms would reach for the slippery yellow water-lilies smelling of almonds. The dances Rose hated, I loved. Rose liked the kitchen and being with mother. Mother was everything to her, yet still she would not kiss her goodnight. "It wouldn't hurt you, such a little thing," I once pleaded with her. Now I see that it would have both hurt and violated her. "Not little!" she cried. "It would be over the whole day if I had to." Yet, *I* loved to kiss her. I loved the smell of her hair and the touch of her. Then, I liked holding hands with young men in taxis and the secret messages of entwined fingers. Rose always clasped her hands together fiercely inside her muff, looking steadily ahead, leaning forward a little. Yet Rose married and I did not.'

Now, Rose was happy at last and Emily sat at the window and watched the wrinkled sea and rarely lifted her sewing to make a few stitches.

*   *   *

On Fridays, lately, Vinny had arrived in the evenings for the weekend. Rose thought that one day he would marry Isabella. She did not know how once, when Laurence was at home on leave, Vinny had felt quite thwarted at having to stay with Isabella again. His desire to be under the same roof as Emily (a desire roused by both curiosity and compassion—two strong emotions in him) could not encompass such frustration. To protect himself from further threats—and Laurence often threatened—he had arranged to bring his mother for a holiday.

Emily had given up her room to her and moved in with Philly. It was the sea-ward room with the rattling door, and Rose had made a long plush sausage and filled it with sand to keep out the draughts.

"We are a full house," she said happily, "with Mr and Mrs Tillotson as well at the weekends."

And it was not natural now for Vinny to stay with Isabella, Laurence or no Laurence.

*   *   *

Mrs Tumulty, stepping out of the big, black wedding-taxi, looked, Rose thought, like Madame Vuillard. Her wide, bony face seemed polished, her narrow spectacles had slipped sideways. She was deeply in black, though black of a rustiness and dustiness that had derived a special texture from its defects. Under her dignity there was jauntiness, merriment on her thin lips. Though old, she was full of gay anticipation; for she loved to be with her son and to make new friends, as she was always confident of doing.

She came nimbly out of the car and stood on the drive surveying the garden and the sea down below, nodding her head in approval of the strong air. The Tillotson children, coming round the corner of the house, skirted her warily, and made a crab-like entry of the porch, watchfully stepping away from her. To them, she looked woefully black.

Rose was in the hall. She took Mrs Tumulty's cotton-gloved hand and made her a speech of welcome. Vinny and the gardener brought in the most curious weather-beaten luggage—an old leather hat-box; a round-topped trunk with labels of countries which no longer existed, hotels which had been shelled in 1916 and never risen again; a gladstone-bag; a wicker hamper. There were also Mrs Tumulty's bird-watching glasses and a

52

black japanned box in which she collected fungi; for she was a great naturalist.

Emily's bare, blowy room delighted her. She loved wild, exposed places and a wind that could make her eyes water; but she was very happy, too, in the flat in London which she shared with Vinny, reading travel-books and cowboy-stories most of the day, or going to Whiteley's (her favourite shop) and asking a lot of questions about things she had no intention of buying. She could not go on a bus without having an adventure, usually brought about by not minding her own business, and there was always some curious incident to relate to Vinny when he returned home in the evening. She had no gift for exaggeration or furbishing up a story and un-fortunately the incidents sounded flat even to herself.

She spread out her old ebony-backed brushes and looking-glass (the glass had once come loose and she had taken it from the frame and found it padded with a piece of brownish newspaper containing, in French, a reference to Napoleon); she took off her hat and combed her thin hair more evenly over her freckled scalp. Then in the mood of a great beauty going to a ball, feeling herself 'all set', she went downstairs to find out about everybody.

She was pleasurably suspicious of Vinny's seaside weekends and intended to sort things out, especially the women. Isabella she had met once before and thought her a poor, silly creature. Rose had made a better impression; Emily a much worse one. Mrs Tumulty had no especial grudge against beauty, as long as it did not detract from liveliness. Anything passive she abhorred, and Emily's dead-white skin, her lack of expression, about which Vinny had found no words to

53

forewarn her, no heart to explain or discuss, annoyed and repelled her. She could sense Emily's life drifting by in an incurious desuetude. This languid refusal of what she, Mrs Tumulty, was greedy for was irritating.

"I hope the children won't worry you," Emily said, with a vaguely polite intention; but this—to be spoken to as if she were immensely aged or an invalid—was more annoying than ever.

"I love noise," she said firmly. "I never have too much of it. I can't even settle to a book without the wireless on. I went all through the Blitz," she added. The phrase, so worn, so ignored, *she* made militant and aggressive. She had met disaster with action; had set out fully equipped, as when on her old travels, for the air-raid shelter; unpacked thermos, gas-mask, knitting; told children to get off to sleep; given information; analysed the war-news; silenced rumours. In the mornings, she had explored the streets; pushing aside broken glass with her umbrella; stepping neatly over fallen masonry. Often, with her brisk words, she had given courage.

"I don't like quiet," she reaffirmed.

Emily said nothing. She put a tray with glasses and the sherry Vinny had brought on a table near to Mrs Tumulty and drew up a chair for Vinny, who was still in his garden-room.

"Were you here all through the war?" Mrs Tumulty asked condescendingly. It was true that the war had given her a new lease of life.

"No. No, I was not."

"In London?"

"For a while."

54

"Did *you* go through the Blitz?" She made it sound like an examination, Emily thought.

"I . . . no, I'm afraid I didn't."

"Nothing to be afraid of—*not* going through it. It was much more the other way round."

"Yes, I expect so."

"Did you get called up at all?"

"For a little while."

"Only for a little while?"

"I was in hospital a long time."

"Oh dear, oh dear, very sorry." Calamity Mrs Tumulty relished. Disaster opened her heart. "Won't you have a glass of sherry, too?"

"No, thank you."

"Oh, you should. It is full of iron, you know. I love it, and the sweeter the better for me. Nothing serious, I hope?"

"I was in a car accident."

"Then I sympathise, for I nearly lost my life once that way. 'Well, this is *it*,' I remember thinking. More amazed than anything. Perhaps that's how, in the end, we most of us meet death. I saw the look of amazement on the faces of the dead during the war. I recall how it all flashed through my mind—not fear, but surprise. 'Surely not *me*!' I said to myself. Too much luggage for those Alpine roads. We skidded and turned over. I crawled out through the sunshine roof, or whatever they're called. 'Ha-ha!' I said to myself. 'Not *me* after all. I thought not.' I left my skirt behind me. We laughed about it afterwards. Oh, we did laugh! Here comes Vincent. I know that cough of his. Pure nerves. I never suffered from nerves, but his poor father did. Always fidgety. Where were you hurt, dear?"

55

Vinny switched on the light as he came in, and Emily's hand flew up to her cheek as if she had been struck.

"My face," she said in a faint, shocked voice.

Mrs Tumulty looked at her with frank interest, as no one had looked at her for years. Sipping her sherry, saying nothing, in her lack of confusion she seemed outrageous to her son.

*   *   *

Mr and Mrs Tillotson arrived just before dinner. Wind-nipped, duffle-coated, they climbed out of what they called their vintage Bentley and unpacked their luggage. Erica Tillotson wore fur-lined boots for nearly all of the year when she was not wearing open sandals, and usually corduroy skirts, and a red cotton handkerchief either over her hair or tied round her neck. She was very flushed from driving in the open car and her face contrasted darkly with her china-white teeth.

Lindsay Tillotson, though tall, frail and pallid, had the almost inhuman indifference to discomfort of many young men who have been at English public schools. In the war, when he was taken prisoner in Crete, he had watched the sturdy, the hardy—bony Scots, Australians, New Zealanders—dropping out on long marches, dying of hunger, of heat, or of cold. He had always managed to endure these things and in his spare moments wrote home to his wife about Greek temples, butterflies, flowers or wine. He so lamented the death of Virginia Woolf that death might not have been all round him: he wrote wistfully of Mozart, as if music were his only deprivation. When he came home he had scarcely altered in his appearance, for he had always seemed starved and fatigued. He looked unlike the rich business-man he was, and Mrs Tumulty put him down at once as a film director.

She was disappointed that they did not appear for dinner. Nannie and the nursemaid sat alone at the big table near the sideboard, among tins of glucose, packets of Ryvita and bottles of Scott's Emulsion. They ate quickly, with their heads bowed, and murmured and whispered to one another in snatches.

After dinner, Vinny walked down to see Isabella, and his mother took her knitting into the drawing-room. Presently, Mr and Mrs Tillotson came in. They said "good evening", settled quietly on the sofa and opened their books. For a while, nothing was said. Mrs Tumulty sometimes, when she started a new row of knitting, gave their side of the room a comprehensive glance, which took them vaguely in, but as if they were no more interesting to her than the William-and-Mary tallboy behind them. Mr Tillotson was reading Colette in French and Mrs Tillotson a war book which Mrs Tumulty had not liked to put on her library-list since reviewers had labelled it 'not for the squeamish'. She was not a squeamish reader, but liked to be a respectable library-subscriber.

She knitted quickly, as if she were limited for time; but nothing ever came of her knitting. When she was alone, she could not waste her patience on it, and she did it now only because she had hoped for conversation, which being buried in a book might have precluded. She was getting nowhere with the silence in the room, when Mrs Tillotson said, as abruptly as if she had not been reading at all: "Constance is much better."

Her husband seemed slowly to draw his attention up

57

from his book as if it were a bucket in a well. He turned a look on her, at first blank, but soon considering. He pondered her statement gravely, but half his gravity was still preoccupation with his book. He implied that it was no light affair interrupting him and he even put his finger on a word to mark his place, like a child.

"Yes," he said.

He waited as if to know whether he should begin yet to reassemble his concentration. Just as he lifted the book again and refocused his attention, she said: "But Baby looked flushed."

"I didn't notice."

To Mrs Tumulty's disappointment, they then returned to their books and Mrs Tillotson seemed absorbed. For reading, she wore some pink-rimmed glasses, which reflected on her cheek-bones, giving her an indignant look. After a while, she said: "He may be teething."

But Mr Tillotson did not reply.

*   *   *

Mrs Tumulty was no feminist. She did not use her vote, believing (although she herself could never have been sexually attractive to men) that public affairs are more effectively and picturesquely influenced behind the scenes; either by what she called 'political hostesses' or by intellectual courtesans. Hardy as she always had been, she insisted on deference to the frailty of her sex and, when she and her husband were on safari in Africa, she had always expected him to make an effort of standing up when she entered his tent, even if he bent double in doing so.

Vinny's manners she had cultivated and cherished,

58

as if they were some animate thing which care and patience would bring to sturdy growth. He had spent a boyhood of running fast across rooms to open doors, was always jumping to his feet, pulling off his cap, giving up his chair; had scarcely ever sat down for more than three seconds in a bus. He was out of cars first and into them last, and could scoop up an armful of silly little parcels and carry them down Bond Street for any lady with an asexual charm. He was too powerfully built ever to seem to dance attendance, and his manner which had been anxious and clumsy in youth had become, under his mother's surveillance, smooth and discreet. He was as calm as a Buddhist. All the same, Mrs Tumulty kept her eyes open for lapses, and several had occurred when Emily had left them before dinner.

Vincent had switched on the light as he came in and, leaving the door wide open, gone to look out of the window. Emily had hurried away. Neither had spoken. He had continued to stare out of the window at the bare garden and had suddenly begun to whistle. Rose, coming in to attend to the fire, had stopped Mrs Tumulty's protests; but as soon as the Tillotsons had gone off early to bed, she began to express her displeasure.

Vinny, still with the coldness of outdoors about him, alert from his brisk walk back from Isabella's, seemed too invigorated to sit down. He paced about the room and, as soon as his mother mentioned Emily, began to fill his pipe.

'So it is Emily!' she thought, noting this sign of discomfiture. She suddenly felt that she did not know her own son—a sensation common enough to most mothers, but new to her.

"So unlike you to be off-handed," she said, having

59

touched on everything—the open door, the lack of a 'good evening', the turned back, the whistling.

"We should not drink sherry without inviting them to join us. It is under their roof, if our own sherry. Refusal or acceptance is a nice point which we must leave to them. The fact that it is an awkward situation will only mean that they will have adjusted themselves to it by now."

"As you were already drinking the sherry, I was sure you had offered it," he said.

Mrs Tumulty frowned. As a boy he had never 'answered back', or expected to have a last word. She was disturbed, and to be more so.

"To ask," he began, wheeling round in a great circle, confronting her, "to ask such questions of her . . . of Emily . . . of Miss Otway . . . to force her to answer . . . surely it was insensitive in the extreme?"

"She had just told me she was in hospital."

"She *tells* nothing. Merely makes replies."

"I couldn't know. I am sorry, Vincent," Mrs Tumulty said with dignity. She took off her spectacles and polished them on her handkerchief. Her handkerchiefs had name-tapes sewn on them as if she were at boarding-school. "I will apologise."

"No."

"Please do not speak so fiercely to me."

"I thought you . . . stared at her," he said in great anguish.

"Nonsense. I merely looked in a kindly way. You are wrong about everything. You know so little about life—shut up at Lloyd's all day, a bachelor. You have never borne children . . . ah, you may well smile, but through one's own pain one learns about human nature."

60

"I am sorry I caused you such distress."

"You are not sorry at all. No one ever is: or grateful, either."

"You were born yourself."

"I am only trying to say that I know more of the world than you . . . there is not a continent I haven't explored. And where have you been? To the Winter Sports," she said scornfully. "I have also lived longer than you."

"That follows from what you were saying previously."

"I know that people would always rather seem interesting than pitiable. I am not suggesting that Miss Otway is abnormal in any way—if you like those Mona Lisa looks she may seem striking . . . she lacks vivacity . . . whether or not as a result of her misfortune neither you nor I can say. . . . If she is sensitive, as likely as not it is on account of other people's reticence; fear of being thought pathetic. I always think that the deformed and wounded must most of all dread to see strangers turning quickly aside, lowering their eyes, from pity or embarrassment. Very hard to bear. A good *stare* shows interest, not revulsion. I've been stared at all my life; by natives; by children. I do not find it disconcerting. Why should Miss Otway?"

He did not reply.

"Why should Miss Otway?" she repeated.

"You have been round the world for nothing if, when you return, you have still only yourself to measure her against."

"It is unlike you to speak so rudely to me, Vincent."

She rolled up her knitting and stabbed the needles through the ball of wool. "It is also unlike you to smoke your pipe in a drawing-room without permission."

His antagonism melted. He began to laugh at her, but in such a way that she smiled, too, and shook her head. She could sense that he was caught up in an adolescent fascination, unbecoming to his years, but perhaps transient.

'He should have married,' she thought. Although worried by his attitude to Emily, she was at the same time revived by this concern and went to bed with a great taste for the morrow.

*   *   *

Vinny did not go at once to bed. For some time, he had longed to have the drawing-room to himself. His mother had left the door open as if expecting him to follow her, and, pacing about the room, pretending to be reflectively smoking his pipe, he managed to elbow the door nearly shut; but dared not deliberately latch it. As if he were being watched, he meandered about the room, puffing and humming; sniffed at a bowl of jonquils; folded a discarded newspaper, and was at last fascinated by a large pink sea-shell lying on the top of a bookcase. He picked it up, swung it about at arm's-length, and then held its freckled lip to his ear as if he were listening to the sea. With the other hand he reached furtively round behind some Dresden figures and drew out two photographs in a leather holder. If the door was opened, he thought he could replace the photographs unseen and would say, in a half-sheepish, half-boyish way, holding up the shell: "These things always intrigue me . . ." or some other trite remark, to show that he felt himself caught out simply in a piece of childishness. The photographs, however, so beguiled him that when he suddenly sensed somebody in the doorway, he spun round guiltily, dropped the leather folder to the floor, snatched his pipe from his mouth and stood facing Rose in consternation, the shell held out foolishly in his hand, as if to propitiate her.

She glanced over her shoulder into the hall, then shut the door. When he had picked up the photographs, she crossed the room and took them from him in rebuke.

His elaborate precautions so often miscarried, because the curiosity and fascination, which made them necessary, also made him preoccupied. Rose, he could tell, was much more annoyed by his prying than was reasonable.

"I can't resist photographs."

It was worse than having to explain about the shell, and it was still not the truth.

'You are a menace to my happiness,' Rose thought. She looked at the folder in her hands and then opened it. Her own face seemed a creamy-sepia blur. At nineteen, her mouth drooped innocently; her eyes were unclouded by the terrors of love. She looked at the camera with a mingling of trust and doubt, as if crying out: "Be good to me!"

The companion photograph had slipped sideways behind the mica covering and she straightened it.

"Who is it?" Vinny asked. His rough voice sounded desperate.

"My sister."

He did not speak.

She handed the photograph to him, with an abrupt gesture as if she were thrusting upon him something disgusting which would hurt him only as he deserved. She watched his shock with hatred.

He wondered how the camera could make such

gaiety static. The expression seemed so fleeting that he half waited for it to change, for the mouth to straighten into gravity and the raised eyebrow to relax. He imagined her teasing the photographer, saw the poor flustered man retreating under his black tent, dazzled and confused. Her eyes did not cry out: 'Be good to me!' but the tenderness of her expression so triumphed over the mischief that instead she seemed to affirm: 'I will be good to *you*.' 'But in a minute,' her eyes added. Then, he thought, the face had vanished; before the minute came.

"Well?" said Rose.

He had so rarely known hatred in his life that he was now overwhelmed by the sensation he felt towards Rose.

"She looks gay and lovely."

"You would not have recognised her."

"No."

"No one could."

"Why do you leave this photograph here?"

"I hid it once, but the day I went to fetch her from hospital I brought it out again. I saw that it was worse for it not to be there."

"Yes, of course."

"When people try to face the truth one must face it with them."

"And the truth, after all," Vinny said, "was only that one kind of beauty replaced another."

"People did not recognise her in the street. I was with her often when it happened. She once said that she felt like her own ghost, coming back, watching everyone she had known, and no one seeing her. She tried to laugh, but it was the only time she spoke of it.

64

I dreaded her going out; and after a very little while she did not."

Vinny, glancing now at Rose's photograph, saw the timid mouth, the rigid way of holding the head. She looked ready to be wounded for everybody, and full of the sensibility which had done her sister such disservice.

"But she appears so high-spirited," he protested. He imagined her laughing (however appalled she had been, she had tried to laugh in her old way); but her little joke about being a ghost had gone astray. Rose had recoiled for her, presented her with little awkwardnesses, and had not allowed her to bring herself back from darkness and isolation. He could imagine the early opportunities going by, encounters prevented, friends warded off, until at last she was left with her own idleness and the society of a half-witted child.

He put the photographs in their place. Unspoken words clashed between him and Rose, but nothing was said save their polite good-nights.

*   *   *

In the morning, he awoke to the sound of sobbing. He seemed to swerve out of his dream, bringing the sound with him—a muffled, guttural crying which he could not understand. His mother would not have hesitated, and neither did he, but pulled on his dressing-gown and went to see what was wrong.

It was early, and light was so far only a negation of darkness in which furniture stood forward menacingly as blocks of shadow. As he opened the door leading to the kitchen stairs Emily turned in surprise. She took a pace back, and as she did so, Philly tried to slip past her towards the garden-door. She wore only her nightgown and her hands and feet were blue. Her face was covered with tears and her lips drawn back on her chattering teeth. Vinny for a moment saw scarlet marks round her wrists before Emily grasped them again, held fast to the girl, who rocked and moaned, trying to lift her arms and dash them free. She made sudden butting movements with her head and, before Vinny could stop her, bent deftly and bit Emily's hand. He took her shoulders and wrenched her away, shook her until she gasped; then, up against his strength, her own gave out, her eyelids sank and she began to weep. Holding her close and chafing her arm, he turned to Emily and took her hand which she had tried to hide behind her back. She was so cold that the teeth-marks were only beginning to redden. Blood sprang from them in bright beads. Tenderness for her, an extreme of feeling, tired him; but it was an exhaustion of the spirit only, and when he had wrapped Philly up in a blanket from his own bed he picked her up as if she were a small child and carried her easily.

Emily went up the stairs ahead of him. She wore an old blue dressing-gown and her hair was spread over her shoulders. He watched, as if it were the most surprising and exotic revelation, her pink heels lifting from her slippers as she climbed the stairs. She held back the baize-covered door for him and followed him across the landing. Still no one stirred. The house stayed in the grip of silence. A wedge of threatening light lay in the well of the staircase, but the landing, with its rows of closed doors, was dark.

Philly's room was brighter: the windows wide open and the curtains drawn back. They could hear the sea, the tide in, right up on the rocks, tumbling into inlets and dragging back with a rattling of pebbles.

"Here!" Emily said, throwing open the bed-clothes ready for Philly. He put her down gently. Still wrapped in the blanket, she lay and shivered, her hands clasped tightly on her breast, the knees drawn up sharply. Saliva had run from the corner of her mouth as he carried her, and he wiped it away on an edge of the sheet.

Emily stood back, watching him; but when he looked at her, she glanced away.

"Is she ill?" he whispered.

She shook her head.

'There is always silence,' he thought. Even downstairs, he had only asked her to fetch the blanket and she had done so without a word. As if she understood his thoughts, she seemed to make a great effort; her lips parted before she spoke. He could see that she was very cold and she struck her hands together, the one smeared with blood.

"This has happened before. She will sleep now."

"Should you fetch your sister?"

"I'll tell her later."

"Or a doctor, perhaps?"

"There is no need."

"May I fetch anything for her . . . hot-water bottles . . . brandy?"

"I'll see to it."

"But you are shivering."

She seemed to sway with the cold.

"Thank you for your help," she said, dismissing him.

Rose, on her way to the bathroom, saw the unlatched door and heard their low voices. Disbelief, then horror,

67

froze her. She locked herself away from them, leaning over the hand-basin as if she were retching, her hands gripping the cold porcelain. She felt as if someone—her sister?—had lifted an enormous sheet of ice and smashed it over her head.

Stealthy and silent from shock, she stood quite still, wondering what to do first to reassemble her sanity, the order of things, how to deal with her non-comprehension, sort out explanations. She even breathed warily. When she raised her head, she saw her reflection in the mirror before her—dazed eyes, and her two plaits hanging neatly over her shoulders.

Then she heard Vinny crossing the landing. The baize-covered door sighed and shut behind him. With absurd vehemence, Rose began to clean her teeth. She went on with this for a long time, as if she were afraid to stop; as if she could think of nothing else to do; dreading all action and suspending thought.

*　　　*　　　*

Vinny dressed and went out into the garden. He made his way down the cliff-steps, and leant over the rustic-work handrail, pretending to be watching the waves slapping the cliff down below. He saw none of it—only a picture of Emily in Philly's room, her hands pressed flat against the wall behind her, her steady look downwards. When she had turned her head sideways, her long hair made a beautiful sweeping line from brow to shoulder. Now, in his imagination, he crossed the room to her and drew back the curtain of hair, kissing her throat and her shoulder. He excused his imagination any prelude to this and in reality he could have arranged none. Inability to cross the gap from wooing to lovemaking and many unconcluded love-affairs, had left him with a large circle of women friends. They bore him no ill-will, valuing his continued attentions—presents, compliments; their pique soon vanished. They married, loved, elsewhere. Only very stupid husbands resented Vinny.

The curious hesitancy in him was caused by his romanticism, his longing for perfection. At the beginning of each relationship, he struck all the right notes; but sophistication, lightness, gallantry, could not carry him through anything so dire as passion. There were changes to make which defeated him. The circumstances were never right—pitch darkness, for instance, was, he felt, essential. Women, having been kissed and stroked, then helped into their coats, were surprised. Sometimes, they went home in such a fury of righteousness to their husbands that they behaved for a while impossibly; having, unexpectedly, no guilt to expiate, they wondered why they should waste their resolutions of kind attentiveness, exonerated as they were by their fidelity (which their disappointment very soon became to them). Next morning, roses from Vinny helped them to forgive.

On one of the few occasions when circumstances were not too daunting—a warm and moonless night in Burnham Beeches—he had been with the woman who became his wife. She took the initiative in everything, and as she detested being 'fussed' as she called it and giggled when he stroked her arms, the transition was soon—and in Vinny's mind far too rapidly—made. He thought it most inartistically done and had nothing to be pleased about in recalling the evening. In his mind, he labelled it an 'encounter', and the marriage which followed was 'buying experience dearly'. He did not so much dislike his wife as pity her for not arousing his love. He thought hers a sterile existence—since he rarely saw her—and guilt mingled with his irritation. He did not blame her for trickery, and saw as a pathetic manœuvre the imaginary pregnancy with which she hastened him into marriage. That she had gained some financial security at the expense of losing his respect for her, seemed to him a tragic bargain. He could not have lived with her or told his mother any of the story. He went to see her rarely and only with proper warning. They talked over business matters amicably. When once, from motherly sensations and a little vague pity for him, she had embraced him, he had moved neatly aside and rummaged for his pipe, hoping he had not given too much offence; but feeling violated. She did not want him in her everyday life, for she was a lascivious woman and his nice feelings shamed and bored her; but she would have missed the idea of him. He sent her picture-postcards whenever he went away, as if she were a child, and often he longed to be rid of her. This morning, he saw her in a worse light than ever before— as an obstacle between Emily and him, a loathed encumbrance in a hazard difficult enough of itself.

To win Emily now appeared to be the great task, the meaning, of his life. At his age, practised though he might be, he felt uncertainties, disadvantages that he would have dismissed in the past. All circumstances guarded her from him—ill-will and perhaps enmity— her own total indifference; his ineligibility; his impatience. For the first time, courtship was not to him an end in itself. He suffered the humiliation of desire, in the day and in his dreams. To reach her would

70

require patient drudgery. Like taming a falcon, he thought—each step forward would mean two more backwards; all progress containing the danger of failure.

'I shall soon be fifty,' he thought, and he turned and went back up the steps very briskly, as if to hurry anywhere would help.

The façade of the house had sprung alive, with curtains all drawn back and children's voices calling. A little boy leant out over a sill and was pulled back roughly by the nursery-maid. Mrs Tumulty stood at her bedroom window looking at the sea through a telescope. As he crossed the lawn, the gong sounded, filling the house with its absurd confusion and followed by the children tearing down the stairs towards the dining-room.

*   *   *

"You look peaky," Mrs Tumulty said. She whipped out the damask napkin with a crack like a whip.

"Peaky?" he said disdainfully.

"Yes, Vincent, *peaky*. As if you slept badly, or scarcely at all. Prunes," she said to the little maid who served them.

A bustle was going on at the big table by the sideboard. Nannie became a different person when Mr and Mrs Tillotson came in.

"Would this little person like a cushion to sit on?" she asked the boy, Benjamin. Puffed-wheat suddenly cascaded out of the packet the nurserymaid was opening. She blushed and Nannie gave her a look. Then she folded a cardigan and put it on Benjamin's chair.

"There now, is that better?"

"No, no better."

"Say 'thank you', Benjamin," Mr Tillotson said.

"*You* should have had prunes," Mrs Tumulty said to Vinny, who drank his coffee and kept glancing out of the window. "What are your plans for today?"

'My plans for today!' he thought. 'My plans for today are to hang about hoping for a glimpse of her, to have my heart eaten away by the thought of her; to feel my blood bounding maddeningly, ridiculously, like a young boy's; to despair; to realise the weight of my misery and hunger with each step I take.' He wanted to shut himself in his dreary room, to try to gather together some discretion; find some mode of behaviour. Every word spoken cut him; he shrank from the glances of other people—unless there was some person who would listen to him all day long while he talked of Emily and dramatised his situation. Only that could appease him.

"I haven't any plans," he said: and then, with a great effort, added: "Anything you would like. A walk," he said vaguely. He was then surprised to hear himself saying: "I think I shall buy a car." He was astonished to hear this and stared at his mother, as if she had spoken, not he.

"A car?"

"It would be more convenient." He imagined driving Emily along the leafy lanes in the summer. They came to the top of a hill and there was a shimmering view and tiny flowers set tight in spongy turf; the smell of thyme; minute faded blue butterflies; dried rabbit-droppings; empty snail-shells. He spread his jacket on the grass (because of the rabbit-droppings and

72

baby thistles) and Emily sat down on it. He began to
unpack the picnic-basket. He still could not find any
suitable dialogue for them. Emily remained mono-
syllabic.

"You remember how expensive you found the
garage," his mother reminded him.

"I heard someone crying this morning," little Constance said in a loud voice. "It was really in the night."

"Eat up, dear."

"I did. It woke me up."

"It woke me up," Benjamin agreed.

Nannie was paying great attention to them today
the children found. Usually, she and Betty, the nursemaid, just talked together and sometimes made strange
remarks, such as 'Little pitchers have long ears' and
'Someone not a hundred miles from here.'

"Was Baby crying?" Mrs Tillotson asked.

"No, madam, not a whimper. Some little people
have wonderful imaginations."

"It wasn't a baby anyhow," Constance said carelessly. "It was a lady."

Mrs Tumulty dribbled out a prune stone into her
spoon, her eyes fixed on the Tillotson table.

"I might find somewhere cheaper," Vinny said, but
she was not listening. Her ears almost seemed to move
forwards like a cat's to catch the children's words.

"I think I paid through the nose before," Vinny said,
willing her to listen to him. "From what I hear," he
persisted. "I was speaking to Fred Jackson about it the
other day . . ."

"Ladies ought not to cry," Benjamin said.

"That knife is too large for him, Nannie. Have this
little one."

73

"I like big knives."

"Do as you are told," said Mr Tillotson.

"I know ladies do sometimes cry," Constance said, glancing at her mother for confirmation, looked doubtful, and said : "At funerals, I expect."

"When their children die a mother would cry," Benjamin said patronisingly.

"May I have some more coffee, mother?" Vinny asked.

"Bible women cry," Constance was saying.

"Bible women are a lot of babies."

"Now, Benjy, we are all waiting for you," said Mr Tillotson.

"Not so much in your mouth, darling," Nannie whispered.

"I was frightened when I heard the crying."

"Thank you," said Vinny. "Shall we go for a walk? Would you like that?"

"Yes, dear, anything."

"Now, no more talking," Mr Tillotson said.

"Yes, no more stories, dear," their changed, weekend Nannie said. "What will Mummy and Daddy think?" ('You are only silly when they are here,' she seemed to imply.)

A long ritual of patent-medicines began, dollops of this and that. Vinny felt nauseated at the sight of dark brown malt being twisted down by one, a fishy cream by the other. Benjamin began to gag, unable to swallow.

"Don't be a silly boy," Nannie said. "Come along, now, woollies on and quick march."

When they had gone Mr and Mrs Tillotson drank another cup of coffee in peace.

"What was all that about, Lindsay?"

74

"One can't encourage them."

"Constance dramatises everything."

"Best to ignore it."

"But such a taste for the sensational. So sensationally inventive."

"All children are."

They spoke for a moment about the weather to Mrs Tumulty and Vincent before they left the dining-room, surveying the sky vaguely. When they had gone, Mrs Tumulty said: "I shall be ready in half an hour. In the garden."

When Vinny returned to his room, his bed was made. A different blanket replaced the one in which he had wrapped Philly. He thought that at some time during the day he would see Emily and she would make some explanation about the morning. But he rarely saw her. His meetings with her were all sudden and disconcerting.

*   *   *

When Emily told Rose about Philly and of how Vinny had helped them both, Rose felt ashamed. All the same, the truth could not quite wipe away what she had first believed with such creative intensity that, against all rationality, her imagination would not be wasted. It left some residue in her mind which had always been a good soil for her suspicions.

From the first, her marriage had been destroyed by her inventive jealousy. Obsessed by sex as only those who fear it can be, she had watched her husband patiently for signs that other women were less disdainful than she was herself. In his simple bonhomie she found plenty to torment her. Once, seeing his pleased glance at a girl sun-bathing, she had pretended a sudden and violent illness. They returned to the house. He was doggedly sympathetic in the practised weary manner so often seen in the husbands of ailing wives. Nothing was too much trouble and her sickness became real to both of them and even, such was the triumph of mind over matter, to her doctor. Some nights later, when they were at last in a convalescent state with one another, she dreamed of the young girl and of what, in the nightmare, was his desire for her. Furiously, yet greedily, in her dream, she concocted for them behaviour she would never have admitted to her thoughts. In the morning, the dream so hung over her that she could not bring herself to look at her husband, or face her own degradation. She had neither the humour nor common-sense to digest frailty or imperfection. She tried to wrench life round into her own pattern. Friends and relations, unable to comply, drifted away, and her own husband drifted away, not with other women, as she had feared; but with excessive drinking. There were always loopholes, she saw, and people fled through them. She fled away from herself in her own dreams, which took revenge on her self-discipline in the most startling and decisive way.

All day, her manner towards Vinny was brisk and evasive. Suspicion seemed to her more logical than the truth and its impact so very much more lasting.

Chapter 5

"Oh, I have always been one of those safe women," Isabella said resentfully.

She and Evalie Hobson had the steam-room to themselves. They sat naked on a slatted bench, knees apart, heads bowed; in an attitude of passive dejection.

"I never endangered anyone's marriage," Isabella continued. "Wives *like* me. You say when you've had enough."

"Another five minutes," said Evalie.

Isabella sighed. "One gets married young. My sort has to, inclining to fatness. As much as one can do to keep up with being a wife and mother, and reading all the magazines, let alone being a menace to the other sex. Now I've absolutely forgotten how to attract them. I wonder how I ever got Harry."

"We look discarded, sitting here," Evalie said. "As if we were waiting for a train which never comes."

"I think it is the most terrible time of my life," Isabella said simply.

"Yes, so terrible."

"I'm sure I've done everything I could think of . . . those beauty articles . . . I could write them myself in my sleep. I tried every pot of face-cream I ever saw. When I was a girl, I was really quite pretty; but unattractive all the same. You've got better bones than me." She turned and had a good look at Evalie. "To your face," she amended. "How arched your insteps are!"

Evalie turned her hands over and over, examining every pore of her glistening skin.

"Sometimes," Isabella continued, "I know that wickeder wives than I liked to have me up their sleeves. 'Why not take Isabella out to lunch?' I am sure they said to their husbands. Perhaps even 'poor Isabella'... no, they would be too clever for that. I can just hear it. Thrusting them towards safety, so that they themselves could run off in the other direction. If they were found out, they could say: 'Oh, but darling, *you* took *Isabella* out.' And because I wasn't so terrible to look at—just undesirable in an undefined way—no one could say anything, though everyone *knew* everything."

"Yes," Evalie said. "My scar comes up so," she added. Isabella inspected it with almost Oriental courtesy, although she wished that Evalie would sometimes attend to what she was saying.

"Shall we go now?"

They rose and drew their wraps round them.

"What I detest is the way our breasts go out sideways when we get older. They look as if they're tired of one another's company."

In the hot-room they sat down in deck-chairs. Slim girls with brown narrow backs and neatly-painted toenails guarded their beauty jealously, with towels carefully tucked up under their armpits. They sipped lemon-juice and knitted, glancing in a bored way at newcomers. An enormous woman in a pink plastic cap slowly stirred and stood up. Her dimpled thighs were like beaten pewter. In the next room, Henry Moore figures were being slapped rosy on marble slabs. The sound was like applause; a terrifying ovation.

78

"We must have lost pounds," Evalie whispered.

"It will all go back on again at tea-time."

Evalie read her newspaper, and Isabella sat staring in front of her, wiping her face with her towel. She felt dreadfully low, realising now why she had been so buoyed-up of late. For weeks, she had thought that Vinny would ask her to marry him. Evalie had been certain that his weekend visits meant this and, indeed, they had appeared so. She had liked to be teased on his account and her manner had grown a little fussy and important. Laurence had become more and more sarcastic. Isabella, acquainted with Vinny's delicacy, had expected to wait weeks or months before she had the pleasure of refusing him. She was not a cruel woman and was sure that Vinny would not suffer from this refusal, or she could not have contemplated the scene with such pleasure. The thought of her gay and tender rejection had been her chief comfort in the last few weeks: it had been constantly rehearsed. She had day-dreamed of a future secure in his gallantry and affection; with occasional luncheons together; always his wistful teasing; the proposal renewed on every—say—St Valentine's Day, half as a private joke, but nevertheless with true pleading. He would shore up her pride and look at her through kindly eyes. Her friends would be perhaps rather envious and she longed to be the subject of conjecture, a thing she had never been in her life. Vinny would be a reason for buying new clothes, 'and one must have a reason,' she thought now. She wiped sweat from her arms and glanced at Evalie.

"Did you see that Jack Frost won at Leopardstown?"

"No," said Isabella.

She thought: 'They will all laugh at me now—

Laurence, Evalie. I have to laugh at myself. I even seem to hear Harry's teasing laugh in heaven.'

Morning coffee with Mrs Tumulty—and she did not like her, had invited her almost as a duty to a rejected mother-in-law—had made her wretchedly depressed. Mrs Tumulty, on the other hand, had had a fascinating day. To begin with, Rose had been so obviously put out by mention of any commotion in the early morning. "Such dreadful crying," Mrs Tumulty had said. "It quite alarmed me. 'Someone is ill,' I said to myself." In reality she had heard nothing. She had merely listened to Benjamin and Constance at breakfast-time and was sure that she knew enough about children to guess when there was a grain of truth in what they said. She could also guess that there was not a grain of sincerity in Rose's denial and puzzled, surprised look.

She and Vinny had gone for a gloomy walk along the esplanade. He was so poor a companion that when they met Isabella and she asked them to coffee she had been glad of a change and not sorry when Vinny had gone off for a haircut.

Isabella was quite aware of the curious glances people gave Mrs Tumulty, whose rusty black skirt trailed unevenly above lavender wool stockings. Dust lay in the folds of her felt hat, which every year she remodelled for the Spring, adding a cockade, or cutting away pieces of the brim. This year, she had stitched on a piece of glacé black ribbon and a bunch of rag violets.

In the café, Isabella had looked down at the table most of the time. Under the glass top, paper doyleys were arranged in a pattern. These seemed imprinted on her mind, as Mrs Tumulty exposed to her the fact of Vinny's love for Emily—so great, apparently, as to make him suddenly churlish, inconsiderate, silent.

"I can't imagine Vinny churlish," Isabella had faltered.

The violets jerked and nodded—very carelessly sewn on, Isabella thought.

"Who *could* have imagined it?" Mrs Tumulty agreed. "Who on earth? Even I was surprised. And I think I know my son. I guessed something amiss from the way he's been coming down here, week after week."

Isabella had raised her eyes and looked bravely across at the old woman. The second reaction from the disclosure was that she would no longer be more than barely civil to her. The first reaction had been a sense of bereavement.

"Never underestimate a cat," a vet had once said to her, and she derived some amusement from this recollection; but it was a lonely amusement and could not be shared.

Now, as she sat sweating wretchedly in her deck-chair, a swarthy woman in a dark woollen swimsuit beckoned her. She went in to her massage, leaving Evalie with her newspapers. Lying on her warm soapy slab as if she were to be sacrificed, she thought: 'How lucky that I laughed at people who teased me about Vinny! But I suppose I have never really managed to deceive anyone in my life.'

"It is like being back at boarding-school," Evalie said, when they were lying side by side in their curtained cubicles.

'For we never grew up,' Isabella thought.

There was even Evalie's conspiratorial chatter about

racing. She now thought very highly of Jack Frost and had a great history of him to tell.

'Saturday evenings are the worst of the week when one is lonely,' Isabella decided. She touched her own arms rather shyly; they felt so newly smooth, so young. All the time, though, a secret damage was being done to her. The wrinkles strengthened and stood; industriously, flesh accumulated from her every little extravagance and indulgence. Her body plotted against her. Evalie took this very philosophically, even negligently.

"Rokeby Venus was scratched," she was saying. "That we must take into account."

'If he married Emily,' Isabella thought, 'there will never be any of the little outings I planned—lunching with him in London. Unless once more because I am thought to be so safe. A harmless treat that wives can well afford their husbands.'

Tea was brought to them.

"The cups are so thick there's no room for the tea," Evalie said. She sat up in bed and poured out. Her damp hair hung snakily round her face. "It is like being in a nursing-home," she said. "Any minute now I feel they'll bring in our babies for the six o'clock feed."

And Isabella had fallen fast asleep with a comb stuck in her hair.

*   *   *

"Whatever inclined you to turquoise?" Nannie asked the nursery-maid, Betty.

"It just looked summery."

She had slipped on her new coat and was turning round before the long looking-glass. The insides of the sleeves felt smooth and new.

"How many months of the year, though, can we take the advantage of a summer coat?"

"Well, I shall wear it this evening."

"It's hardly weather for a pale colour. Far better save it for a nice day. A real scorcher you need for that shade."

But saving clothes half wasted them. To get their true magic one must snatch them at once from their box, shake tissue-paper all over the floor, put them on and go out. Anywhere, to be seen. Her mother called it 'hacking things on the minute you get them'.

"Well, you look nice," Nannie said kindly. "I only thought it was different to what you'd set your mind on. I wondered whatever made you turn to that shade. You've got a nice choice, though; I'll say that."

She gathered up all the discarded paper and Betty ran to her room where her stockings steamed in front of the gas-fire. She put them on carefully and they steamed on her legs for a few minutes more. She thought that the dangers of damp clothes were easily over-emphasised. Nannie made her hold the children's vests to a looking-glass, searching for the faintest film; but she never did when she was on her own.

She tied a silk scarf over her hair and gave her reflection an odd look or two. Her eyebrows lifted; her nostrils dilated. 'I beg *yours*!' she seemed to be saying. 'I'm afraid I haven't had the pleasure.' 'I certainly am *not* going your way.'

'To be out of uniform! To be out!' she thought, as she ran downstairs.

*　　　*　　　*

Laurence arrived unexpectedly and the house was empty. Isabella was still at the Turkish baths. The fire was laid, but not lit. The evening paper was on the doormat. He took it into the kitchen, spread it out on the table and carefully worked out his day's winnings, which came to two and threepence. Then he made himself a cup of tea; but he really liked Army tea, orange-coloured, with condensed milk if possible. The empty house made him feel restless, and after a while, he wrote a note to his mother and went out.

The shops were beginning to close. He did not often look into shop-windows; but now he examined them carefully for want of much else to do. Rhubarb on bright blue paper, pork-pies cut in halves to show the pink, marbled meat and grey jelly, piles of black-puddings, faggots, all suggested a cosy domesticity which he missed at Aldershot, where no one went out to choose and buy the food they ate. The florist's disturbed him—the cool, scented interior. He breathed deeply, standing by the open door and looking in at the pots of ferns on the damp wooden floor and then at a green-and-brown orchid with a hanging jaw. He would have liked to buy some flowers for his mother—even the orchid—and his hand touched his money in his pocket; but then he did not know how he would ever give it to her, and feared lest she should be too pleased, so that he would be made guilty and embarrassed. He wandered on.

At the end of the street, where the gardens were, he could see trees with pale pink blossom, and this he thought very pleasant after all the chestnuts and the raspberry-coloured May at Aldershot. He was not unhappy there; but he never again cared for chestnut-trees; just as, although he had not been unhappy at school, Lombardy poplars, which had bordered the

84

playing-fields there, now had a discouraging effect upon him.

The lovely violet light over the town, flowing down the streets, stirred him; even—for he was a guarded and cautious youth—excited him. A weekend at Portsmouth, with his best friend, Len, had begun the unsettling. Len's mother had constantly talked of what she called 'Len's young lady'. The young lady had come to tea on Sunday. She sat on the arm of Len's chair and kept slapping his wrist. They were the centre of attraction and much indulged. Laurence had envied Len the lordly way in which he sprawled in his chair, grinning, fondling the girl, being waited on by his mother. "Bye-bye, Laurie," the young lady had said. She kissed Len's mother, and she and Len went out to the back-door to say good-bye. They were a long time gone and Len loafed back, scratching his head, smiling to himself. Laurence, trying not to show curiosity, had become grumpy and silent. He would dearly have liked a young lady of his own, even if like Len's she said only 'So what?' and '*I* should care!' He could not imagine ever having anyone of his own who would have such an easy relationship with his mother, kissing her goodbye, winking at her, joining that confederacy against the foibles, the conceits of men. The idea staggered him: yet it was not impossible to see his mother playing much that kind of role—chiding, affectionate, woman-to-woman. The imaginary young lady assumed any part he liked to allot her; only he himself was intractable.

The most bitter thing for a child is to see in another just the kind of son his mother deserved, and Laurence was always doing this. Whenever boys teased their mothers, flung about their homely banter (American youths in films did it most of all), he realised how exactly they complemented Isabella, and he mourned for her; then longed to leave her, before some terrible and alien phrase was forced from him in pity.

All of his friends made better efforts—unless it was no effort at all—the Lens and Syds and Rons, whose names sounded so strangely to Isabella, used until now to Hay-Hardy and Ross-Amberley and Bagshot-Hepburn Minor. ("Surely, dear, you don't call them by their Christian names?") At no cost to themselves that he, Laurence, could see, they fell into the necessary chiding, rallying and rudenesses required of them. This rather contemptuous attitude which mothers seemed to delight in from their sons, was strongly resented when coming from their daughters. "Don't you speak to me like that, miss!" Laurence had been interested to hear Len's mother snapping at her daughter. "Fancy wearing red at your age!" the girl had said—a remark which, when made by Len a little earlier, had elicited chuckles, mock fury, and a flustered: "Oh, get along with you," when he had tried to kiss her. Laurence was fascinated by this scene and wondered if a sister of his own would have eased his lot and made him behave more naturally.

He stopped outside the cinema. He saw so many films that he could never remember them. The poster of a girl in a topee and breeches, with blonde hair to her waist and an unbuttoned shirt, seemed familiar, but the warm puffs of air coming from the foyer enticed him. He liked the smell of carpet and smoke and disinfectant. The film was half-way through; but, like so many of his generation, he was adept at piecing together two parts of a story offered in the wrong order. No difficulty occurred to him. It was only a matter of 'seeing it round'. "I stayed to see the film round," he would explain to his mother.

He followed a girl in a turquoise-blue coat and stood behind her at the ticket-office. Len would have thought her a fine young lady, and when she asked for one two-and-fourpenny, Laurence did the same.

He trod clumsily after her, tripping on carpets as yielding as feather-beds, into the darkness which a great, vibrating film-voice dominated. Unaccountable (since he could not look at the screen without stumbling) silences fell, followed by gusts of laughter. He plunged steeply downhill after the girl, drawn forward by wavering torchlight, then brushed past a row of resentful people, who put their knees sideways, or half rose, clutching bundles to them. He sat down next to the girl, who immediately untied her silk head-scarf and smoothed her blonde hair with her hands. She settled down in a businesslike way, unbuttoning her coat, combing her hair and putting her gloves into her handbag. All the time, she stared ahead. He stared at her, until the smart click of her bag when she shut it brought him to his senses. He folded his arms and looked at the screen. After a while, he was quite sure that he had seen the film before. He recognised crocodiles launching themselves into the muddy river and monkeys behaving satirically in trees. The story he could not have distinguished from many others so much the same—the humbling by love of a too rebellious young woman—and it was drawing towards its reassuring conclusion that, even if she triumphs over the rigours of the jungle, no woman escapes the doom of her sexuality: a satisfactory conclusion; no surprise to anyone.

Films never surprised Laurence, who sat through all of them in a daze of acceptance, not looking for them to have reference to any life he had known—school, or home, or Aldershot; certainly not that revelatory glimpse of life at Len's in Portsmouth. Although the cinema could never surprise him, his surroundings often did, and he was now astonished to find that the girl beside him, whom he had forgotten while he was adjusting himself to the film, was leaning heavily towards him, as far away as she could gather herself from the man on her other side. The air seemed to throb with uneasiness. Laurence could see the back of the man's hand against her thigh, his foot groping for hers. Both man and girl looked almost desperately ahead of them at the screen: he to disguise his intentions; she, Laurence was sure, to hide her humiliation.

"Would you like to change places?" he suddenly asked.

Once, at school, he had extricated a younger boy from an unequal and bloody fight. The look of gratitude, the upward glance of relief and disbelief, had sickened him. Irritated by pity, shamed by feelings of grandeur and reluctantly appalled by the child's suffering, he had for ever after avoided him, though the expression in his eyes he could not banish. The young girl looked at him now in the same way, but this time he felt excited and almost reckless.

They exchanged seats. He enjoyed enormously a feeling of having dominated a situation. He sat up very straight, his arms folded again across his chest. He looked stern and protective. The man beside him slumped away, sighed, and presently got up and went out.

When the lights came up for an interval, Laurence stretched his legs and yawned, taking no notice of the girl, as if to assure her of the disinterestedness of his chivalry. Organ music swelled up and he began to hum.

"Thank you ever so much," the girl said primly.

He turned and smiled. He had never felt so confident.

"You get more embarrassed than anything," she explained.

Under her eyes, her skin was a foxglove colour with golden freckles. The rest of her face was thickly powdered. All the same, holding her opened handbag up high so that she could peer into some cracked glass on its flap, she began to touch herself up with a grubby puff. Looking down over his shoulder, he observed the brisk, dispassionate way in which she repaired imaginary damage. She reminded him of Len's young lady; but younger, more timid, prettier.

*　　　*　　　*

Philly slept until the afternoon. When she awoke, she was afraid, as she was always afraid of any alteration in her day. The roughness of the blanket in which she was wrapped frightened her. The light on the ceiling was not the light to which she usually awoke. Shadows, falling differently, gave a different look to the room, and she could not explain this to herself. Rose, not Emily, sat at the window. She turned her head, hearing Philly whimpering, and came over to the bed.

"Are you better, darling?" she asked in her bright, unloving voice.

89

Philly put her face pettishly to the pillow.

"Do you want to get up?"

"Shall I dress you?"

"Would you like tea in bed?"

Her questions were like neat flicks of a whip, and they cut her, as well as her daughter, so that she longed to return to inanimate things—the scrubbed afternoon kitchen; trays ready for the drawing-room; kettles to be filled.

Philly had turned her head a little from the pillow and watched her mother suspiciously. Her unfocused eyes looked scarred, as if from incessant weeping. There had always been a faint downiness on her jaw and round her mouth and this was beginning to coarsen and darken. Rose could see no trace of the empty prettiness Philly had had as a young child. Because she could not think of more to say, she knelt down beside the bed, and with a sensation of overwhelming revulsion laid her cheek against Philly's and took her hand. She did not need to formulate her despair and anxiety. For the thousandth time she simply cried to herself: 'Oh, *why*?'

Philly's eyes did not move.

'How sad!' Emily thought, coming into the room. She tried to go away again, pretending to have seen nothing; but Philly, sensing her there, stiffened, listened, then called out, moving impatiently from her mother's arms as if the embrace were of no consequence.

For the rest of the afternoon, she was with Emily. In Rose's sitting-room, she sat slackly by the fire while Emily cut patterns in folded paper to amuse her. Philly liked to shake out the lacy mats and to watch the scissors turning in Emily's hands. Fans, strings of paper dolls, lay over the floor. Cosiness produced silence, inertia, a deadness of spirit.

At five, Emily fetched their tea. They often comforted themselves in their strange isolation with picnic meals at odd times, trays brought in by the fire, little snacks of toasted cheese, cups of chocolate. It was as if they were very old and could achieve a slumbrous contentment from a warm fire and sweet drinks. Yet sometimes Emily would suddenly rise and go to the window. She would strike her hands together and, for an instant, close her eyes. As this day wore on towards evening, she needed more concentration than ever to still her restlessness. She heard the voices of the children in the garden and a cascade of bird-song before it grew dark—a haunted hour, goading, overthrowing. She both wanted to go out into it and never to be pained by it again.

"You see!" she cried gaily, holding up a paper lantern. Her nurse had shown her these things on rainy afternoons long ago. Rose had not remembered.

When it was at last dark, Emily drew the curtains thankfully. 'That is that!' she thought, meaning the day was gone. It had promised nothing and given nothing. She let Philly stay on after her usual bedtime, hoping that she would sleep more soundly.

"Why did I get up so late?" the girl asked, frowning with vexation because she had torn one of the paper mats.

"You slept badly. You had a disturbed night."

The fire had fallen low and there were no more logs in the basket. Philly dropped the torn paper on to the dull ashes and watched it flare up. She shivered and then began to throw everything Emily had made into the grate. Flames reached up and consumed them.

Emily, who had spread out a game of Patience on the table, left it half-finished and went to sit by Philly.

"Bed in five minutes," she said.

She sat on the rug with her elbow on Philly's knees. The charred paper on the fire creaked; white ash had mounted up. To feed the shortening flames, they began to tear up Philly's scribbling books—old magazines, fashion-papers. Philly's face darkened with exertion. As they cast the pages, one by one, on to the fire, the flames raced up, and brightened the room; shadows suddenly arched up the walls. It seemed to matter, even to Emily, that they should keep the fire going, and she tore up the paper dreamily, her eyes narrowed lazily, against the wavering heat. 'How absurd,' she thought. 'I must have some great gap, defect, in my own mind, that such things can absorb me.' And she hoped that Philly had those long stretches of peace and lethargy. At last they had no more to burn and Philly looked about disconsolately. They felt their spirits diminish with the fire; the light flattened; Philly sagged with fatigue.

When she had put her to bed, Emily came back to the cold room. The grate was stuffed with layers of black paper which moved tinnily in the draught from the chimney. She went to the table and began, from habit, to move the playing-cards about. Her hand was very quick and deft; putting up aces, shifting kings. 'If it comes out,' she told herself, 'if I can finish it, I promise myself . . .' But she could see that the game would not come out. She stared at the cards for a moment, then swept them up and paced about the room, shuffling them restlessly. She shuffled them over and over again, without knowing that she did.

Hearing a door slam, she started, and let the cards fall to the floor. They flew in a bright shower from her hands, but she did not heed them. Knowing that it was Vinny's door she had heard, and now recognising his footsteps on the gravel, she went quickly from the room and out of the kitchen entrance into the dark garden. As he came from the shrubbery, she moved away from the house towards him.

He had thought of her all day, looked for her, wondered how they might meet, made elaborate plans. All of those plans, the artifice, designed accidents, continued coincidences, were made to seem absurd now by the simple and resolved fact of her coming to him, hurrying from the house to intercept him, with no coat, her cold hands clasped on her breast and saying—stammering, hesitant, her words so unprepared: "I should like, if you will . . . may I talk to you?" Then she looked round the unfriendly garden at the shrubs bowing in the wind, thought of the chilly, untidy room with the scattered cards, and laughed. "But where?" she asked. "I don't know *where*."

*   *   *

When, once or twice, during the short film, Laurence laughed aloud, the girl beside him laughed too. On their own, neither would have made a sound or seen so many jokes.

The big film, coming round again, was a signal for a general settling-down. Everywhere, couples subsided; heads came together; arms went along shoulders; deceptively slumbrous, lovers seemed an immune audience. Introductory music surged over them and drove them closer together; but beneath the inertia,

93

Laurence was conscious of a covert business; of hands exploring, of breathing quickening.

He wondered how Len had begun with his young lady, how he had initiated the affair—slyly, or impulsively; with some encouragement, or none? All of the couples in front of him appeared already to have an understanding; they sank towards one another as naturally as if to their accustomed places. He saw no beginners.

The girl at his side sometimes gave a prim little cough and he had an idea that this was a reminder to him of her presence, as when she shuddered at the sight of a python knotted round a branch and swaying its spade-like head above the heroine's.

Laurence decided to take his very next opportunity, and when hostile natives began a frenzied war-dance, he put his arm through the girl's, and clasped her hand, as if to reassure her throughout the heroine's predicament. She seemed not to notice his action: her hand simply lay in his, giving no answering pressure; but when he once untwined his fingers, testing her, she did not draw her hand away; she let it rest on his, palm upwards, trustingly. Her skin was rough, her nails so short that he wondered if she bit them, and hoped she did. He did not want a young lady too tranquil, too defined.

"I just picked her up at the pictures," he intended to tell Len; but beyond his pride in the adventure, he felt wonderfully as if he were throwing out a canopy of protection over her: tenderness mingled with triumph, an uncomplicated tenderness such as he had never known before, a triumph elevating and serene.

She narrowed her hand and drew it from his, began to button up her coat, not looking any more at the

94

screen. She glanced at him uncertainly. "Where I came in," she whispered.

"Where I came in, too."

He got up quickly and followed her out. Beyond the bright foyer, the street was dark now. The commissionaire leant informally against the ledge of the ticket-kiosk talking to the girl inside. Their yawning, desultory conversation echoed dully. ("You don't say" . . . "That's right" . . . "Fancy!" . . . "Makes you think, eh?" . . . "You're right" . . . "What a life!" . . . "Well, we live and learn" . . . "You're right!") They caught yawns from one another. The commissionaire pushed back his hat and scratched his head. The cashier scratched hers more daintily with a pencil.

"Well . . ." Betty said, glancing up and down the dark street, shivering. Nannie had been right in one way—the coat was not warm enough.

Laurence put his arm through hers and very masterfully guided her down the road to the milk-bar. Inside, under the fluorescent lights her golden hair looked greenish. A late-at-night untidiness prevailed. Waitresses with dirty aprons shouted crossly at one another, wiped down tables resentfully, brushing crumbs on to the littered floor.

"Two coffees," Laurence said.

"Two coffees," bawled the waitress.

"Anything to eat?" Laurence asked.

The girl shook her head, and in any case the waitress had gone away.

"Where do you live?"

"I'm staying up on the Cliff Road. I'm a children's nurse and we brought them here to get over the whooping-cough. I'm not in quarantine, though, or anything like that. Anyhow, I had it when I was four. Did you ever have it?"

"Whooping-cough? I couldn't say," Laurence replied carelessly, as if children's ailments were rather beyond his scope. After a while, feeling that he had offered nothing about himself, he said: "I'm in the Army."

She glanced gravely at his uniform, not smiling.

"My name's Laurence Godden."

She admired this name for a moment or two. Taking the evening step by step was like going over the tracks of a daydream. She thought that she had experienced just as much as she would be able to remember in bed that night. Bliss so crowded in that she was sure her memory would contain no more. She was in some ways —emotionally, at least—a cautious, hoarding girl. Feeling herself incapable of further happiness; wanting to save, not waste, her pleasure, she refused a second cup of coffee. Instinct urged her to hurry home with her treasure and count it over in solitude.

"What is *your* name?" Laurence asked.

"Betty Logan."

"How long will you be here, in Seething?"

"I don't know. They don't tell you. Until Baby picks up, I expect."

Laurence hoped that Baby would not pick up for months. He did not care if—he? she?—lay at death's door indefinitely.

"Will you come out with me again?"

"Well, yes, I'd quite like to."

"Sure?"

"Yes, I'm quite sure."

Laurence dropped sixpence on to the table as they

went out. He did not slip it genteelly under his saucer, she noticed.

The streets were almost empty. An obviously betrothed couple stood looking in at the lighted window of a furniture shop at a three-piece suite labelled 'Uncut Moquette'. Doors of pubs swinging open sharply let out wedges of light, a gusty, Saturday-night hubbub.

They crossed the open space to the sea-front and Laurence said: "That's where I live," pointing to the row of houses by the pier.

'Quite a little house,' she thought.

Laurence imagined his mother alone there—unless with that Vinny—behind the drawn curtains, and he felt a curious triumph, a hardening against her, standing there with the girl beside him.

They walked on. "But aren't you going home?" she asked.

"When I have seen *you* home."

She settled again to her contentment. Passing the Italian Gardens, where the Public Conveniences stood at the entrance, hedged with euonymus and laurel, he pulled her close to him and kissed her. He did it a little roughly and clumsily and not as he had intended, and he hoped that she would not notice or compare the embrace unfavourably with others. In the light from a street-lamp he saw her blink; she looked jolted, as if the breath had been knocked from her.

Incredulity surmounted all other feelings in her. In first love—and to some people for ever after, too—the long-anticipated is strangest of all; the inevitable cannot be believed; the familiar daydream becomes the most unfamiliar reality. Love had seized her as unexpectedly as would sudden death.

Having seen this look on her face, he drew her head to his shoulder again, moved his cheek tenderly against her hair, kissed her eyelids. A half-drunken man stumbled towards the lavatory, unbuttoning himself, muttering stupidly. Laurence held Betty tightly to him as they walked on; as if to keep her quite safe from the ugliness in the world.

*   *   *

"But it is done from kindness," Emily insisted.

They were walking along the esplanade and Vinny's condemnations of Rose kept checking her as if, standing still, she could protest the better. Though they had walked with a wide space between them, each time she stopped, he went closer to her by the sea-wall and they looked over the sands together. When she had finished her argument, they would move on until the next provocation.

"And I do not mind," she added.

Her hands, which rested on the stone wall, were bare of gloves, of rings. The darkness suited her looks, he decided; deciding also that a woman would pretend to misunderstand, hearing that. It was simply that the contrast of her pallor was now more dramatic and that, having no colour by day, she lost nothing by darkness.

He said: "You give her more than ever she gave you —her peace, her security; you compensate her for all she lacks; you shield her from her own child."

"I do it gladly."

"And if one day you began *not* to do it gladly, you began to chafe against imprisonment. . . ."

"Imprisonment?" She laughed, and looked at him scornfully.

98

". . . And wished for more scope and something of your own?" he continued smoothly.

"I should not."

"You *could* not."

"Why 'could' not?"

"You are shutting doors one after another which you will soon find are *finally* shut. Shut fast. You inside, the world outside."

"I shall want nothing different," she said impatiently.

"We never know what we shall want from one year to another—every age a dangerous age in so many ways. . . ."

The discussion had begun at the beginning of the esplanade. As they had come off the sands, he had suddenly invited her out to luncheon the next day, to hire a car, he suggested, and drive into the country. She had half-a-dozen reasons for not going—her dread of being in public places; the interest which would be aroused in Mrs Tumulty and the other guests; the embarrassment of explaining to Rose; the fact that Sunday luncheon was a busy time when Philly must be kept out of mischief; her own deep disinclination for anything different. She gave one or two of the reasons, but neither the first nor the last. The idea could not appeal to her because she did not allow the possibility of acquiescing: it was dismissed at once for her, but she could not so easily dismiss it for him. He saw that the hardest job would be to make her ever consider such an invitation (once considered, surely he could persuade her by one method or another?); but her objections were ready-made and unconditional. She was so sure, that she was not offended by any of his remarks, and only faintly surprised. She denied his most personal onslaught coolly. That he was a stranger could make no difference to her, since there were only strangers in her life. In Vinny's experience the one possible alternative to enjoying talking of oneself was to shrink from doing so. To be calmly unconcerned, as was Emily, as she appeared to him to be, was something he had not met before.

"It was kind of you to come and explain to me about Philly," he had said earlier.

"I owed you that, at least," she had replied.

There had been nowhere in the house for them to talk and she had fetched her coat at once when he had suggested this walk. He waited for her in the garden and, seeing her come running out of the porch with her light step, he had been filled with pleasure and anticipation; but conversation between them had turned out differently from his expectations. Her frankness and friendliness only underlined the fact that she was beyond his reach and had no need to be guarded with him.

On their way through the garden, they had passed the drawing-room window. As they trod softly on the grass, they could see into the uncurtained room where Mrs Tumulty and Mrs Tillotson were in earnest conversation. Mrs Tumulty had dropped her knitting. She sat upright in a winged chair, her fingertips just meeting across her stomach. Mrs Tillotson leant forward, her chin on her fist, an intense expression about her mouth, as if she were talking sensibly about something emotional—such as sex or religion. Yet Vinny guessed that his mother was only telling her how to bring up children; describing how she had reared him; sat up all night through scarlet-fever; taken him to

Weymouth for his holidays; fed him on wholemeal bread; been mother, father, nurse, wife, god-parent, teacher, confessor, psycho-analyst to him. Mr Tillotson sat on the sofa, staring at her in wonder, his finger on a word in his book.

Vinny rather disloyally described such a monologue to Emily and heard her laughing softly beside him as they went down the steps to the sands.

"So you never married?" she asked.

"No," he said sadly.

She thought his sadness was because he had not; but it was really because he had lied to her.

"Why do you bother about people?" she now asked him. "I never do."

"Oh, I am too interfering, I know," he said. "But from the same standard, you are not interfering enough. In my own defence, I must say that to be curious *is* to be at least in the outgoing stream. An inquisitive man cannot help but touch life at many points, be drawn onwards, as one should be—from whatsoever motive. The danger isn't from lack of discrimination, but from choosing nothing at all . . ."

"Danger?"

"Danger of death."

"I have chosen nothing," she echoed lightly. "Yet some in the same circumstances might say that they had chosen their duty."

"You made *no* choice," he insisted. "Your days are filled now with things chosen for you."

"And all that I lack was rejected for me." She thought of her old life, of her lover who had left her. "You have been very censorious."

"Only for my own sake. I so wanted you to come

with me tomorrow that I could not accept any of the excuses you made. If you had said: 'I do not care to,' it would have been my own private loss and I should never have questioned you; but your saying that you may not leave that child or do anything to displease your sister; that you meet no one, go nowhere, reveals the sort of life I can't contemplate for anyone, you least of all."

Coming to the end of the sea-wall, she touched the last stone as if it were a superstition of hers, then turned and began to walk homewards; but she did not answer him.

"I hope Philly won't try going for walks tonight," she said tiredly. "Or Rose will be losing all her visitors."

"Is it wise for you to keep her there?"

She looked at him sharply, and he added: "The responsibility . . . the fact that she might do herself harm."

"Away from me, I think she'd die anyhow."

Across a grassy space with shrubs, the Victoria Hotel was floodlit—lamps hidden in rockeries flung up such a glare upon the façade that balconies, gables, verandahs were bone-white. Dance-music floated away from the building.

"Would you like a drink?" Vinny asked her.

"Oh, no, thank you."

She recoiled from the idea, even to taking a pace, physically, away, nearer to the sea-wall.

"You'll accept nothing from me—no drives in the country, luncheons, sound advice. Not even a glass of brandy."

"I accept the kindness which lies behind all the offers."

" 'Kindness' implies condescension. If I were ever allowed to give you anything, the only kindness would be yours to me. The gift could only be a tribute . . ."

"You are very good at this sort of conversation," she said.

". . . a tribute to your beauty," he added.

She looked away.

"In which no other woman I have ever seen equals you."

"You pay so many compliments."

"I have paid them all my life, not realising until now how I threw away my words."

"Shall we go by the road or sands?" she asked, pausing at the end of the esplanade.

He thought the sands more romantic, but regretted the choice as soon as they began to climb the cliff-steps. Although in good health always—as most inquisitive people are, since curiosity whips up the circulation and gives an appetite—he had begun of late to feel breathless when going upstairs. He became silent and tried not to breathe too loudly, but he could hear an annoying buzzing in his head, and his temples throbbed. Emily went up so lightly. Her hand scarcely touched the rail. At the top, he was desperate at the thought of saying goodnight to her with no promise of seeing her again.

"At least you came for a walk with me," he said. "I can remember that."

She said: "I had to explain," then quickly added: "It was a lovely walk."

"Shall we go for others?"

"I couldn't promise."

They came to the back entrance of the house, the door set in the flint wall. A fir-tree sawed the air with its creaking branches. Nettles and rank grass grew among the mossy cobblestones, dust-bins, foot-scrapers, gratings. It was a dreary part of the garden where only tradesmen went.

She stood with her back to the door, but had already opened it, letting out a slit of light. He guessed that she hoped not to see Rose. Saying good-night to her sadly, he went through the shrubbery towards his bedroom. 'I am nowhere with her,' he told himself dejectedly. He wanted to break into her isolation, rouse her, bring her out of the briers, present her to the world. 'But why?' he asked himself and, glancing at the mirror, thought: 'A fine sort of Prince to break the spell—old, out-of-breath. And why? Why?' he wondered. 'What do I want with her in the end?' He sat down suddenly on the bed. "I want to marry her," he said aloud.

*   *   *

But he was, in fact, somewhere with her. Going into Rose's sitting-room, seeing the dead fire, she thought that the afternoon seemed far away in some old life. She knelt and picked up the playing-cards, frowning at herself because she felt pleased and excited, as if the walk had dispelled a stale languor. She went over to the table and drawing up a chair, neatly laid out a game of Patience. She played carefully, as if a great deal depended on the result. If she could have glimpsed her own stern set look, she must have laughed.

*   *   *

"Darling, I was so sorry I was out," Isabella called, hearing Laurence come in. "Did you go to the cinema?"

"Yes."

"I must have got back almost as soon as you had gone out. What a pity."

Laurence, who thought it nothing of the kind, agreed. Isabella was reading the catalogue for the Auction Sale of her furniture, and it made strange, sad reading for her.

"How oddly they group things together!" she said. " 'Lot twenty, shepherd's crook and Gladstone-bag.' Do you recall a shepherd's crook, Laurence? And Gladstone-bag? We may be Liberals, but I didn't know we had a Gladstone-bag."

"I remember the shepherd's crook. It was in the loft."

"I never saw it. How does one get such a thing in the first place? I don't recollect any shepherds in the family. Or sheep, either."

"Are you going to the sale?" Laurence asked, hoping that she might avoid some remark about black sheep.

"Or only *black* sheep," she said merrily. "Yes, I shall go. Vinny promised to take me. He goes to Market Swanford sometimes on business, and says that day will do as well as any. I think he has property there of some sort. The butterfly collection's in the catalogue . . . you *did* say . . . I hope you haven't changed your mind about it. Or about the rowing-machine? They've put the little carriage-table into thick, black print, like the Persian rugs. I didn't know it had any value. The china I feel worst about. I ought to have it stored, so that I could give some to your wife."

"My wife?"

"Unless she's given some, no bride can get nice china nowadays. Of course, I'd never let the Rockingham go.

I couldn't—not even to a daughter-in-law. But I ought to have kept the blue-and-white Worcester for her."

"I may never marry."

"Of course you'll marry," she said crossly. "Don't start that sort of nonsense."

"Or my wife might not care about blue-and-white china."

Isabella took off her spectacles and looked at him most suspiciously. "I hope you won't marry *that* sort of girl," she said. "I shouldn't like that at all. Have you had any supper?"

"No, but don't worry. I'll get myself some baked beans." This preference of his had outlasted the years, seen him through high-tea at Prep-school, study-teas at Public School, Naafi snacks in the Army. Isabella sighed. 'But perhaps it's as well,' she thought, 'that he's what he is, the world being what *it* is. And I don't suppose he has very nice friends, not being an officer.' Once, taking him out to dinner on his birthday, his father had offered him oysters. "I'd rather have the money," Laurence had said. Harry had behaved quite equably about it and at the end of the meal said : "Well, fourteen-and-six less two shillings for the soup you had instead is twelve-and-six," and handed him a ten-shilling note and half-a-crown, and Laurence had said "Thank you, sir" and put the money in his pocket. 'It was no way to develop his taste,' Isabella thought, and the next day the boy had bought three Fats Waller records, and played them to himself, hour after hour.

'I don't understand him,' Isabella thought. To understand misunderstood boys had at one time seemed easy to her : she had sympathised with them in novels and on the stage—boys who were introspective, sensitive,

106

unhappy at school, misfits in the Army; who hated games, who wrote poetry and fell in love with older women. But from such characters to Laurence was a big step indeed. 'Yes, it is the world we live in,' she decided, hearing him opening the tin of beans in the kitchen. 'Nothing has *style* any more.'

Laurence ate his beans sitting at one end of the kitchen table. He ate slowly and with enjoyment, all the crusts first, then the buttery, soggy middle part. When he had finished eating, he sat for a little while and thought about Betty; not going over, as she at that minute was, what had so far happened between them; but planning their next meeting from beginning to end. Erotic visions he had often had, but these, and Len's and Fred's and Norman's stories, seemed now to have nothing to do with the truth; for, in all the visions and the stories, tenderness had been missing, and this, as he now found, was a foreign ingredient, negativing other ingredients, such as callous triumph, cruelty, lechery, rude laughter; transforming lust to love, sensuality to sensuousness. He was vaguely conscious of change and although he would not resist telling Len of his adventure, he would leave out his feelings about it, which Len, with his simple appetite, could not appreciate. (It did not occur to him that Len ever left out some part of *his* stories.)

He thought he would make himself some cocoa and, upset by the evening's happenings into sudden unselfishness, made some for his mother, too.

Isabella, who was trying to slim, faced by the hated, strong, sweet drink in the thick beaker, was extremely touched. No champagne could have made her feel more cherished.

Laurence went to his room, feeling inspired, suddenly dizzy with ambition. From the bottom of his Prepschool tuck-box, from under old magazines, he brought out a sheaf of newspaper-cuttings. He spread them over the table and with devotion, as if he were writing a poem, traced back, from one snippet to another, the breeding, history, performance, achievement of April Madrigal, which was to run on Monday.

Chapter 6

ISABELLA's guess that Vinny owned property in Buckinghamshire was incorrect. He merely paid the rent of his wife's flat in Market Swanford. The floor above it, which was one long room once used by the Spiritualist Society for séances, was now rented by his wife for her dancing-studio. Large pockmarked mirrors covered one side of the room, opposite the *barre*. Above the piano hung a pair of old ballet-shoes. The pupils were told that these had belonged to Pavlova; but they had belonged to no one of the kind.

To say that Vinny's wife was not above telling a lie—and she would not have been his wife at all if that had been so—would be to underestimate her inventiveness. She had, in fact, a great distaste for the truth and was for ever tidying it up or turning her back on it. 'How can I present *this* to people?' she would at once ask herself when faced by anything shameful or alarming. Vinny's desertion she had disposed of by moving to a new place and saying he was dead. She even changed Vinny himself into a Fighter Pilot and gave him a D.F.C. with bar.

As the Rita Shinfield School of Dancing sounded so well, she retained her maiden-name and would have been surprised to be called Mrs Tumulty—for that had become, in her mind, merely her mother-in-law's name. When Vinny came to see her, she told anyone who would listen that he was the family solicitor. This amused him, for he saw that her description of their relationship was one of the instances when, in trying to tell a lie, she stumbled accidentally towards the truth. Sitting at her table, going through her books, her ncome-tax forms, he sometimes thought how odd sex was to lead him to such a situation, to such a woman. The most fleeting loosening of his control, that faintest experience of pleasure, had as its result all these years of going over her accounts, the secret journeys, the letters he drafted to the landlord, the advertisements he worded for the local newspaper, the cups of tea and the macaroon-biscuits with which they sedately rounded off the occasion.

He had not found time to see her since the early Spring and his first visit of condolence to Isabella at Seething: he felt, too, a new disinclination to be with her, and put off the journey from week to week, planning to see her if he could slip away from Isabella for a few hours when he took her down to her old home in Buckinghamshire for the Auction Sale.

Isabella was staying in London, and the evening before the sale Vinny took her to dine in Soho. The outing was only fairly successful. He made mistakes due to heedlessness, said: "Darling, what a gay little frock!" and touched the black silk fringe which swung against her plump arms when she moved.

"Gay?" she said dubiously. "I bought it for Harry's memorial-service. It was not meant to be gay."

He ordered a sweet, sallow wine she liked and which made him pause in the middle of sentences while he smothered little belches. She ate *mille feuilles*, then regretted them. Waiters constantly interrupted to ask if the meal was all they desired.

Afterwards, they walked some way through littered

streets, hoping to repair the effects of the wine and pastry. It began to drizzle and Isabella's heel caught in a grating. Women at street-corners stared past her at Vinny and this embarrassed her.

In the morning, when they met at Marylebone station it was raining hard. They dodged the fishy-smelling puddles on the platforms. A deluge of rain drummed on the glass roof of the station, and when the train moved, it seemed to beat its way through the sodden landscape, smoke flapping back at the misted windows. The brilliant green woods of early Summer took the full weight of the rain.

"This doesn't help your day," Vinny said.

She wiped the window with her newspaper and peered out at the familiar scenes—the backs of houses, strips of garden, sheds, allotments. Then striped fields unrolled; a barge went slowly up a steamy canal; the rain was white against dark fir-trees. This journey had played its part in her married life. On Wednesday mornings she had taken what Harry called 'the matrons' train' for her day's shopping in London—an entirely feminine day with visits to hairdressers and dress-makers; luncheon at one of the stores; delightful trackings-down of gloves to match a blouse, a belt to match a bag; tea at Fortnum's, enviously watching a mannequin weaving her way between the tables with a quick step that seemed to cover no distance. ('A mink stole is slimming,' Isabella would think, breaking open a chestnut meringue with her fork and wishing that she was not about to eat it and hoping that she would not have another when it was gone.) In the holidays, Laurence would often be with her, going sulkily to the dentist, or to Gorringe's for school clothes. "How nice to be home!" she would greet her friends as they got out of the train in the evening; but she would not have missed her Wednesdays for the world. This morning, taking the journey the wrong way round, she felt an alien, and knew that she was on her way to see a home disintegrate which was already lost.

The rain slackened, and had stopped when they got out of the train. Drips fell from the spiked shelter, and out in the road all the suburban trees sighed and shook down showers of raindrops and wet petals. Behind the drenched laburnum, the pink may, the ornamental cherries, stood large brick houses with curving drives. They had deceivingly rural names, like Red Barns and Little Orchard and Old Thatches, and all were familiar to Isabella—for she had dined here and played Bridge there—and she leant forward and noted the smallest change—each lick of paint or mended fence.

'How absurd to have come!' she thought. She had little imagination and had not, until this moment of approaching the house, visualised the ordeal of witnessing her home stripped down before her neighbours' eyes.

Cars stood in the lane already. The white farm-gate was open between the glassy laurels. 'For Sale' boards were thrust into the hedge.

They drove in, over loose wet gravel, and Vinny touched her clasped hands steadyingly.

"It was vulgar to come," she whispered. "And embarrassing. I shall bid myself for the little lacquer bureau. Not that I want it; but I suddenly recall that Mrs Mitchell always did. I could not bear for it to be in her home, with her papers in it."

The garden looked untidy and trodden about. The white-washed house, so looped with purple clematis and wistaria, looked a transitory residence, a place taken over and furnished for summer months; bought and re-sold over and over as speculation, a house without reality or experience, from which mothers went to nursing-homes to give birth to their children, out of which no coffins had been carried. 'Nothing has happened here,' the leaded diamonded windows assured, 'nothing left its mark.' The garden had been laid out once for all at the beginning; a polite cycle of social exchange had been maintained—he who was host one week was guest the next—envy was a commoner emotion than jealousy; tiny unkindnesses were done; the lacquer bureau aroused deep feelings. 'Nothing wild,' Vinny thought, 'nothing beautiful, tragic, terrifying took place. No one threw open those smug windows to feel the cool air on his burning eyes.'

The car stopped. The porch was full of gravel; footmarks were all over the parquet-flooring of the hall, Isabella saw with dismay.

'But I do not like terror, violence, beauty,' Vinny told himself. He helped Isabella out of the car. She kept her gloved hand on his arm as she entered the porch, supported by him, upheld, in her neighbours' eyes; prepared to meet their sympathetic glances and their tact. 'What I love is charm, grace, discretion, order.'

This villa, which did, or had done, well enough for Isabella, would not have done for Emily. He imagined some desolate moorland, a house rock-hewn, mist-wreathed, haunted.

Isabella stepped over a rolled-up carpet to greet an acquaintance. Vinny looked at his catalogue. He had planned to leave Isabella and return for her later, when he had been to see his wife at Market Swanford, fifteen miles away. He hoped that the lacquer bureau would come up within an hour or two: for, to buy it himself, to snatch it from under Mrs Mitchell's nose— whoever Mrs Mitchell might be—was, he decided, the best comfort he could contrive for Isabella that day.

*   *   *

Buckinghamshire contains all of England—suburbia, industrial squalor, great estates, even valleys remote and rural where most of the families have the same name. Some of the market-towns change little—coaching-inns and old-fashioned drapers surround the squares where the buses end their journeys. On market-days Market Swanford is crowded, with stalls and village-people. Waitresses run to and fro in the dining-room at The Bull; bus-queues line the pavements.

Early-closing day makes another world of it. Vinny came into this blank world, in the dead part of the afternoon. Navy-blue blinds covered the shop-windows, reflecting the empty streets. He saw no sign of life, but pigeons walking about under a statue of some great Buckinghamshire figure—Disraeli or Hampden, perhaps . . . he had never been close enough to be sure— in the middle of the square.

Rita's flat was in a street off the square, and over a cheap tailor's. The shop-window was full of overcoats and suits on dummies which had large price-tickets in place of heads. From the top floor—so quiet was the street—came the sound of a piano and the staggered thumps of children practising a *pas de chat*. He felt that the pianist should have been in time, having, probably, more control over her instrument than the children had over their limbs.

"Stand!" said Rita's dancing-mistress voice, and the music trailed off and a humming and shuffling arose.

The door at the side of the tailor's shop was open, and Vinny went up the stairs. These were narrow, and had rubber treads. At the turn of the stairs there was a little board on the wall, with a pointing hand and the words 'Rita Shinfield School of Dancing. 2nd Floor.' On a bench beneath this, Vinny sat down to wait.

The music began again—one of those ageless, dancing-class pieces which he could hum but give no name to. "Hold!" Rita called. "Oh, dear, dear! Arms, Cynthia!" But soon she said "Stand" again and then clapped her hands. "Thank-you!" Her high, actressy voice came floating down. 'Thank *you*!' thought Vinny. In a minute or two, his ordeal began. Little girls came clattering down the stairs, swinging ballet-shoes by the ribbons, flicking back their plaits, glancing at Vinny—all tremulous, secret, personal. "Good afternoon, Miss Shinfield," they had chanted. 'Perhaps they adore her,' he suddenly thought.

The pianist followed them down; slowly, for she was rather lame. She had a sad, reproachful look which Vinny well understood, and he could think of no more irritating way of earning a living than hers, no mode of living more dim or fruitless.

"She'll be down directly," she said as she passed, and, as he watched her descending the stairs, clutching her music-case, leaning her weight on the banisters, he could imagine the house she would return to and the whole of the life that she had led and must lead; submerged and unnoticed; crying in vain, he thought, for a kind word.

Rita came running downstairs, her feet, in old ballet-shoes, turned outwards; her hand holding some ropes of pink and grey pearls to her breast. She was still humming the *pas de chat* tune and did not stop when she saw Vinny. She patted his cheek and in an excess of gaiety put her face to be kissed, going up on tiptoe to reach him. She then did a little glissé, took her key from her handbag and opened the door of the flat. "Entrez!" she called after her.

'There is only one thing she can settle down to without lighting a cigarette,' he thought, watching her going round from one empty box to another, even lifting the clock and looking behind it. He handed her his case. Although she smoked so much, she did it in a fussy way as if it were the first cigarette of her life. She blew out smoke and waved it away with her hand, narrowed her eyes, shook ash off her pearls, made a fish's mouth and forced out smoke-rings. "Well, darling!" she said.

He moved a fluffy cat off a chair, revolted by the creature's lumps of uncombed fur. He brushed hairs off the velvet cushion and sat down. Rita took the cat on her lap and stroked it. He remembered with disgust that she took it to bed with her.

"That poor woman—your pianist," he began—for he could not escape from his old ways of pity.

"Poor?"

"I mean the poverty of her life. It is in her face and her voice."

"She's perfectly happy."

"None of us is that."

"I am," Rita said in surprise. "Darling puss!" she murmured, holding the cat up to her face. "We are

116

very happy, aren't we? Being busy's the secret," she said in a brisker voice. "So as there's no time to think about yourself."

"It is a poor happiness that can only exist that way."

"What's the good of unsettling everyone and making them think they're badly off? Poor Miss Walker, as you call her . . . supposing you manage to convince her she's missing something by not living in Mayfair and drinking champagne every day . . . that's you all over . . . you like to make people feel dissatisfied . . . I wouldn't put it past you to take her out and give her a taste for fine things, so that she'd fret for them ever after . . . long after you'd forgotten her, or gone away feeling good, thinking you'd given her a glimpse of high-life and something to look back on. . . . You really are a silly old fool," she concluded, in her most friendly voice. "People have to live those lives."

Against his judgment, he asked: "What does she *do*?"

Although this flat and Rita's own life made him feel claustrophobic, his last intention was to unsettle her. His wish was quite the reverse; but curiosity always endangered him.

"How do I know what she does? Goes home and cooks her father's supper, I suppose. If there was anything so very terrible in that, half the world would starve, wouldn't they?"

"Yes. Yes, of course."

"So you see!" she said gaily. "And *there* you are, Puss angel, and down you go, sweetest, while mother puts the kettle on."

Vinny went to the window and looked into the wet

street. He had meant to rehearse some dialogue before-hand, but had found the difficulty of being unsure how her half of it would go. 'If I say this and this, *she* may answer me thus,' he had thought. Now—not only had he not made his own set speeches: he had set her off along quite opposite lines—trying to make what she would call 'the worst of it' for her; allowing her cause for self-pity, none for gratitude.

The vacant white light of a wet summer's evening filled the street, was reflected in dove-coloured slates. No one went by. In the butcher's window across the road, sheaves of paper hung on the meat-hooks; on a clean tray two pallid pig's-trotters lay side by side as if in supplication. Next door, piles of dusty junk cluttered the window and swept back into the shop: broken furniture, old books, pictures, antlers, fire-irons. That Rita should be happy living here in this little town (facing, day after day, the pig's-trotters—which he thought of as permanent décor—the tobacconist's full of dummy cartons, the junk-shop, a jeweller's window with shelves of tarnished silver) seemed astonishing and reprehensible to him, though also useful and accom-modating and much to be encouraged.

Puss walked between his feet and round them in an unending figure-of-eight. Rita brought in the tea and Vinny watched her as she poured out. She was very thin and her satin frock showed up her little rounded and uncorseted stomach: even the indentation of her navel. Her face was carefully tended as it had always been. No one would mistake her age, but they might think that she was wonderful for it. Only her neck was deeply creased and she had a way of putting her hand to her throat as she talked or when she felt attention upon her. He stared gravely at her and she began to chatter distractedly to Puss. Vinny remembered that her cats started off when kittens with elaborate names—he thought that this one had been Cleopatra—but all became Puss before long.

While he drank his tea, he read some of the business letters she had handed to him; but for once he scarcely grasped the meaning of any of them and in the end he laid them aside without comment and suddenly said: "I came here, Rita, to ask you to divorce me."

When he found the courage to look at her, he saw that she was blushing. He had never seen her blush before and he knew that the causes were anger and surprise, emotions that he had not previously aroused in her.

"Our marriage cannot mean much to you—it does not deserve its name," he said gently. "And any harm I have done you was years ago. There is no more to be done."

She pulled out her handkerchief and clapped it to her mouth, looking at him with wide-open eyes. She seemed unable to answer him.

"Are you so shocked?" he asked.

"No."

Then she raised the handkerchief to her eyes and broke into tears. "I thought it would happen years ago. Not now. I used to dread you coming here in case you asked it. Then I began to think you never would. And all the worry seemed over."

"What have I ever done for you that you should care, or be anxious?"

"You married me," she said with dignity.

"It was the worst mistake. We both decided that. If I had not . . . if we had not . . . you would have married

119

someone else who would have been a real husband to you, made you happy, supported you."

"You've supported me."

"I didn't mean money."

"No more did I."

"I have never made you happy."

"But I can't divorce you. Everybody thinks you're dead. I couldn't bear the disgrace. Why must I? Why change at our time of life? It seems so silly and unkind. Surely you haven't fallen in love with someone else—with someone, I mean? At your age?"

"No," he said sharply. "I only want to end this meaningless relationship." ·

"You're ashamed of me."

"I'm ashamed of having married you. It was a great disservice I did you, though I did believe it to be quite otherwise at the time."

He thought this barb might embed itself in her conscience, but her trickery had long faded from her mind. That imaginary pregnancy which had brought him to the registry-office was quite forgotten. For years, she had put down the failure of their marriage to his mother. She had seen films about possessive maternity and she thought that the dominating Mrs Tumulty, whom she had never been allowed to meet, had jealously, morbidly, stood between them. Vinny's fleeing back to her was knowingly associated with uncut navel-cords and apron-strings. She had let him go with some relief; for she thought him too superior and could not live under his eternal and silent criticism. Every time she said 'pardon me' or 'excusez-moi' his face twitched as if he had neuralgia. No one before had ever thought her unrefined—quite the reverse—and she disliked seeing herself in the distorting mirror of his snobbery.

'She cannot say that she has given me the best years of her life,' he thought. 'She has given nothing. And taken only a very little.' She then confounded him by saying: "You meant everything to me. You were always at the back of my thoughts."

"The back?" he smiled.

"Because I was sure of you. There was no need for you to be in the foreground, as people are who can't be relied on. The letters we mean to keep for ever we put at the back of the drawer."

'She *would* keep her only interesting observation until now!' he thought.

"But we know they're there," she went on, and began to cry dreadfully, so that her lips could scarcely shape the words. "All the time, I knew you were there and that comforted me. Because it's been so lonely. You talk about Miss Walker!"

"From my point of view," Vinny said coldly, "to be some hoarded-up thing, kept lest I might come in useful . . ."

"I hadn't meant it like that," she said, and he knew that she had not. He had tried to work up anger, for pity would weaken him: but he was not used to anger, and pity was his old trouble. He put his hand over his eyes.

"Who should I have left?" she asked.

He could not say, although he had never believed she led the chaste life she described. Once, when he had stayed longer than usual, writing letters for her, she had glanced a great deal at the clock and kept taking her powder-puff from her handbag; but no one had ever come while he was there. As if against this very day, she had preserved the illusion of loneliness and martyrdom.

Her words followed all his thoughts as doggedly as if they were always in view.

"When you would not live with me, I did not complain; though my pride was hurt and I was in despair."

He looked for a second at her collapsed face and she said: "To wait until now when I'm getting old, not attractive any more . . . you try so hard to stave it off . . . looking old, I mean . . . all the effort . . . and you think you'll manage to conquer it, or delay it, and be different from other women . . . all the expense of keeping yourself young . . . the denials . . ." She glanced at the plate of cakes. Like most lonely people she had a sweet tooth. "And it's never any use . . . just like the tide coming in . . . and one day you just feel scared and you give in."

"But don't cry," he begged.

"It's different for men."

"No. I don't think it's different."

"All the time when I didn't see you, I was planning little things so that I wouldn't seem any less attractive when you came next time." She was beginning to believe every word she said.

He looked at his watch. Scenes take up so much time. So much emotion makes the minutes fly by. Nothing was settled, nothing accomplished, and if he did not catch the next bus, he would be late for Isabella, who was waiting for him in the ruins of her old home; tired, too, he supposed, and needing comfort.

He began to walk about the room and Rita sank to her weeping again.

"I shall have to go. I hope you will reconsider all this and try to be sensible. I want to assure you that, of course, there would be no loss to you financially," he said stiffly.

"That's of no consequence. I can work. I never asked you for money." Her great blaze of rage astonished him. He was often amazed that money—to him a trivial thing—should arouse such overwhelming emotions.

He began to button his coat and walked towards the window, dreading his goodbye to her. Still sobbing, she stacked up the tea-cups and plates with one hand, holding her handkerchief to her forehead with the other.

He began to speak but, glancing down into the street, forgot what to say. Across the road, looking into the window of the junk-shop, was Isabella. She was examining a little dark picture, holding her head sideways to avoid the shine of the window. Then she leant forward and must have bumped her nose on the glass, for she put her hand up to her face and straightened her hat. He drew back quickly when she moved and walked on down the road. He was relieved and bewildered. Then suddenly, as if ending her indecision, she turned and hurried back to the shop-door and tried the handle. She rattled it crossly, he could see, and frowning with disappointment or impatience, came out of the doorway and looked up at the window where Vinny was still standing. As if she had not seen him, she looked away again and then, her brain seeming to receive an unexpected message, looked back. He had tried to step behind the curtain, but when she waved uncertainly he was forced to do so in return.

At once, Rita, holding the teapot, came over to the window and showed her swollen, tear-stained face between the curtains.

*   *   *

When Isabella, embarrassed, had sauntered on along the road towards the square where the buses were, Rita, still clutching the teapot, began to sob more than ever; but sobbing of a different quality.

"How dare you bring her here, and let her walk up and down in the street while you are begging for your freedom?"

Scorn swept over his protestations, but her scorn moved him less than her pleading. She would not listen to him. "To have her walk up and down outside, to wait across the road for you to give her the signal, because she could not constrain her impatience."

He went to the door. "I will have to go. I will write. I will come again."

"Bring her in next time. Don't leave her outside in the street. Bring her up to tea. Let us all be cosy together. Walking up and down outside, peering up at the windows, flaunting her new summer hat!"

It was not a new hat at all. It was last year's pink felt and, later, sitting on a bench at the station, Isabella pulled it off her tired head and raked her hair with her fingers.

"I shouldn't have gone," she said once more.

She felt a miserable separation from and embarrassment with Vinny, having caught him out in what she supposed was something shady and unsavoury. A distaste for men and their grossness put a distance between them which she had felt the evening before in

Soho when women had glanced at him from doorways and street-corners. She had once thought him such a fastidious, tender man, and now she saw that she did not know him at all. Over and over she made her explanations for being in Market Swanford and he listened courteously and smiled.

"As soon as you had gone, I felt exposed, so dreadfully exposed: no one made a bid for Harry's Butterfly Collection and someone giggled when they held up the Garden Figure."

Vinny put his hand over hers and they both sat staring in front of them at their private miseries. The little station was quite deserted. The colours of the evening were intense rather than brilliant as if before rain. Swallows flew low, showing their pale, neat bellies. In distant woods, cuckoos answered one another at long intervals, haltingly—one with its June stammer already, its explosive, broken cry. At the backs of gardens along the line cumulus lilac was banked up against a navy-blue sky; roofs beyond had sharp outlines.

"So I thought to myself, soon after lunch, 'I'll get away from all this,' and then there was nowhere to go but to find you."

"Those damn cuckoos!" Vinny said restlessly.

"I knew the bus you'd catch. I thought: 'I'll wait about in the square for him. And we can go straight back by train. It will save him coming all that way to fetch me.' "

"It was very thoughtful."

"I love poking about little towns, though I hadn't bargained for early-closing."

'How far can I trust her?' Vinny wondered. But he decided that he could not trust her at all.

'Was she what they called a kept woman?' Isabella asked herself. 'Or just a common prostitute? But why go all the way to Market Swanford for a prostitute? And surely prostitutes don't cry? Harlots, still less.' To Isabella, the two words suggested a great difference—there were common prostitutes, sly and squalid; and there were painted harlots, defiant and not unromantic. A paramour was far removed, in elegance and education, from either.

Vinny glanced at his watch. A porter crossed the lines in a leisurely way. Then a signal came down sharply, like a guillotine, and Isabella started.

"Your poor nerves!" Vinny said and smiled at her. "You are quite right. It was a mistake to have gone there today." One mistake had followed another all day long. 'The woman on the stairs—poor Miss Walker—led me into my worst mistake of all.'

"To see all one's *things*!" Isabella cried. "People staring. One's own friends staring. I felt they would put *me* up before long—Lot 29. Middle-aged widow, birdcage and roll of coconut-matting."

The train came into sight, its smoke buffeted between the high banks of the cutting. When they were sitting in their empty compartment, Vinny said, looking out of the window: "The day has been too much for both of us. You *and* I. I had a very trying ordeal . . . with someone with whom I have business connections . . . in great trouble . . . great personal trouble . . . one feels so powerless to help."

"You take on too many people's burdens," Isabella said, glancing at him shrewdly. "Oh, now, it's beginning to rain again. What a mercy it held off most of the day!"

Long threads of moisture hit the window. As if released at a sudden command, the rain bounced and danced on rooftops, fell like knives into the flower-beds of the suburban houses below the railway-banks. The fields steamed. Down bowed all the clotted blossom; the drenched lilac, the guelder-roses, looked ready to collapse; the air was full of grubby petals.

"I never want to come back to Buckinghamshire again," Isabella said; and when she spoke her breath clouded the window.

'Nor I,' thought Vinny wearily.

"Except for just one thing."

"What is the one thing?"

"A little picture of a steamer painted on glass. I saw it in that shop, when I . . . however, the shop was shut. That made me want it all the more, naturally. It is exactly like the one I have in the parlour; only slightly different, of course. I must go back one of these days and see if it's still there."

'It is none of her business,' he thought. 'She might be my wife, she is so curious and possessive.' He did not offer to buy the picture for her, as he did not believe it to be her real reason for returning.

In a great flurry of rain, they were borne on towards London. Everything rural lay behind them; trees thinned, the fields were gone and now the windows of houses looked only an arm's distance from them. They flew across bridges above roads busy with traffic, and, at last, into the tunnels.

Lightly, lightly Vinny's thoughts went—wary, delicate; as if Isabella were reading every one. He was on tiptoe with fear. Too tired to trust his judgment, he wondered how much to explain to her and again decided that he could explain nothing. 'I have taken too many risks already,' he thought.

She smoothed on her gloves and smiled at him. "It was nice of you to buy the bureau," she said. "That was the best part of the day. It was wonderful to see Mrs Mitchell not getting it."

The bureau, hours earlier, he had intended as a parting-gift to Rita—to hold the papers he would no longer be dealing with. Isabella turned away, seeing his look of exhaustion.

"Well, we are back again," she said, trying to be gay, as they came to a standstill under the discoloured glass roof of the station.

"And the day is ending as it began," she added, looking up at the dirty panes vibrating with rain.

But to Vinny the difference between setting out and returning was the whole of the measure between hope and despair.

Chapter 7

SOME dazzling days came after the rain. Betty wore her
mauve-and-white striped uniform and no coat when
she took the baby for walks. If Laurence were home for
a weekend he often arranged to meet her at the top of
the cliff and sometimes pushed the pram for her, with
great energy as if it were a lawn-mower. His mother's
dismay would have been mixed with incredulity had
she seen him; for he appeared quite unselfconscious and
even took an unmanly interest in the baby. Betty's
uniform delighted him, especially the little frilled bands
over her rolled-up sleeves. It was his first time of being
happy for years, and he saw that manhood was indeed
a wonderful escape from boyhood.

Both he and Betty felt at variance with their elders
and far from at home in their homes. Her problems
were more easily explained than his; for they were
difficulties of poverty and shame; insuperable, but
avoidable.

"You couldn't take anyone there," she explained,
"so it wouldn't be any use having a friend." But he
felt that she *did* take him home, and saw, as vividly as
if he had been there, the family eating their bloaters in
the kitchen. The scene fascinated him and although he
knew that he would dislike them all except her mother
—who unfortunately for herself had high standards of
behaviour as her daughter had—he would have enjoyed sitting down to a bloater with them. Betty's nice
feelings were like his own mother's, faddish, feminine;

but he was always pleased to hear about them for, retailing them, she exposed the rest of the picture.

"You can't imagine how disgusting it is—having to go to the lavatory at the bottom of the garden, and washing at the scullery sink. Then the kitchen's too hot and smells of Grandma's Germolene, or else she's soaking her feet. And Dad not particular about saying 'pardon' when he belches."

He could not envy her this home as she envied him his: he thought of Grandma as a filthy old party, but was not repelled by her. "She doesn't belong to you," Betty said. "If she did, you'd long for her to die. She keeps talking about her corns and her false teeth and her wind—at mealtimes, too." As a family, they seemed to be exceptionally troubled by wind. They also had rows. Father rowed with Grandma; Mothe with Father. They quarrelled with their neighbours and relations. Sometimes, Betty got her ears boxed for answering back. Yet, to Laurence, hate, disgust, indignation seemed easier emotions to bear than guilt and embarrassment. In his world, the elders were disgusted with the young —tactlessly and illogically disgusted that they should manage to live in the sad conditions bequeathed to them. No apologies were made for having handed on such a world, and Isabella, for instance, gaily blamed her son for taking what he found. She lamented the old days and often told Laurence what he had missed. He thought that he inherited all her generation's sighs, as well as the fruits of their foolishness.

More and more she made difficulties for him. She frustrated, with her last-minute questions and suggestions, his plans for meeting Betty. Since the sale, she felt herself back again to the days after her husband's

130

death, face to face with a grief as sharp as it had been at the beginning, with a sense of loss almost complete. Vinny had tided her over; but, once he removed his support, she saw that he had only helped her to pass the days: the pain had been allayed, but the malady itself persisted. Vinny had indeed seemed to remove his support, and the romantic friendship she had envisaged continuing into old age had already dwindled. Sometimes she wished that he had left her alone; for, added to her loneliness, there was now the pain of feeling herself excluded. This had always been the most hurtful experience to her and one that repeated itself throughout her life. She was so often the instrument of bringing two of her dearest ones together, while hoping humbly that they would manage to think well of one another, if only because she herself thought so well of both. After a time—whether it was school-mistress and mother, brother and husband—she would begin to feel herself too much a third party, too unnecessary to them. Although there was often sexual jealousy entangled in her emotions, it was not always an ingredient and could not much worsen what was so bad already. The chief agony was to feel herself outside—jokes were made which she did not understand, or understand quickly enough; she would feel that she was making no mark: her innocent little tests of their affection always turned out negatively—if, on walks, she went a little ahead, no one hurried to keep up with her; if she lagged behind, no one turned to see where she was. Having once had two friendships, she would suddenly find that she had neither.

She had been much less than in other affairs the instrument of bringing Emily and Vinny together; but she wished she had sent him to The Victoria in the beginning, and not taken him to Rose Kelsey's; for now only courtesy and kindness ever brought him to visit her and she knew that he dissembled rather than confided in her, which would have been the only—though faint indeed—salve to her wound. Moreover, since the day in Market Swanford, she realised that Vinny had always been a stranger to her. Apart from feeling the impotence of her own personality, she was forced to suspect that, unlike herself, who had no mystery, no secrets (save her little flutters on horses), behind the façade of other people lay a labyrinth of mystery, a vast terrain of secrecy, which resulted in unaccountable behaviour. If Vinny, then why not Evalie Hobson too (who always seemed so simple); why not Laurence? Perhaps Harry, too, had had his hidden life.

For this reason, when Vinny next called, she turned over to him all of Harry's files of papers and letters.

"There is no hurry . . . but if you could be so good . . . you would know better than I what I should keep . . . and you could throw away the rest."

Vinny felt stifled with the weight of other people's papers.

"I feel it is not my business," he began.

"It might not be mine," she said simply. "I am always hearing that men have their secrets. Harry and I were happy together—or, rather, I believed that we were. It would be a pity to begin wondering things."

He thought that she must have begun wondering already and he sat down there and then, rather fearfully, and began to untie the bundles of papers. Isabella could not help hovering about. She fidgeted round the room, trying not to glance at him. 'Heartache is *real* pain,' she thought. 'We ought not to be made like this —always wanting what we mayn't have—and then getting pains in the chest because of it.'

Harry could not have left things tidier and there was nothing personal, except Laurence's school-reports, and a little bundle of letters Isabella had written when they were betrothed. Vinny was relieved to recognise the handwriting.

"Well, I find nothing but political letters," Vinny said, "and how should I know whether one should keep them or not? I know nothing about politics. There are just these . . ."

When she took the old letters from him, she felt that the thread of her past was stretched out to its very beginning. The letters seemed to have been written far, far back, much longer ago than her childhood; yet not written by her at all, but by some eager, bold young woman, who could say all the things which even a year of marriage made impossibly embarrassing.

Vinny had looked solemnly away.

She had not yet read a line of any of the letters, but the sight of the handwriting, the old-fashioned stamps on the faded envelopes, reminded her of the incautious contents. She remembered, too, her state of mind, in which she had wanted no one but Harry—the desert-island stage of their infatuation—yet a fortnight's honeymoon had really been enough after all.

"Being in love is a great inconvenience," she suddenly said. "The world can't deal with it, and one can't oneself."

"How true," said Vinny.

"I don't know how some people can go on doing it

again and again all their lives. One says such ridiculous things." She slid a letter from its envelope. It was full of wild reproaches. Harry had had to work late and "I am not made of stone," she had written. "So unjust," she added.

"Unjust?"

"Oh, flying into a bate, as we used to say at school ... I believe that is really something to do with falconry ... rather interesting ... and then purposely misunderstanding. Seeing no faults, then suddenly seeing more than could ever be there."

Then the air in the room seemed to contract with apprehension, as her heart did. 'He is going to say something dreadful,' she thought.

"I am in love," he said.

He stood up and with immense dignity awaited her reply.

*   *   *

When Vinny returned to Rose's it was an hour of change and bustle. The lovely weather had prolonged the afternoon in which the house had lain under a spell, with only Mr Tillotson's white tennis-shoes drying on an upper sill to show that anyone had ever lived there. Now, suddenly, the spell broke. Mrs Tumulty, in black alpaca, and carrying an enormous black butterfly-net, came down the drive. Lindsay Tillotson appeared, yawning, at his bed-room window. He felt rather enervated, having spent the afternoon making love to his wife and then reading the *Manchester Guardian* while she slept. The evening loomed before him. He told himself that it would soon be over: then he saw that to-morrow loomed, too, and—such was his mood—all the days of his life.

Mrs Tumulty entered the house. Someone in the kitchen began to chop herbs on a board. The children came up from the beach; first, their voices floated towards the house: then Constance burst through the macrocarpas in her pink sunbonnet.

"We never hear a cough now," Lindsay said over his shoulder. His wife yawned till her eyes watered and she wiped them on a corner of the pillow. "As soon as the decorators are out, they can come home," she said.

"I'll be glad."

"It has seemed endless," she agreed.

Sometimes, the days seemed endless to the children, too. In the mornings, they scarred and dug the sands and at luncheon-time the tide smoothed it all out again, erasing for ever Constance's castle and Benjy's name which he had scraped with his spade. Occasionally, they made tentative approaches to other children, edging close to their moated castles or pools, running to fetch a ball for them if it came their way. Then Nannie called them back. Not to get sandals wet. Not to be rude and stare at others. To mind their own business, if they pleased, and time in any case for their milk and biscuits.

Betty, returning with the baby, who thrust his arms and legs from under the fringed canopy, met Nannie as she came round towards the front of the house, and sharp words, Lindsay thought, ensued. He could not quite catch what Nannie said, but her displeasure was evident, from her gestures and the brisk way in which she bundled the children into the house.

Lindsay turned back to the room, so that he did not see the most dramatic scene of all and would not have understood its drama if he had.

Vinny, returning, saw Lindsay take in his tennis-shoes from the sill, heard raised voices, baths running, pans clattering in the kitchen. The garden looked deserted, but somehow only just deserted. Then Emily came out of the house, carrying a basket of gooseberries.

His love, since he had spoken of it to Isabella, had become more settled and permissible. A step forward had been taken, and with new confidence he accompanied Emily to a seat beyond the shrubbery where perhaps she had sat all the afternoon, for her book, her sun-glasses and knitting had been left there, and Philly's cutting-out magazines.

The sea, winking with light, was stretched taut like a piece of silk. Confronted by this and the enormous expanse of sky, Vinny felt much less able to talk than indoors, in, for instance, Isabella's parlour. His lack of words panicked him: he had no time to be patient. At any moment one of his enemies might come round the bushes—Rose, Philly, his mother. His mother seemed just now his worst enemy. Having seen how things were with her son, she had determined to take away the excuse of her presence and was returning to London. She also made his love seem ludicrous to him and talked spitefully of glandular disturbances which his father had suffered at his age.

"Your mother is happy this evening," Emily said. "She found a butterfly she had been after for years. A kind of fritillary, I believe."

Vinny sighed; Emily glanced at him in surprise. For a moment, she thought that the butterfly-hunting must depress him. Then she realised that his mother did.

"She is a remarkable woman," she said slyly.

"Yes. Remarkable."

"And very forthright. You know where you are with her."

"Yes, but you don't want to *be* there."

"How convenient, though—and for you, too, because old people can be a burden—that she should still find so much interest in all those hobbies—looking at things, collecting things . . . oh, I collect things myself—all those shells—but only because I am bored when I am out for walks, and to please Philly, too, perhaps. Your mother, though, is really absorbed in the things for their own sake. She was telling me of some wagtails she was watching. . . ."

"She simply can't mind her own business."

"I thought you were a loving and attentive son. . . ."

"And so I may have been," Vinny said slowly.

"Surely, people don't suddenly change . . .?"

Her head was bent as she topped-and-tailed the gooseberries and dropped them into the basin. He felt that she kept her eyes downcast, not to be drawn into a glance at him.

"But of course people suddenly change," he protested. "Newspapers are full of stories of *how* suddenly they change—timid men all at once take a hatchet to their wives; happy people go off and hang themselves; cowardly people do something incredibly brave; clergymen's wives surprise themselves by doing a bit of shoplifting. I have surprised myself by finding my mother intolerable. I have quite changed. And you have changed, too. You told me so yourself. I cannot imagine what you were like before you cut yourself off from other people and became your sister's prisoner. No wonder you are bored . . . you said you were bored just now," he reminded her for she had caught in a breath as if she were about to protest. "Bored when you go for walks."

She ran the gooseberries through her fingers and frowned. Because he knew she meant to ignore all he had said, and was desperate for some reaction from her, he put his hand into the basket and touched hers. She made no response; but the negation of it, the *not* responding, was more revealing. He felt the involuntary tremor before the tension, the shocked leap of her blood which she could not control. 'Even her arms are blushing,' he thought. But her face had its usual pallor, was turned aside, so that he could not see—but he *did* see—her eyes enlarged by tears which would have fallen if she had moved her lids. 'She *cannot* blush,' he thought.

He took her hand from the basket and held its palm to his mouth, knowing that she could not speak for tears. Her fingers were roughened and stained, grubby from the fruit, her nails short and unvarnished. Her wrists were very flat and narrow and along the inside of her arm—and he had always thought this part of a woman most touching and exciting—the long veins looked drawn there simply as decoration.

"I cannot make excuses any longer," he said. "Having my mother here was an elaborate ruse. It has cost me my reputation for being a good son." He saw that her tears had receded and that she dared to smile. "Now she has seen through the ruse and is indignant with herself, and me; though, after all, she has watched all those birds and caught her famous butterfly, which she could not have done in London. But she is already packing the trunk. She has some work to do at the British Museum, she says, and she wants to go to the

Summer Exhibition of the Royal Academy. She goes every year to see all those portraits of princesses. She dotes on Royalty. She would peer at *them* through field-glasses if she had half a chance. She sits all night on a campstool waiting to watch them being married or crowned or buried. She once touched the Duke of Edinburgh, whom she loves to excess. He didn't turn a hair. Do *you* love the Duke of Edinburgh?'' he asked, in a haughty and suspicious voice.

"I rather like fair young men," Emily said demurely. "I used to be disgruntled because, after all, one never did meet anyone looking in the least like Rupert Brooke. I expect he is the cause of a lot of disgruntlement among women of my age."

"Rupert Brooke," Vinny said and laughed disagreeably. "I suppose your fiancé was golden-haired."

"No."

"You think I am presumptuous to mention him?"

"Only in the way that psycho-analysts are presumptuous—for one's own good. I am sure you think it is for my good to be made to discuss what pains me, and be forced to stare at what makes me flinch."

"I am tired of being likened to psycho-analysts. I am just interested in people."

"You are not so unlike your mother, after all. You merely have the wit not to use field-glasses."

"My mother doesn't care one jot for all those birds she pries at. A psycho-analyst doesn't care about the answers he gets; he only uses them. He does not mind bitterly what he is told, or feel personally rejected when he is told nothing."

She had finished the gooseberries, and she picked up the basin as if she were going back to the house. He took the bowl from her to keep her there longer and, staring gloomily ahead, continued: "He doesn't have to say to himself: 'I am too old for this patient. She must find someone who hasn't grey hair.' I hate this damned psycho-analyst. I am jealous of him, whoever he is. I am sorry we ever made him up."

"Then I am sorry, too," she said gently.

"When my mother has gone home, it will be clearly apparent that I come here only to see you."

"But will you come?"

"Naturally."

"Darling, don't be so formidable!" She was laughing; then became confused when he looked up in surprise. "Oh, forgive me! I used to say things like that to people . . . you know how, for some women, everyone must have an endearment. I suppose I was a woman like that . . . very silly, I think, don't you?"

He had glimpsed in that instant the chattering, gay, perhaps affected girl she had been; frivolous, diffuse, impulsive. He said: "My darling, be happy again. And *my* 'darling' is not like yours—not for anyone but you; not a slip of the tongue; but premeditated and rehearsed and willed. You can't evade it. It is said now, for the rest of your life, even if you forget it in half-an-hour."

She looked at him and he realised then how often before she had lowered her eyes or turned aside. Though she said nothing, he could tell by the flickering of her eyelids, her quick frown, that she was searching for a phrase—yet none was right; none could be trusted to meet the occasion: and he was sure, too, that she would not forget his words in half-an-hour, that she might even go up to her room to turn over and consider what had been said to her.

He picked up the basket and, as they walked towards the house, he was hoping that everyone would see them, so that his courtship could be acknowledged and his enemies informed.

*　　　*　　　*

"I didn't come down with the last fall of snow," said Nannie. "I know all about it. I can tell the way things are trending."

"How?" Betty asked, artlessly.

"From various sources." But that was untrue. The only source was Mrs Tumulty.

"No doubt you think Madam is employing you for the sole purpose of getting yourself taken advantage of by soldiers during your working hours." Anxiety and indignation made her exaggerate harshly.

"You must have carried on alarming when *you* were young, to have such ideas in your head about *me*."

"Very well then, miss," Nannie said threateningly.

"Very well what?"

"If you incline to sauciness with me, maybe Madam's the one to deal with you. Going out with men when you're in charge; soldiers, too; letting them lay hands on baby's pram. I shall wake in the night and go cold at the thought."

"What's the harm, even if he did?"

"What harm? Don't you ever read the paper? I sometimes wonder where you've been all these years. When I first went into a nursery we weren't even allowed to join up with other nannies in the Park. My mistress said to me: 'I hear as you were out with Nannie Pankhurst this afternoon,' she said. 'Please remember to keep yourself to yourself, and Baby to hisself. You won't see the Royal nannies gossiping along with others.' And here are you up on the Cliff Road with soldiers. And sitting down on the seat, letting him hold the pram in his filthy hands, and jigging it up and down to keep Baby quiet. I felt my ears were deceiving me when I heard that."

"His hands are no more filthy than yours. He happens to be a gentleman."

"I hear differently. I know to my certain knowledge that he's a soldier."

"And can't a gentleman be a soldier, then?"

"No."

Nannie handed her a nightgown off the clothes'-horse. "Is this supposed to be ironed or what? Did they never teach you how to respect nuns-veiling in that so-called college of yours? No, as I was saying before, a gentleman would be an officer and as such not likely to be seen pushing a pram or sitting about on benches in broad daylight. You better remember, my girl; and if you can't, we'll see if Madam has any way of reminding you. When you take Baby out, you *take* him out. On your own. Now you'll kindly go down and ask leave of Mrs Kelsey to borrow a shammy-leather to give the pram-handle a wipe over. And mind there's no future cause for complaint."

'It's that damned old Mrs Tumulty,' Betty thought, running downstairs. 'I feel really upset,' she told herself; but she knew that the course of true love never does run smooth and tomorrow was her evening off when she could tell Laurence all about it.

Chapter 8

IT WAS absurd to make love at the beginning of the outing. Vinny knew that he should have waited for the return journey, or at least until after they had drunk the bottle of wine. They were observed, too; though in a desultory way by a man on the skyline carrying a large black butterfly-net.

The air was unsteady with heat, for the chalky path went down to the sea between steep hills; an enclosed and sensuous place with its long grasses and butterflies. When Emily sat down to take a stone from her shoe, Vinny sat down, too, and would not get up again.

It was a great triumph that she had come with him after so many refusals, and part of the triumph had been that Rose had now joined issue with him. He had brought into the open his love, and she her hate; and at breakfast she had told him that she would need his room now, for other purposes. "I cannot afford this weekend letting at the height of the season," she had said rudely.

When Emily had fastened her shoe again, she sat up very straight and looked ahead, waiting for him to finish his rest. Yet in her heart she dreaded their ever walking on again and, though she tried to look aloof, she was worried that it was in response to her, to her ill-disguised inclinations, that he put out his hand and drew her round to face him. Perhaps it was too much in accord with her own feelings, which she was not used to having interpreted; and she looked at him anxiously, and then up at the man on the skyline.

143

"He reminds me of your mother," she said hesitantly.

"I don't mind if it *is* my mother."

"These are all very common butterflies round us—Cliveden Blues and marbled whites. I don't think they are very rare. But it is a famous place all the same, and there are always very strange people here—strange men, I mean—with those large nets; not at all the sort of butterfly-net I had as a child. . . ." Her voice trailed away.

He kissed her arms, and she still looked nervously about her.

He said: "Will you please forget that man up there. There is a time and a place for everything and even if this isn't the time, it is so beautifully the place. And I have never been anywhere before so seductive. The very grass breathes seduction, and all the silly little butterflies give an erotic charm to the air. I could not find anywhere better to make love to you. It was delightful of you to bring me here."

"But I do not want you to make love to me," she protested, lying down in the grass and crossing her arms under her head in a beautifully submissive movement.

When he kissed her, she betrayed more of her past life than she would ever have done in words, and he sensed what deprivation she had endured in these recent years: once avowedly amorous; perhaps promiscuous as well. His was the acceptedly womanish role of romanticism, his passion a by-product of his passion for *her*. Desire, of itself, had scarcely existed for him, obstructed, or obliterated, as it so often was, by his exaggerated sense of personality. But she—he guessed—had taken her love less seriously, delighting in carnality for its own sake; had probably become light-heartedly engaged to the young man who had made love the best: and, although such marriages often turn out stormy, there is always, he reflected, the answer of the marriage-bed.

The man with the butterfly-net had moved out of sight.

"You *will* marry me?" Vinny said. "I have waited a long time for my first love."

She looked incredulous and then laughed.

"It is true. I could never contrive to *make* love and *be* in love at the same time."

She only vaguely saw a difference, and smiled again.

"If I loved a person, I was too inhibited to—initiate anything . . . I could not take that step forward. . . ."

"How strange! Because *I* find you very bold."

"Yes, it is strange. Strangest of all is that this is the daytime. Before, I have kissed people only in the dark, and certainly not done such a thing as this—at midday, out-of-doors," and he opened her frock and slipped her clothes down from her shoulders.

Her body was creased with shining scars, drawn up into white whorls and ridges. "You see!" she cried; and she turned her head until her face was hidden against the long grass. She feared lest he might cover his revulsion by some sentimental and insensitive act. 'If he should kiss me now,' she thought, 'I should feel like a leper. I could not endure his charity and condescension, or his making a gesture at my expense.'

"My love, I am so shocked for you," he said; and he pulled her up closely to him, as if he could not bear to see.

* * *

145

Mrs Tumulty's luggage stood in the hall, like a testimony to the cumbersome excuses love makes—and they had been most cumbersome and expensive in Vinny's case, this fetching of his mother, and all her curious handbags and paraphernalia, from London to the seaside.

Coming down to luncheon and passing the luggage on her way to the dining-room, Mrs Tumulty told herself that she had been used. 'I did not know I had an artful son,' she thought, spreading her napkin over her knees and nodding at the Tillotsons across the room. 'I thought I read him like a book. But, no, he has *used* me, and made me to look a fool, sitting here alone at my last luncheon, while he gallivants about the countryside.' Other people's outings she always called gallivanting or gadding about. Only if she were included did they acquire the dignity of an excursion or a visit.

At breakfast, he had calmly explained that he would be out all day. "With Miss . . . with Emily," he had said firmly. "It is such a lovely day that we are going for a picnic." He had not invited his mother, or made any mention of how she was to spend her last day in the place to which he had inveigled her. Her whole holiday now took on a look of trickery, and, although she had, in her innocence, enjoyed herself, now she could only feel monstrously ill-used. While she was catching her butterflies, her son had escaped. It was enough to turn her against butterflies for ever, and more than enough to turn her against Seething and all to do with it.

While she ate, phrases kept coming up to the surface of her mind—'bare-faced effrontery', 'as cool as a cucumber', 'without so much as a by-your-leave', 'at his time of life'.

146

"I am rather short-handed this morning," Rose Kelsey had said very tartly when Mrs Tumulty had gone into the kitchen for a piece of string to tie together the camera-tripod, umbrella and butterfly-net. Really, the work was going beautifully, but Philly was moping, sitting by the kitchen-window and looking out, as if for Emily's return. She feared her mother in her present mood of frantic hurry—the spiteful look as she cut up vegetables, the way she crashed down the lids of saucepans. For Rose was in torment. She saw Emily slipping back into her old ways, remembered the reeling horror in which, she, Rose, had learned, when they were girls, that her sister was not chaste. Emily had laughed impatiently at her distress. Now Rose wondered if these peaceful, virginal years since Emily's accident had been in truth most wretchedly against her nature. The apathy, the lack of laughter, the reserve, the stammer and hesitancy in her speech, were surely the result of pain and long illness? Rose had believed that and had foreseen no end to their gentle days together; no reason why they should ever change. 'Life, stop still here!' she had prayed; and she had no means of expressing her detestation of Vinny for threatening this. Lacking a wax image to pierce with pins, she could only be rude to his mother; tell him she required his room; slam down the saucepan-lids and take her revenge in a martyrdom no one observed.

Philly sat in the kitchen because, unused to being alone, she did not know where else to be. Her mother, in this mood, terrified her. She waited with intensity for Emily's return, believing that she must come at any moment; for she never was long away.

When it was luncheon-time, she went reluctantly to

Rose's sitting-room, where they sat together in silence. Rose's cheeks were flushed; her hands trembled as she cut up Philly's meat for her. 'To be here alone with her!' she was thinking, feeling the girl's reproachful look. 'If Emily ever went away! To wait, all alone, for the next fit of tantrums! To be watched and watched in this way, until there is nowhere left to look! And what are they doing now, and saying? She and that man? I dread seeing her come back. When we were girls, I always knew when she returned—knew by the look of her what had been happening . . . when she was laughing and easeful; teasing; bright. I could not bear to stay in the same room with her. But to leave me today! My busiest day—with Mrs Smith not here; Mrs Tumulty going; all the teas to get; and Philly on my hands.' She went on more articulately in her mind with this last complaint, knowing it was the only one she could ever make aloud.

"You should eat your fat," she said sharply to Philly. "It is good for you."

Philly looked across at her with the boldness of terror, saying nothing, and fearfully Rose stood up and put the plates together.

Mrs Tumulty went out to a deck-chair with her Sunday newspapers and read the Horoscopes. Her own —Gemini—was very uninteresting, with financial difficulties and tension in the home on Tuesday. She turned to Vinny's—July the third, Cancer—and was filled with annoyance to find that the affairs of his heart would prosper, with obstacles removed and help forthcoming from an unexpected quarter.

'He is making a laughing-stock of himself,' she thought. 'Helping lame dogs over stiles is one thing.'

"Pandemonium!" she said aloud, frowning, as Benjy Tillotson began, for some reason or other, to howl.

"Benjy!' shouted his father's warning voice. "Give Constance her spade immediately."

The way of giving it was to whack her over the head; so Constance began to cry.

'A tenement,' Mrs Tumulty thought. 'He might just as well have taken me for a holiday in a slum. I shall never trust him again. Such a whited sepulchre. His father would turn in his grave to see me treated so. Chivied from pillar to post, to suit his slightest convenience. At my age.'

Love is a disturbing element, as Isabella had said—disruptive, far-reaching. The world cannot assimilate it, or eject it. Its beauty can evoke evil: its radiance corrupts: and Vinny and Emily alone on the rocks, drinking their wine, feeling the sun touch their very bones, had bred, from their own bliss, fear, terror, indignation, shame and hate.

*   *   *

"Oh, it is bliss," Emily said. "The word is like a new one to me at this moment. I feel that we have just invented it."

The sun had warmed the wine and she dipped her madeleine cake into it. The rest of the wine was put to cool, the bottle wedged into a crack in the rocks, where the sea ran in. Clear water was like glass above white pebbles, blood-red seaweed.

They were alone in the cove except for, across the rocks, a woman knitting and a little girl in a sun-bonnet, who approached the sea's edge uncertainly, staggered, her little spade waving, suddenly sat down.

On their—Vinny's and Emily's—side of the cove, ledges of rocks descended in layers, limpet-encrusted. On the lower ledges, the sea washed over them, fanning out soapily, going scrupulously into the corners like a good charwoman.

Vinny reached for the bottle. The label floated away and he caught it up carefully from the water and put it to dry on the rock.

"To keep for ever."

She smiled, with her mouth against the wineglass, and raised her eyebrows in a puzzled way. When she had drunk, she said: "I can't see the point."

"Have *you* kept nothing?"

"Nothing."

"Not from anyone?"

"Nothing."

"No letters, pressed flowers, champagne-corks?"

"Not a thing."

"You are a very funny girl."

"I feel rather drunk."

"Yes, it is wonderful to sit in the sun and feel blurred with wine, and drowsy."

He put his hand on her thigh and at once she put down the glass she was holding. Something prompt and lacking in coquetry in her made him laugh. When he leaned over her and embraced her, the woman across the rocks rolled up her knitting, and called sharply to her child.

The difficulties of their future had risen and fallen all day, like a fever-chart, receding with each kiss, each glass of wine, vanishing altogether now. Only later, when they began to pack up the basket, did those problems loom again and, going home as the shadow stretched and thinned, they looked once more, to both their minds, well-nigh insuperable.

But Vinny felt full of courage and energy, ready to plead with Rita again. 'I will go next week,' he thought. 'Then, when everything is settled, as it must be, I shall tell Emily; be sure of her understanding.'

They seemed, going up the drive, like creatures without shells, dreading any impact: lovers returning to the world. When Betty, hurrying away from the house, said 'Good-evening', they flinched; for all day long they had heard only one another's voices.

Chapter 9

"Mother," Laurence had said. "That friend I went to stay with at Portsmouth, Len, I wondered if it would be any use asking him down here the next weekend we can get off."

"Any use, darling? How do you mean? I like to meet your friends," Isabella said encouragingly.

"I just wondered *would* you, though? He's a bit of a rough diamond. I mean, the men you meet in the Army aren't always too fancy, though very nice."

"I think it is wonderful of you to be so adaptable."

He blushed.

"But I cannot understand why they don't give you a commission like everyone else."

"So this Len, you see, now the summer's here said he felt like a breath of sea air." Then, remembering that Len's home was also on the coast, he quickly added: "He likes a change."

The truth was, Len was curious about Betty, of whom Laurence talked so much, and wished to give her, and Laurence's home, as well, what he called the once-over. Laurence, though nervous of the impact of Len on his mother, was tempted by the picture of himself with Betty clinging to his arm: they would indulge in teasings and little familiarities in front of Len, as Len had before Laurence with *his* young lady. Laurence would assume a proprietary attitude for which Len would respect him enough to make coarse allusions before the other men on their return.

On the other hand, he could not help being a little uneasy, and when Isabella said: "It will be lovely, darling," he was not really convinced that it would.

"You will remember what I said—not to make him feel awkward?"

"I think I know how to behave," Isabella said crossly.

"Yes, I know, but you might think *he* doesn't."

"Shall you just leave it to me?" she suggested, icily smooth. "Remembering that as your father's wife I think I showed myself equal to most occasions."

'Well, if she is going to be like that for a start!' Laurence thought, his apprehension growing.

When the weekend arrived, she was not at all 'like that'. She rather enlisted Len's services in correcting Laurence; for Len was, unmistakably, the fatherly type. One glance at his red, good-tempered face reassured her. He would lead her son into no harm. All the same, she could not resist a little lecture when Len asked if anyone could tell him what had won the three-fifteen at Chester.

"I'm afraid no one here would have any idea," she said. "I do hope you, Laurence, don't back horses. Except for the big races."

"What are the big races?"

"Well, darling, the ones everyone takes an interest in. The Derby, and the National. And," she added doubtfully, "perhaps the Lincoln."

"Nothing at Ascot?"

She looked suspiciously at him, feeling he was making fun of her. "I am really serious," she said to Len. "My father lost so much money on horses. He was a born gambler, and sometimes it runs in families, so that one must be on one's guard. It ruined my mother's health

153

and happiness." That was a grand way of saying that her mother had nagged.

"What, Granny?" said Laurence, seeing her in a new light.

"On our pay, we can't afford to have a bet," Len assured Isabella.

'We can't afford not to,' Laurence thought.

"It's the bookmakers who ride in the Rolls-Royces, in my experience," Len said, speaking from it.

"How right you are, my dear boy!" Isabella said. Len she recognised as being a man-of-the-world, beside whom Laurence seemed a schoolboy still, with his sulks and impatiences.

"Good *Lord*!" he was always saying, and flinging himself into an armchair. But every time Isabella came into the room, Len jumped up and fussed with the chairs and had his cigarette-lighter ready, if not his cigarettes. 'Showing-off!' Laurence thought, wishing that he had never invited him. His mother was showing-off, too, with her 'dear boy' and her sycophantic advice-asking. She was also smoking too much. . . . He looked forward to tomorrow, to Betty's half-day, when he could do a little showing-off himself.

"Not a very nice evening for you," Isabella said, joining Len at the window. People were coming up from the rain-pitted sands wearing mackintoshes: some of them held wet newspapers over their heads. All the deck-chairs were abandoned. The boat-littered water by the pier faintly steamed. A young boy came pelting along the slippery esplanade and stopped to push the evening paper through the letter-box.

"The paper!" Isabella said.

No one stirred.

"Laurence, dear, would you fetch the paper?" (No 'dear boy', though; just the 'dear'.)

"I will," said Len, and was out of the room first.

"*Such* disappointing weather," Isabella continued. "Ah, thank you, Len." She glanced carelessly at the headlines. "Oh, dear, another bus strike! What is the world coming to? I'm sure they don't know when they're well off. Everything done for them and they're never satisfied."

Len, whose father was a bus-driver, seemed not to be listening. Turning from Isabella, he grimaced at Laurence, his thumbs going down dolefully. Laurence looked steadily back. Isabella continued to chatter her way through the news. She looked at each page in order and only glanced at the stop-press.

"Do you want the paper, Laurence? Or Len?"

"No, thanks," Laurence said.

Len took it, as if for politeness' sake, and read out the weather-report.

"Now, let's have some sherry!" Isabella said, suddenly gay.

Evalie Hobson seemed gay, too, when she arrived for dinner—to help Isabella out, as they had arranged.

After dinner, the boys went for a walk.

"It was all right, then?" Evalie said. "You *did* do King Humphrey?"

"Not only. I had a double with Dumb Blonde."

"Oh, you didn't *tell* me!"

"And how could I, with Laurence and his friend in the house? Every time I went to the telephone, one or other of them came into the hall."

"I was only *teasing*," Evalie said frostily.

*   *   *
155

"Whose tip was that?" Len asked, as they pushed open the swing-door of the Saloon Bar. "Anthology, or however you say it?" He stressed the third syllable.

"Anthology," Laurence said. "Ginger had it from one of the apprentices at Newmarket. Next time out, he said."

"Two small milds," Len said.

When it was Laurence's turn, he ordered their usual mild-and-bitter.

"I was economising," Len said. "In the circs."

"Well, I had a saver on King Humphrey."

"You might have passed it on."

"I thought I did mention it,"

"You bloody know you didn't."

"Well, I'm sorry."

They drank in silence.

"Don't look round," Laurence said later. "Boy-friend of my mother's just come in."

Vinny, seeing Laurence pretending not to see him, crossed to the other side of the bar, drank a whisky and went out.

"What, serious?" Len asked.

"I daresay."

"Quite a decent-looking old codger. He put that down fast. Does he drink?"

"Everybody drinks," Laurence said crossly.

"Do you mean he wants to marry her?"

"I shouldn't wonder."

"Very queer," Len mused. "Thinking of such things at that age."

"Gives me the cold horrors," Laurence said.

"Must be fifty if he's a day. What does your mother think of him?"

156

"Oh, Lord, don't ask *me*."

"Well, I don't blame them," Len said tolerantly. "They'd be company for one another." He was interested in Isabella and her affairs. "In their old age," he added.

"Shall we move on?" Laurence asked.

* * *

Vinny had needed his whisky. He had walked along the sands with Emily and Philly after tea. Philly had kept stubbornly apart, edging too near the sea and getting her sandals wet, to draw attention to herself.

"Can we never be alone?" he had asked.

"Rose is busy with someone new arriving. I had to keep Philly out of the way. It is almost all I do. Come back, darling," she called.

"I hate to hear you sigh, as if you were tired through and through."

"I cannot be that, for Rose lets me do less and less."

"To have come all this way and never to see you alone! Nothing ever again like that one beautiful Sunday we had."

"Which still has its repercussions."

"But if she won't let you do any work, how can she miss you when she says she is busy?"

"I have told you, I keep Philly out of her way. Someone must be with her, or she mopes, and hangs about the kitchen. I can understand how Rose feels. She is frightened of the child, of what she will do, and how to deal with her—for she is really incalculable."

She picked up a shell and called to Philly, holding it out in her hand; but the girl turned her head exaggeratedly and walked on.

"When you've seen her to bed?" Vinny suggested. "She goes much later now that the evenings are light."

"I can wait till night."

"Yes, well, then . . ."

"I will meet you at the bottom of the steps."

"The tide will be coming in later."

"Then I shall be cut off, if you don't come in time. I shall have to go up the steps into the garden."

"Please, don't."

Then Philly had slipped on a rock she was climbing and had cut and grazed her legs. They helped her up the steps. She made no sound, looking with vague interest at the blood starting through Vinny's handkerchief, and trickling down towards her ankle.

"Oh, can't you take more care of her?" Rose said sharply, meeting them as they came to the house. Philly leant back against Emily, pinching up a fold of her sleeve, as if to hold on to safety.

When Emily had gone for a bowl of water and bandages, Rose had said to Vinny: "Can't you please leave us alone? I am forced for all our sakes to speak to you in this way, because you interfere here and make us wretched, and I have to think of Emily's happiness. She has had so little."

"You know I want to marry her."

"You are only sorry for her. You cannot resist your feelings of compassion."

"No, I am, after all, only sorry for you."

"You shan't pity me!" Rose said, in a furious, small voice. She stroked Philly's untidy hair and her hand was trembling. Philly's unmoving eyes were filled with terror; but she sat very still, as if to move would be fatal. "How dare you!" Rose whispered.

"After all, what pity I feel, and for whom, is beyond my control. And beyond yours, too. Neither of us can stop it."

When Emily returned, he said goodbye and went fast down to the town where he turned into the first pub he came to and bought a large whisky.

*　　　*　　　*

"Belmont," Evalie suggested, going through the *Morning Advertiser*.

"Belmont?" said Isabella. "But we don't know what weight it's carrying."

"It did well at Thirsk. Oh, do you remember when we did our first crossed doubles—how nervous we were? There ought to be evening-classes for those things. Would that be someone at the door?"

"Perhaps the boy's back home again." Evalie folded the paper and stuffed it in her handbag.

But it was Vinny.

"How nice!" Isabella said. "We will all have a little drink. I feel rather gay tonight. I can't think why, but I expect because the boys are here. This doesn't look very nice whisky . . . so much tartan all over the label. Oh, I always wanted two sons, and a daughter, too: but after Laurie, there was all that bother with my Fallopian tubes, whatever they may be. I am so sorry there's no soda-water."

"I feel gay, too; but not so gay as Isabella," Evalie said meaningly.

"And I should feel gayest of all," Vinny said, which was far from true, "because I had a little flutter today."

"A little flutter?" Evalie said.

"A bet. On a horse."

"Oh, I see. And did it win?"

"It did."

"What was its name?"

"Its name," said Vinny, raising his glass, "was Dumb Blonde. So ridiculous."

Isabella looked down, and Evalie from her to Vinny.

"You must tell us what will win at Ascot," she said, "then we can have a little flutter too."

* * *

Len said: "I like your pubs, old boy."

Laurence felt personally congratulated and looked with modesty about the saloon-bar. They were in The Anchor now.

"I like the beer," Len added. He was more of a connoisseur than Laurence, who found all beer much the same and now felt very sick. The barmaid receded, then swam up towards him, enormous and not quite, he thought, straight on her feet. Small things caught and held his attention. He concentrated his mind and his eyes on the wet rings his glass made on the counter. When the barmaid swept a damp cloth over them, he still stared stupidly, feeling unsafe, as if some prop had been removed.

"Haven't," Len said, "ever enjoyed myself so much with my clothes on." This was one of his favourite sayings and Laurence hoped he would not be using it indiscriminately.

"A pity the blonde couldn't be with us this evening."

Laurence could not imagine Betty on such a round. When he was with her, they went to the milk-bar and, under the fluorescent lighting which turned the food an uninviting colour, they ate and drank the childish fare which Len despised—sundaes, shakes, parfaits, whips, melbas.

The proprietary word 'blonde' had made Laurence feel nervous that Len might try to take over his girl as he seemed to have taken over Isabella, perhaps aligning himself with her with little jokes at Laurence's expense.

'People are different in different places,' he thought hazily. 'And if they're all right in one place, it's best to leave them there.' Len at Aldershot was one thing; but in Laurence's home he was too clearly making his mark —helping to wash-up; complimenting Isabella on almost everything she did, or had; condescending to Laurence.

"Nice when she calls 'Time' and we don't have to go on enjoying ourselves," Len said. But that was one of his sayings, too, and meant as a joke. "You look a bit under the weather, old boy," he told Laurence.

"I bloody well feel it."

He did not see any reason why he should be competitive about drinking, when he had always disdained to be so about everything else—games at parties as a child; school athletics; getting his commission. He had never won, or tried to win, any of those little silver cups which his mother seemed to think part of the décor of a schoolboy's bedroom. He said: "I've been quite drunk for at least half-an-hour."

"Well, I don't know how you manage it," Len said, but not in a congratulatory voice. "You've only had the same as me."

"Then we must come to the conclusion that I get drunk quicker."

"No cause to get shirty."

"I am shirtanly not certy.'

"I feel fit as a flea myself."

"Then you can deal with my mother when we get home."

"Of course, old boy, make it all right for you."

"She has never seen me sewn-up before."

"She won't know, I promise you."

"Got to *get* home first," Laurence said gloomily.

"Better make a move then," Len said and, to Laurence's indignation, put an arm along his shoulders and steered him out of the pub.

Vinny was just leaving Isabella's when they arrived; but one look at Laurence made him step back into the hall.

"Have you had a nice stroll?" Isabella asked them.

"Never enjoyed myself so much," Len said. "Nasty shower about nine, so wè stepped in for a glass of beer. Very quaint little pub. Once used by smugglers, so the Landlord was saying. I always like anything with a bit of history about it."

"Come and have a whisky," Isabella gaily said.

Vinny thought both she and Evalie were over-excited; their first drink had gone to their heads. He stood slightly in front of Laurence while Len talked. Laurence bowed and swayed, trying to keep his back against the wall and then, whitening, began to make for the staircase as if treading air. Vinny followed him.

"Whatever is wrong?" Isabella asked.

"Poor old Laurie doesn't feel too great," Len said, and he fended her off, into the parlour, where Evalie was sitting, straining her ears.

"In what way?" said Isabella.

"He wasn't too good on the journey here. We got a lift part of the way in a lorry, and what with the jolting and the fumes . . ."

"Laurie not too good?" Evalie enquired.

"I thought he looked pale at luncheon," Isabella said. "What is the Army food like really? He always says 'not bad', but I have doubts."

"We don't get caviare above every other day."

"And you have to work so hard, though I am not quite sure what *at*. Does *your* mother worry?"

"All mothers worry," Len said with a fond smile at her.

"Perhaps he needs a tonic. But I am sure you think I am fussing. You mustn't tell him. Won't you have a drink, Len? Do help yourself."

"I wouldn't mind a small whisky."

"Do! It's all on the tray."

"What about you?" He looked from her to Evalie, his hand on the decanter.

"I can't see why not," they agreed.

"Thank you, Len," Evalie said, taking hers, and looking up at him.

"Well, I certainly am enjoying myself," he said, and drank. "Sorry about poor old Laurie, though," he added with a pious expression. "I'll go up and see how he is."

"I should leave him," Vinny said coming into the room. "He's gone to bed."

"Oh, but I must take him up some hot milk," Isabella said.

"He doesn't want to be bothered. I asked him."

"I wonder what is wrong?" Isabella said.

"Lot of gastric 'flu about," Vinny said.

"He may have eaten something," Len suggested.

"Thank you for your help, Vinny. Have a drink."

"No. I must go."

Isabella saw him out and then went up to Laurence's room.

"He's pretty well had it, hasn't he?" Evalie asked Len.

"I'm afraid so. He doesn't want his mother to know."

"I can't see how she can't. You reek of alcohol. Do you go on like this at Aldershot?"

"We couldn't, on our pay."

"He's fast asleep already," Isabella told them. "He must have been completely exhausted, poor boy. No wonder he's been so cross all day."

"He'll be better in the morning," Evalie said without conviction.

"He's been over-working, I can tell. I don't honestly agree with all this drilling and marching . . . even guardsmen faint sometimes . . . and Laurence simply hasn't the physique. You're different, Len, I can tell. Much sturdier."

"Oh, I don't know."

Evalie thought: 'He looks like a purring cat with cream all over its whiskers.'

*   *   *

Rose, when she saw Emily glance at the clock, was sure that her sister meant to go out again that evening. They were in the kitchen, shelling the peas for the next day and, as soon as they were done, Rose gave a great tired sigh and began to get out the pastry-board.

"Oh, surely you aren't going to begin cooking at this time of night," Emily protested.

"It has to be done."

"You always make the pastry in the morning."

"I shall have more than enough to do tomorrow."

"But why more than usual?"

164

"You seem to forget we have extra people here."

"Only one."

Rose measured the flour.

"I can do it in the morning," Emily offered.

There is no impatience like the impatience of desire thwarted. To be out of Vinny's arms one moment more was so intolerable that she felt like a spoilt child, ready to stamp her foot. It was difficult to hide her disappointment at the delay even this argument had caused; and she did not hide it. Rose, looking so disdainfully into the mixing-bowl as she poured in water, became a ridiculous and hated person. She would have liked to do her some physical violence, push her roughly, shake the look of suffering from her face; as often, when they were children, she had been driven to snatching things from her or pulling her plaits. Then Rose had run in and told tales. Now that there was no one for her to tell, Emily could imagine the lingering air of injury, the muted offendedness she would carry about for days.

Rose, knowing her sister's hands were clasped tight with exasperation, would not look in her direction. She knew herself the misery of such over-riding passion, though in herself it had sprung always from hatred and not love, from disgust and never from desire, and she dealt it out as a punishment, knowing its discomfort and shame.

The pastry had gone too far now to be left till morning, and Emily, in a voice she had not used since girlhood, could only grumble. "You were always a martyr."

"To have to work so late and then to be abused as well . . ." Rose began; but, fearing that Emily would

165

use a quarrel as an excuse for walking out of the room, she caught her breath. It was caught on a sob, and she leant heavily against the table, and then put her floury hands to her eyes.

Emily, on the wing almost, about to defy, was trapped.

"I cannot go on," Rose cried.

Again, Emily was tempted to shake her, knowing that Vinny must be waiting already and only Rose was in her way.

"Are you tired?" she asked coldly. "I told you not to begin all this work."

"You don't understand. It is useless to explain. You know nothing about running the house."

"Because you will never let me help."

"I don't want your help. I haven't ever wanted it and I am not asking for it now. But I have to plan my work ahead, and you won't understand. I have to get *forward*, or when I wake tomorrow I cannot face the day."

Her driven look, her desperate voice, began to alarm her sister. The streaks of flour on her face were so un-Roselike.

"You are over-tired," she suggested.

"It is this terrible pain."

"Are you ill, then?"

"I feel as if my inside were being dragged from me," Rose said, so graphically that she indeed began to feel this. As, when her husband was alive, it seemed that her body would not let her tell a lie and immediately caught up with whatever she described.

"Then you must go to bed."

"How can I go to bed?"

"I can finish all this."

166

"I know your pastry," Rose said, and sank down into a chair and began to cry.

*   *   *

"He was always delicate," Isabella said to Len, speaking of Laurence. "When he was a baby, his digestion was such a trouble. Diarrhœa, and so on."

Len nodded. He was tired himself now and wanted to go to bed.

"I thought we should never rear him. I know my mother-in-law openly said so. I would creep into the nursery at night and wonder if he could ever live till morning. He had a sort of mauve look."

"Horrible!" said Len.

"Does he seem to stand up to Army life?"

"He mucks in like the rest."

"Well, of course; but does he seem to you to get especially fatigued?"

"I daresay he gets a bit browned-off. I know I do."

"There was that terrible experience he had when my husband . . . I expect he told you."

"Yes," Len said quickly. He looked away while she was searching for her handkerchief.

"His matron," Isabella struggled to resume, "at Prep-school used to say to me: 'That boy is living on his nerves. He wants taking out of himself more.' But we never seemed to manage it. We could never hit on anything that interested him. Were you strong as a child, Len? I imagine you were."

"I was all right once I'd had out my adenoids."

"Were you? Yes, they said that would make all the difference to Laurence, but we didn't notice any change. He's still a mouth-breather I'm afraid."

167

'Poor sod!' Len thought. 'I expect his ears burn as well.'

"Only children are always a problem. I should have liked a large family, but I could not—for internal reasons."

"Quite."

"Laurie tells me you are engaged to be married."

"That's right."

"It's very young to be making up your mind, you know."

"So her dad said; but I don't know. My brother had been engaged twice by the time he was *my* age."

"Twice?"

He blushed when she laughed.

"But I'm different with this girl," he said simply. "I really love her, with all my heart and soul."

"How heavenly for you!" Isabella said. Her warm voice masked the foolishness of her words.

"I'd rather you didn't repeat it to Laurie, though. I never told anyone before, not even her—my young lady. You don't want them feeling too sure of you," he added, with a return to his usual swagger, "or they get above themselves. My way is to always have them guessing."

"Is *that* what men think?" Isabella asked him with great interest; for she was always ready to learn. "I could not be more fascinated."

Chapter 10

VINNY left by an early train next day. As if there were not enough obstacles in his way, Rose had now thrown in a nervous collapse, convincing to all, endorsed by her doctor. Philly's grazed leg had become septic. It was a good thing, after all, Emily said, that Rose had insisted on getting 'forward' with the work, for Rose was not merely in bed; but fretting in bed, with a great deal of bell-ringing, reminders, and advice.

"I ran out to the steps last night," Emily apologised, when Vinny called in the morning, "but it was too late. The tide was right up, and you had gone."

He sat down in the kitchen, watching her while she worked. He said: "I waited until I could scarcely get back over the rocks." He was cross at the memory of scrambling over the slippery ledges, once or twice having to put his hands down to steady himself; and a wave had washed right over his shoes. He had appeared ridiculous to himself, an elderly man behaving like a love-lorn youth.

"I was sorry," Emily repeated. She would not explain how inadequate a word this was for her sense of dismay and deprivation, seeing the water churning about the foot of the steps and knowing that he could not have waited.

"You asked me not to come up to the garden," he said reproachfully.

"It would have seemed strange, so late."

"To wait about in the dark anywhere at my age is

strange. It is not at all seemly. You will have me clambering up balconies very soon, and that is not my way of doing things. I should like to have a proper courtship, and an announcement in *The Times*."

"*Why* do you want to marry me? Is it from pity? Rose says it is."

"I don't know what is meant by such a word. Perhaps 'pity' is one of those beautiful and debased words, like 'charity'. Ruined by condescension. If there is condescension, one-sidedness in it, I could not feel it for you. Yet if you are hurt, I should pity you, surely—as well as admiring your loveliness, which was the first thing I knew of you—when I watched you walking on the sands that evening, and the time when you ran into my arms in the dark."

"You could not know whom you took into your arms."

"Yes, I knew."

"I had given up love. I had gone into a nunnery."

"You had that hood over your head and those wide sleeves to your coat. Yes, a nun."

"But no nice thoughts, no good deeds or living for others."

"You did not live."

"This week I did something to try to please you. I went into the town one morning. I was just finding the courage to walk into the café and sit down at one of the tables among all those shopping women, when a man I used to know came out. I said 'good-morning' to him and he looked quickly over his shoulder thinking I must mean someone behind him. Then he raised his hat and fled."

"Did you still go into the café?"

"No."

"I wish you had."

"I felt that I was blushing; but I cannot blush. Did you know that?"

"Your arms blush."

She looked down at them with great interest, then said: "The moment in my life when I felt really destroyed was the moment when everyone thought I was well again. For the first time, the doctor allowed me to have a looking-glass. He handed it to me with such a pleased smile and stood back to watch. I can see him now, his hands clasped over his stomach, leaning back a little; confident, so triumphant—like . . . like one's favourite uncle who has given one a present. I stared and stared, but no words came. I knew I was lost. Until then, however in pain, bandaged, in darkness, despairing, I had been myself. But in that looking-glass there was no vestige of me."

"The poor doctor!" Vinny said, and turned quickly and looked out of the window.

"Oh, I remembered in time—that I had been properly brought up and would not be ungracious about a gift. Before his smile could fade, I managed to say thank you. I went on staring at myself, saw the lips move, *my* lips; then tears rolled out of the eyes. When the Sister came in, I had dropped the mirror and was crying with rage and terror. I thought that I would never again have the courage to look at myself. 'It's the relief,' she told the doctor, and he went happy away."

She put some dishes into the oven and slammed the door. "Rose said last night: 'I know your pastry,' and look at it, quite grey. So I am useless as well."

"Next week you will walk right into that café?"

"Yes, I will," she said in a hurried voice.

"Which day?"

"Perhaps Wednesday?"

"Wednesday. At eleven. It must be exactly at eleven, because in my mind I shall be going in with you."

Those games, to outwit time and distance, all lovers play—the rose that the hand touched, the kisses on paper: so that the earth is spun about by invisible threads, a tangle of enchantment.

In the train, the enchantment flattened out, coming up against the dullness of Sunday evening. He shut his eyes and tried to compose the conversations that he might have with Rita when he arrived at Market Swanford—a less alert, defensive Rita than he had last encountered, when she had tartly disposed of any suggestion of her desertion—an idea he had begun to cherish—with letters to prove her point, she said. He wondered if she had been given some legal advice, so adroit she was, in phrases not her own. To have resorted to solicitors at such a stage disposed of his wan hopes of a dignified agreement. He saw that he could expect no reasonableness, mercy or generosity; that she was resolved to cling fast, in theory, to what she was happy never to have.

At Market Swanford, he walked from the station under scented lime-trees. Grit swirled on the pavements, and he felt tired and dirty. In the Square, a Salvation Army band was playing at the foot of the central statue. Youths leant against the blank shop-windows, watching the band and the girls strolling in twos, and the pigeons. Utterly enervated the place seemed, stupefied by the brassy hymn-tunes. Interiors of public-houses were dim and muted. Cool darkness was cast over the pavements from the wedged-open doors.

Inside, shafts of light looked strangely bilious and out-of-place, striking across rows of beer-handles or bottles, or illuminating dust-motes down varnished walls and on linoleum. Voices inside were only murmurs at this stage, and the band, occasionally punctuated by the brief clash of money being rung-up at a bar, dominated and depressed. Its sound, hardly attenuated, followed Vinny down the street, past the drab jewellers, the shop where Isabella's picture on glass was still propped up against an old fender. The door at the side of the tailor's was shut. When he rang the bell, the sound seemed to come from inside his own head, so tired was he, so much beyond—at his age—enduring the exhaustion and complication of his affairs.

'We can afford to be undignified only when we are young', he thought, waiting in the street, staring at his dusty shoes. 'And love, alas, has so much indignity attached to it.'

The bell sounded far away from its source, winding up the stairs, along passages, carrying his urgency to her; but she did not come. He wondered—for it was the first time he had ever come to see her without a warning—if she were shut in there, hiding, whispering, with a lover. He yearned for this lover for her with all his heart, and stepped back on the pavement and looked up, as if he might see him peering down from between the flowered curtains. The windows were shut and blank. For a long time, he could not believe that she might be away from home, that he had made this impulsive but tedious journey for nothing. The streets had so filled him with ennui that he could not imagine them tempting anyone forth from indoors.

He rang again, but hardly waited. He walked dully

away, and Emily was in another world from him at that moment.

'I shall keep coming back,' he thought. 'Again and again. Ringing the bell until my train is due.'

A man went by carrying a trombone, and Vinny realised that the band had stopped playing. In the Square, they were packing up, dispersing, watched still by those youths who leant against the shop-windows and the iron grilles across doorways. Women, sitting at opened upstairs-windows, gazed down hypnotically. 'How can they be so bored, and live?' Vinny wondered, feeling so permeated himself by the slackness of the atmosphere that he might just as well, he thought, expire along with his fading hopes. 'Fading desire, too,' he was forced to admit, sure that if he had Emily in his arms at that moment, he could feel nothing but dullness. Yawning, he caught a glimpse of himself in a big navy-blue shop-blind. His bowed shoulders looked thickened, bison-like. He was walking as if over-burdened by the small case and the hat he carried. His grey hair was greasy and combed into furrows. Untidily, his jacket swung open, his tie flew out. To escape any other reflections of himself and the despondency of the streets, he turned into a pub. This was the cocktail-bar of the only big hotel. Rather appalling, he thought (for he inclined towards old-fashioned pubs with frosted, engraved glass and photographs on the walls of boxers, actresses, rosetted dray-horses), with raw-hide and chromium.

On one of the stools at the bar, Rita was sitting.

"Well, look who's here!" she called. Her two companions glanced with interest at Vinny. "Hello, stranger! What brings you here?"

Vinny thought that she must be drunk and wondered why she spoke with an American accent.

"What are you doing around here?" she rattled on. "Oh, pardon! Mr and Mrs Wilcox, Mr Tumulty. What are we all having?"

"No, please!" Mr Wilcox leant authoritatively over the bar, trying to engage the attention of the barmaid. "What's yours, old man?" he asked Vinny.

Mrs Wilcox handed round a large gold case of cigarettes. The case was so slim that the cigarettes were squashed. They were scented from her handbag and after the first draw Vinny held it down at his side. Mrs Wilcox had purple-auburn hair and a black suit covered with dandruff. She examined her fingernails a great deal, cleaning one with the tip of another, pushing back her cuticles and staring crossly at the chipped varnish. As she moved her hands, all the seals on her bracelet slid heavily together. Rita, still chattering brightly, stirred the ice and fruit in her drink with a sprig of borage.

"Were you passing through?" she asked. "Why ever didn't you phone up?"

"I . . . came to see you."

"Well, why ever not let me know? How did you know where to find me?"

Vinny thought: 'She asks two questions at a time, hoping to get only half the answers.'

"It was rather urgent. I wanted a chat with you."

"It's lucky you found me then. Oh, Davey darling, don't line up another one for me. You know my head. I've got all this already. Oh, you *are*! You simply *are* the end."

She finished one drink and then began to eat all the
175

fruit from it. The American accent kept changing into nasal Mayfair. "I'm so hungry!" she wailed, spearing a cherry.

Mrs Wilcox drank calmly, professionally, as if disposing, without fuss, of some contemptible chore. When she had tired of fidgeting with her hands, she began to pat her hair, and more dandruff fell.

"Good luck!" Vinny said before he drank.

"All the best," said Mr Wilcox.

"Cheers!" Mrs Wilcox murmured offhandedly, in a warding-off way as if throwing spilt salt over her shoulder.

"Well, here I am," Rita said. "All ears." She looked engagingly at Vinny, her head on one side. "What have you got to tell me, pray?"

"Perhaps later you could spare me a moment."

"Later?"

"I don't want to interrupt you now." He glanced uncertainly at her friends and then down at the floor in time to see her foot pressing against Mrs Wilcox's.

"But later we're going out, you see. We can't not, because we've promised."

She put her arm through Mrs Wilcox's, as if she were afraid that Vinny would drag her away.

"Don't mind us," Mrs Wilcox said, and she opened her handbag and stared into it, leaving them in private, she implied.

"May I get you a drink?" Vinny asked her. "What would you like?"

"La même chose, thanks."

"I can't think why ever you didn't phone," Rita said again.

"Yes, I should have done."

"What train are you catching?"

"There is one in ten minutes. No point in staying longer."

"No. What a pity. Not another drink for me! No, you shouldn't."

"All the best," Mr Wilcox said.

"Cheers," said his wife.

"Such a shame we are going out. Next time you come, remember and phone, won't you?"

"Shall I come next Sunday?"

"Really weekends are a bit tricky. I usually go out. Much better ring up."

"Goodbye, then."

Mr and Mrs Wilcox smiled bright, relieved smiles.

"So don't forget," Rita said. "Then we can have our chat."

He imagined, as he crossed to the door, their silence eloquent with grimaces, the two women rigid with smothered laughter.

"Thank you, darlings," Rita said, when he had gone.

"What did he want to talk about?" Mrs Wilcox asked.

"Without unduly flattering myself I think I might say that he didn't want to talk at all."

"How long have you known him?"

"For years and years."

"The rejected suitor," Mr Wilcox said.

"My husband used to say he'd take a horse-whip to him if he didn't leave me alone."

A look of bereavement then saddened her face. Her mouth tightened. A splendid little creature, Mr Wilcox thought. So sunny always, though inconsolable. He patted her shoulder encouragingly. Mrs Wilcox drained her glass. No one ever knew what she was thinking.

Chapter 11

THE next weekend, Vinny drove to Seething in his car. This was a maroon Daimler, twenty years old. When he had fetched it in the middle of the week, Mrs Tumulty had been both scornful and suspicious. It was hearse-like, she complained, and smelt of fungus. She had pictured herself, tied up with veils and wearing goggles, driving in a fast, open car; had hoped for something like the Tillotsons' Bentley. Vinny drove her out to Richmond Park and she found a great deal of fault. "It isn't manœuvrable in traffic," she observed. "I shall have parking difficulties."

"Mother, I don't want you to drive this car."

"You think I am too old, I daresay; but if I lived to be twice my age, I should never choose such an elderly-looking motor as this. I feel like the Queen Mother perched up here. But it would be extremely useful to me to have a car during the day. I could get over to Whiteleys more easily and to Kew and Buckingham Palace."

"You tire yourself out with this Buckingham Palace nonsense."

"On the contrary, I find it very restful."

"Standing about for hours merely to see a car slide in through the gates."

"I had a very clear view of the Queen yesterday. I saw her chin and her pearls. And beautiful dove-grey gloves. I like nice well-fitting gloves." Her own were mauve cotton and needed a wash. "Besides, I don't

178

stand, Vincent, I sit down on the steps of the Victoria monument."

"Oh, mother, no!"

"I buy an evening-paper and sit on that. Vincent, you must stop the car at once. Surely you see that dog over there worrying the sheep?"

"It's only running up and down, and it isn't our affair. There are some people with it."

"It isn't under proper control. I shall have a word with them."

"Mother, please!"

"I have asked you, Vincent, to stop the car."

He had to watch her trailing across the long grasses, her skirts powdered with pollen. At last the dog was brought to heel. The sheep moved away, a querulous, undulating mass. Mrs Tumulty returned to the car, quickened with both annoyance and satisfaction. "So rude!" she said. "Without conscience or civic responsibility. I cannot understand such people."

When they were home again and she was in her room, divesting herself of all her strange outer garments, Vinny had an impulse to telephone Emily. He had thought of her that morning, making her second attempt to enter the café, and he wondered how she had fared. He gave the number and waited impatiently, hoping that his mother would not join him too soon. He felt nervous—and angry with himself for being nervous; feeling sure that Rose would be the one to answer. This happened. The voice was faint and tinny along the singing lines.

He asked: "Are you better?"

"A little, thank you."

"May I speak to Emily?"

"I am afraid not. She isn't at home."

"Then I shall telephone later."

"She has gone out with friends."

"And you don't know when she will return?"

"I'm sorry, I don't."

He sat by the telephone, trembling with anger, believing that Rose had not spoken the truth; for Emily had no friends and there was nowhere for her to go. When he heard his mother coming, he moved towards the open window, looked down at the dusty plane-trees in the gardens of the square. The flat, with all its oriental furniture, travel-trophies and knick-knacks seemed no longer a place that he could bear to inhabit.

"I think I shall write to one of the newspapers," Mrs Tumulty said.

"What about?"

"About people not keeping their dogs under proper control. You seem depressed this evening, Vincent. Is it because you have made such a bad bargain over the car?"

"I am perfectly satisfied about the car."

"Well, I am glad that you are. I am very glad you are."

"You have some weeds stuck to your skirt," he said in exasperation.

"Mouse-ear chickweed," Mrs Tumulty said, stooping to pick it off. "Not uncommon."

*　　　*　　　*

Emily, when he arrived after dinner on Friday, was delighted with the car. She saw him draw up before the house and hastened out to meet him.

"Such a sedate and lovely car!" she said, walking round it.

"I am afraid my mother makes a mockery of it."

"Will you take me for a drive?"

"I bought it for no other purpose."

"All the mahogany and ash-trays and flower-holders. One might almost expect to find a commode. What is this cut-glass decanter?"

"I think it is for smelling-salts in case of an accident."

"Oh, yes, of course." She smiled brightly. He stood looking down at the gravel.

"Please don't worry!" she said. "I know what you are thinking. Surely there are not people anywhere so sensitive that those allusions could distress them? How can words hurt that have no cruel intention? Especially when there are so many of the other kind."

"They sometimes might be cruel simply by being a reminder."

She touched his cheek with her hand. "Don't be sensitive *for* me! There is Rose to be that. Two is too great a burden. Shall we go now? I will run quickly and say goodbye."

Rose, sitting at the sewing-machine, treadling frantically, looked frightening and obsessed. She had a fringe of pins between her lips and was bowed, frowning, as if over some infernal machine. Close to her ear, Emily said—and hoped to run away at once—"I am going for a little drive with Vinny in his car."

The whirring slowed down. Rose put her hand at the small of her back and straightened herself. Quickly, Emily said: "You know that Ralph told you to rest. I could have done these sheets this afternoon, if you had asked me."

"Oh, I know your machining. And what doctor ever explains how one can get all one's jobs done without doing any work? Words come too easily to them."

181

Rose knew that Emily was being solicitous and quoting the doctor from a sense of her own guilt; passing the buck; in fact laying blame to ward off reproaches.

"I shall not be long."

"In a car, did you say?"

"He has just bought one."

"I hope he can drive it properly."

"I hope so."

"Sometimes," Rose began and put her hand hesitantly on the sewing-machine, "sometimes I wonder if . . . I think you must be in love with him."

"Don't sound so accusing."

Her protesting laugh was full of affectation, Rose thought. She was sheltering behind insincerity.

"Where is Philly?" she asked.

"She is drying her hair. I had just finished washing it when Vinny arrived."

"Then I shall have to see her to bed," Rose said.

Emily looked away. 'You *are* her mother!' was a ghost-phrase, unspoken; but perhaps reflected in her eyes.

"Will you help me to fold this sheet before you go?" Rose said.

'She was like that in her married life,' Emily thought, as she went out through the hall. 'Always speeding him on with her martyrdom, sighs, reproaches, the little last jobs before he went out, though implying that they could hardly help. A great one with a welcome when he came home at night; a past-master at not having sat down all day, or touched a morsel of food. Most days started with bleak descriptions of not having slept a wink all night; remembering every quarter having struck, lest proof were needed.' Even as a girl she had had her splitting heads, allergies, indispositions and the

182

perennial travel-sickness. To retaliate, Emily herself had assumed an exaggerated robustness. Because Rose finicked with her food, Emily ate everything—once, standing at a stall in the street, ate jellied eels, the skin as well—and had for a while kept as a pet a grass-snake, overcoming her revulsion as Rose could not.

"Why are you smiling?" Vinny asked, opening the car-door for her.

"I am rather surprised if I was. I was remembering something disgusting."

'It is wonderful,' he thought, 'to see her sit down in the car beside me, as if we have driven out together for years, seeing her smooth her skirt over her knees and settle down.' He said: "Tell me about this disgusting thing."

"When I was a child, I had a pet snake. One day I saw that he had a large bulge in his middle, so I tapped it with a ruler—I was showing-off to Rose—a dreadful ripple ran all along the poor old snake—whose name was Fabian, by-the-by—and a little frog popped out of his mouth."

"I hope you won't keep snakes when we are married," Vinny said in consternation, feeling that one naturalist in his life might be enough.

"I detest them."

"Then why have them about you?"

"Because Rose detested them, too," she said simply.

He drove out on to the Cliff Road, and every car which raced past them he felt with her nerves, though she sat beside him seeming relaxed and indifferent.

Inland, the fields of wheat were a dark blue as clouds raced over them. Vinny drove slowly along the narrow lanes, between hedgerows hoary with chalk dust.

Emily was looking about her quickly, from left to right, as if noting changes in and remembering this country-side which, Vinny supposed, had been for years beyond her limits. At the top of a hill, he drew the car into a field gateway. The view was of a valley, all parkland, dark elms with slanting oval shadows, and a grey house smothered in trees.

"How many years since you drove in a car?" Vinny asked, lifting her hands from her lap and kissing them. "You seem to me to be a very nonchalant and low-strung girl."

"Not years. Last Wednesday." She laughed, but seemed uneasy and then added: "That was my surprise for you."

He leaned away from her and fetched out his cigar-ettes. When she refused one, he stared into the case, as if he could not decide which one to choose.

"I went into the café at eleven," she went on. "You were thinking of me?"

"Of course."

"I knew. I was sure. It was truly a second chance; for, as I went in, the same man was paying his bill at the cash-desk. Instead of hurrying by, because I felt you with me and very brave, I said good-morning to him. This time he smiled and said good-morning, too. We had a little conversation and he apologised for not recognising me that other time. I could tell that since then he had made enquiries about me. He was very charming and made his excuses in a charming way. He even came back into the café with me and sat down at my table. I thought 'How pleased with this Vinny will be!'" She glanced at him uncertainly. He thought that she was smiling too often.

184

"What is his name?" he asked.

"Hughie Cooper."

Vinny looked as if he could not trust a man with such a name.

"And you've known him for years?"

"We used to go to dances together."

"It was nice for you to talk about old times," Vinny said, trying to keep unhappiness from his voice. "How old is he?"

"My sort of age, I suppose."

"And not married?"

"Oh yes, married. His wife had gone to America. I forget why."

"I am very glad you were rewarded for your courage," Vinny said tonelessly. "Well done! You see, it wasn't so bad, was it?" He patted her hand.

"No, it was not bad at all."

"And so he drove you home and you were brave about the car, too?"

"No, he didn't take me in the car then. I had the shopping to do. But in the evening he called for me and drove me out to the Golf Club. I met a lot of people. He must have warned them first. They . . ." her voice trembled and she put her fingers to her eye-lashes . . . "they were very kind to me. So I am a different person from last week. I have got friends again. I have gone out into the world, as they used to say at school in prayers for the old girls."

'But without me,' Vinny thought. 'She has managed it all without me.'

"I could not have managed it without you," Emily said.

"Of course you could, and did."

"If it had not been for you, I should have stayed shut up at home for the rest of my life. You know that."

'I wanted her to escape, be really free,' he thought, 'and that must mean to other people, not just to me—to everyone; the Golf Club; this wretched Hughie Cooper.' He asked: "What did Rose say?"

"Rose, to my astonishment, was not displeased, especially when I got back and she could tell me you had telephoned. She said: 'It will do you good to see other people occasionally.' She had to add 'occasionally'. She seems to feel threatened only by you, nowadays; though once she guarded me from everyone, and I was glad enough for her to do so."

"It is splendid that she realises that I am a serious menace."

"Dearest, am I . . . oh, tell me . . . turning into something different from your first ideas of me? I am afraid that it is only myself I am turning into—though I cannot be sure, or help myself. You may be disappointed."

He leaned over and kissed her mouth and at once she put her arms round him, turning with relief from words. Often, in these last few years, pacing about Rose's sitting-room, or playing Patience, she had suddenly covered her face with her hands as if she were giddy. She did so now, when he had kissed her.

But Vinny was speaking of marriage—a remote arrangement, she felt; and not to do with this minute. "Yes, when you say," she cried. "At any date you like—next month, next week, tomorrow. I am desperate to go away from Philly and Rose and my bounden duty, and all other sad things." She was desperate, too, for his embrace, and impatient with his scruples, and wondered in moments of panic if her scarred body were

186

an alarming test of his love for her, so nice were his principles, so unshakeable was his respect for her.

"And you will always love me?" he insisted.

She nodded.

"And not Hughie Cooper?"

"Certainly not Hughie Cooper."

When he kissed her again, she said: "We will marry tomorrow. The day after at latest." He could see that their betrothal must come to an end, and her own frank impatience could not add to his own, which was complete.

"I cannot think why you love me," he said, as all lovers say; but with more anxiety in his voice than is usual.

"Oh, I am nothing without you," she said. "I should not know what to be. I feel as if you had invented me. I watch you inventing me, week after week."

Chapter 12

"I HAVE just had the most curious letter from Laurence," Isabella told Evalie Hobson. "He hates to write letters, and at school he never did unless he wanted something. I know that he has to want a thing very badly for him to put pen to paper."

She shook out from her library-book a narrow piece of lined paper with backwards-sloping writing. "You don't get much for your money at those schools," she explained. "There are several spelling-mistakes—see how he spells 'epistle'—and it is very facetious in tone. 'Excuse haste!' Why should I excuse haste?"

She handed the letter to Evalie, who took out some blonde tortoiseshell-rimmed glasses from her sewing-bag and began to read.

Isabella picked up her tapestry-work again. This was their latest enthusiasm, and she often nowadays sat down to it in her dressing-gown as soon as she had finished her breakfast.

"Who is this girl?" Evalie asked.

"I never heard of her. Betty Bags. It doesn't sound much of a name."

"Betty Page, I make it."

"Oh, good! But who she is, is more puzzling. 'A girl I met one weekend.' How could he meet a girl? There are none here."

"What will you say?"

"I shall invite her to tea on Sunday, as he asks me. To refuse to is to drive him into her arms." Isabella's sagacity was learnt from the problem-pages of the women's magazines, which she and Evalie found so amusing. They had often wondered if the readers ever took the advice they were given—to see no more of the married man; to take mother into their confidence; to seek other interests—and now she was taking it herself; but without knowing. "No harm can be done," she said, "by my meeting the girl."

'Except to the girl,' Evalie thought. She was surprised at Laurence's sudden lack of secrecy. To bring girls to his home was the last thing she would have expected of him. She did not know that Len's success with Isabella had made him over-confident. As a woman, and a mother herself, she could have warned him that the situation was not the same; that some of the ingredients for success were absent.

"Well, we shall see," Isabella said, and she pressed her hand on a tapestry rose whose stitches stood up unevenly.

Evalie stretched her neck and kneaded her dowager's-hump. "I get so stiff. Are we, perhaps, with all this sewing, giving ourselves such double chins as we shall never get rid of?" She suddenly slapped under her chin with the back of her hand until she made herself retch. Isabella took no notice of this surprising behaviour. It was part of their friendship that they could behave oddly without rousing comment or offering apology.

"You know that Vinny is engaged?" Isabella said carelessly, and she frowned and pressed very hard upon her tapestry. "I have done it too loosely, and I don't think I have the character to unpick it and do it again."

"Have you enough wool?"

"Plenty of wool."

"Let me see!" Evalie put on her spectacles again, which seemed to be worn more for passing judgment than for work. Isabella watched her anxiously. "Yes," Evalie said consideringly and handed the work back. Isabella took up her scissors—they were shaped like storks: she had had them at school—and began quickly, before she changed her mind, to poke and snip at her sewing. She felt tired and angry. Everything went well for Evalie: her needlework was smooth, and neat at the back; her son did not write illiterate and disturbing notes to her; her husband did not get drowned; her best friend did not become engaged to another woman and not even invite her to the wedding.

"You mean with a ring and an announcement and everything?" Evalie now asked.

"No announcement. One would think he is ashamed, or she is ashamed. They could not be more secret about it all. But a ring certainly—sapphires of such a size one doubts them. Although, knowing Vinny . . ." And then she broke off; for she did not know Vinny. She had never known him. That had not been his wish.

"You sound quite upset," Evalie said.

"Upset? Why should I be upset?" She had now cut through a thread of the canvas and could have cried. Then she was alarmed that Evalie would answer her questions; and to stop her she began to say what she had meant for ever to keep to herself. With an instinct for self-preservation she threw away Vinny's secret so that she could keep her own. "I am only worried," she was saying. "I do not know what to think or where my duty lies."

Evalie murmured encouragingly.

"But I must tell someone." Isabella discarded her sewing and sat looking anxiously in front of her. "You won't breathe a word?"

"Of course not," Evalie said, as if this were a mere formality, easily agreed to.

"You do promise?"

"Surely you can trust me, Isabella?"

"Yes, I know; but this is something serious. I lie awake at night and worry about it."

"What is it?" Evalie asked, not unreasonably.

"Do you remember that I went up to Buckinghamshire to that christening—when I was godmother to the Mitchell baby?"

Evalie nodded.

"I stayed there on the Sunday night . . . and the next morning, instead of catching the train from there, I drove with Mr Mitchell into Market Swanford, where he has a factory . . . they make things out of plastic . . . soap-dishes, fruit-bowls, beakers, everything you can imagine. . . . I thought I would catch the train from there—it is one station down the line, you see. I had some time to spare, because he gets away early in the morning . . . It seemed worth making the effort in spite of so much champagne at the christening . . . the taxi is eight shillings, to say nothing of the tip . . . and so I went into a tea-shop and had some coffee which I didn't want, and then I suddenly remembered that when I was there the last time I had seen an amusing picture, on glass—like that one above the bureau—in some scruffy little shop in a side street. When I saw it before, I couldn't buy it or ask the price, because the shop was shut. . . ."

"Yes?" said Evalie.

"Would you like a drink?"

"Not at the moment."

"When I saw the picture, it was on the day of the auction-sale and Vinny had gone in to Market Swanford on business, he *said*, and he promised to come back for me at the sale. But I could not bear to stay there any longer . . . you can't imagine how distressing it was . . . *never* go . . . and I decided to go to Market Swanford myself and meet Vinny by the bus-stop."

"Yes?" Evalie said.

"You mustn't breathe a word of this."

"Of course not."

"It is always a mistake to change plans. It was only because of changed plans that Harry went out in the boat that day. I knew it was a mistake, as soon as I arrived in Market Swanford. I felt more wretched than ever. Early-closing day. I wandered about, knowing where I could find Vinny when the bus was due, but wondering where he might be meanwhile. I looked at the picture in the shop-window and rattled the door-handle, and then . . . I don't know what made me . . . I glanced up at a building across the road and there he was—Vinny—looking at me out of a window, but not as if he were trying to attract my attention."

"Yes?"

"I didn't know what to do, for I knew that he had seen me. I just waved, in a silly sort of way." She did so now, to show Evalie. "He lifted up his hand in answer, but he looked put out. Then a woman came to the window, too, and stared at me. It was all in a flash, but before I looked away I saw that she was crying. She had frondy sort of hair, very elaborate. I would have known her anywhere after that one glance.

And I did know her. The next time. The morning after the Mitchell christening."

Evalie put down her sewing and rested her hands in her lap.

"I was just going into the shop to ask about the picture when I saw her across the road. She came out of the side-door of a shop and went off down the road, leaving the door wide open. She held her hand over the curls on her forehead to stop them blowing about." Isabella could rarely describe a gesture without making it herself, and these gestures Evalie found more illuminating than the verbal descriptions. She now felt that she saw the woman perfectly.

"I forgot about the picture," Isabella said. "And as soon as she was out of sight, I crossed the road and looked into the doorway. I could see a notice at the top of the stairs and I thought that it must be the way up to some offices. My curiosity overcame me and I began to climb the stairs. The notice was the name of a dancing-school—Rita-Something School of Dancing. I turned to go down the stairs again . . . my heart was banging . . . I had a bit wondered if it was a notice about a brothel . . . and suddenly I heard someone running up the stairs and when I turned round this woman was there, rather out of breath, as I was."

"What did you say?"

"I asked her if it was right for the Estate Agent's," Isabella said with a look of pride; but this expression faded at once. "She stared at me, my face, then my hat, then my pearls, very slowly, and rudely. Then she said: 'There is no Estate Agent.' I apologised and said I was wrongly directed. I wanted to pass her and go down the stairs; but although she didn't in the least bar my way, I could not take one step forward. She leant against the wall and kept swinging her door-key to and fro on one finger and watching it, then staring again at my clothes. She said 'What do you really want? It is something to do with my husband, isn't it?' I told her I did not know her husband and she said: 'Oh, yes, you do, and I think he has sent you here because he does no good by coming himself.' "

"Her husband?" said Evalie.

"Oh, you won't tell a soul? You do most faithfully promise?"

Evalie's lips moved impatiently.

"It would be so dreadful. What would Vinny think of my spying in that way? Or does he already know what I have done? But if he knows, he could not have told me that he is marrying Emily so soon."

"This woman was his wife, then?"

Isabella nodded in a terrified way. Although they were alone in the house, their voices had sunk to whispers.

"But perhaps they are now divorced?"

"No. That is one of the things she said to me. 'I will never divorce him. You can go on your bended knees, and so can he.'"

"You?"

"She seemed to think that I was in love with him and hoped to marry him."

Evalie's eyes rested on her.

"She had put two and two together and that hardly ever comes to the right answer. Because she had seen me that morning from the window, because I had gone exploring up those stairs . . . she made no allowances for curiosity."

"Then what are you going to do?"

"Yes, what?"

"You must tell him that you know."

"I never could."

"For Emily's sake."

"Her sake is no affair of mine."

"But it is a crime which you are condoning," Evalie said pompously.

"I know nothing for sure."

"You will let her marry him?"

"I must. And then for ever hold my peace. Once they are married, I am bound to do that. It is in the marriage-service. And I am not invited to the wedding —no one is—so the other thing does not arise."

"I am not surprised that no one is invited."

"He said: 'At my age, I want it to be a simple affair.'"

"What about at her age? She is not so very old. And every woman naturally wants to be a proper bride and wear white."

"She is very retiring since her accident," Isabella said, in defence of Vinny. "Although lately I have seen her about the town more. That is how I glimpsed the ring. He suggested bringing her to tea on Sunday."

"And you will have Laurence and this girl as well. Everything of interest coming at once. Does his mother know his past history?"

"I should think no one does. And we should always remember that that woman may not have told the truth."

Countering one conjecture with another, they passed the evening pleasantly. Often, Evalie was reminded of Isabella's trust in her, then sworn again and again to

195

secrecy, as if the trust lasted no more than a moment or two. When she had put away her sewing, Evalie glanced round the walls. "Did you ever buy that picture?"

"Oh, no!" said Isabella.

Chapter 13

THE children could not disguise their impatience. The thought of going home enchanted them. "But you have loved your holiday?" Mrs Tillotson said. Constance, before Benjy could deny this, said of course, but home was nice, too. She had an instinct, always useful, though often contemptibly used, of knowing what answers went down well.

"We don't want to forget our home," she said.

"I have already forgotten it," said Benjy, who had not the instinct. "I can't remember my bed. Perhaps Baby thinks he always lives here. It will be a fine surprise for him."

"Babies have no memories," Constance said. "Or they might remember being born. And no one remembers that."

"I do," said Benjy, and then looked away from his mother in embarrassment.

"What was it like, then?" his sister asked sarcastically.

"Oh, nothing much," he mumbled.

"You will never recognise the nursery," Mrs Tillotson said gaily, "with its new curtains and wallpaper."

"How lovely!" Constance breathed sycophantically.

"I would like to have seen it once more as it used to be," Benjy said, "then I could know if I had remembered right."

"But you *have* enjoyed your holiday?" their mother asked again. A great deal of money had been spent and she wished to wring every advantage from it, even down to gratitude.

"Oh, yes!" Benjy said this time. He over-did his enthusiasm, lapsed into roughness, hit his sister and was taken away, crying, by Betty.

Betty was the only one grieved at the thought of leaving. To Nannie, it was a matter of indifference where she carried out her work and she had done so in Egypt and India and Singapore. Her travels had not enriched her and she brought nothing back but grumbles at the difficulties of obtaining the right brands of gripe-water, groats or rusks. She made no friends and needed none, but bent all her energies upon her charges, as no mother does upon her children. She felt no emotion for them, so they did not tire her. They were a hobby she pursued single-mindedly. Her true backgrounds were the beach and the public gardens: her excitements the occasions such as dancing-classes and children's parties where she entered—though hoveringly—into competition with others of her kind, standing to be envied or disgraced. When Benjy cried at the conjuror, or Constance found no partner for the polka, the best consolation was in recalling other small charges who had fared better—for was not little Lady Ariadne always first on the floor, and Dominic Haig-Drummond every conjuror's right-hand man? Seething had never been really satisfactory, except as a test to her professional skill. There had been difficulties—about Baby's washing; uneasiness about Philly and the unsuitability of having her under the same roof—however much out-of-sight—as the children; and the whole problem of Betty and the soldier.

"I don't see your rising to the top of the tree if you

are going to be man-mad," she told her. But the top of Betty's tree was a small house surrounded by laburnums, in a quiet neighbourhood, far from her parents, with Laurence returning home to her in the early evening, in early summer, which it would always be.

To go back to London with everything so vaguely left endangered her dream, by which she had lately lived her very lonely life. She had a terrified vision of herself—so frantic is the impatience of the young—rejected and forlorn, with nothing, indeed, better to do than to get to the top of that bleak tree Nannie had mentioned, where those like her reigned in virginal old-age, forced to busy themselves in their declining days with other people's children in other people's houses.

This thought had brought her to weeping when she told Laurence the date of their departure. Her tears, contrary to all he had expected, filled him with distress. Len had spoken with contempt of girls weeping—'turning on the water-works,' he called it; but Laurence felt tenderness, not disdain, and he was surprised to discover that the locality of this was his heart. The emotion had a definite situation—well to the left side of his breast, and not in the centre where clever people now insisted that the heart must be.

The occasion was a Sunday afternoon. They were out on their usual walk and were having what Len would have called 'a bit of a lie-down in the long grass'. Laurence moved over and rested his cheek against her bosom, and he could hear her heart-beat, muffled and hurried like an expensive little watch.

"Yes, it's well on the left side with you, too," he said.

"What is?" She pushed his head away and went on crying.

"Your heart."

"Well, of course. I'm not deformed."

"You certainly aren't," he assured her.

'I wouldn't mind being a man for a little while,' she thought, in the middle of her tears. 'They get the best of it, us having these nice bosoms, and they having nothing comparable to offer.' In a detached way, she put herself in his place and almost felt her own flesh with his hands. This put her into a mood of great condescension, but the tears still flowed.

"You mustn't cry," he soothed her, though he did not mind her crying. "I shan't see you so often, it is true; but sometimes I can get to London."

She saw herself translated to the Corner House, but to the same sundaes and parfaits and milk-shakes. There would be nowhere to make love except the cinema.

"We can go to the cinema and places," he said vaguely.

All the time they talked, his love-making was progressing from one stage to the next; although, this evening, she seemed scarcely to notice. As soon as he lay down upon her, she said: "I haven't even met your mother yet."

"You shall," he quickly promised.

"You brought that friend of yours down—Len—but you never even asked me to your house to tea."

"I was shy," he said, struggling with her underclothes.

She raised her hips from the ground to help him. "I thought he was really common," she said. "I didn't think you would have friends like that. Some of the things he said!"

"You meet all kinds," he murmured, his lips on her brow, his eyes shut fast.

"I can't think why you're not an officer," she complained. Then—as if for the first time realising his immediate intention, "You know it's wrong to do this," she grumbled; and her limbs tightened to him, fastened hard. She said no more, and the tears dried at the corners of her eyes.

*　　　*　　　*

She was nervous on the afternoon of the tea-party, recognising it as a crisis in her ambitions; but one which must be faced. They walked for a little while on the cliff, and each time Laurence touched her she brushed his hand away. It did not occur to her that Isabella might be nervous, too.

"What did you tell her about me?" she asked.

"Nothing. I just said you were a girl I had met."

"Didn't you tell her where I worked?"

"No, of course not."

"Why 'of course'?"

"That can be later. You don't have to say what people's jobs are to someone they haven't even met."

Laurence felt a moment of terror as he took Betty into the house. He was, at first, relieved to see Vinny and Emily already there. He did not recognise Emily and would not do more than glance in her direction, so embarrassed was he that Vinny should have overlooked Isabella for her. He had not wanted Vinny for a stepfather; but no son cares to see his mother jilted.

Betty's dismay at sight of Emily was profound. 'How could'st Thou, God!' she cried in her heart. She sat down where Isabella told her, trying in a

201

confounded way to sort things out, feeling ensnared, but by whose trickery she could not decide. Isabella sat behind the tea-tray and chattered. Emily turned her great engagement-ring, to which she could not grow accustomed, round and round on her finger, and catching Betty's eye, gave one fleeting, meaningless smile.

"How nice!" Isabella kept saying. How nice that the wedding should be so soon, that they had found a little house in Chelsea, that Betty looked after children, that it was her half-day, that she was soon to return to London. Passing the rather slopped cups of tea, she said "How nice!" once or twice too often, when it was nice for no one but herself.

"Did you meet Laurence's friend, Len?" she asked Betty.

'She need not have chosen that moment,' Laurence thought. Betty had just bitten off some very dry sponge-cake, so could only nod.

"I thought he was so nice, didn't you?"

Betty swallowed and looked stubborn, while Laurence prayed that she would not call Len 'common'. He could imagine his mother's wide-open look at that, putting nothing past her this afternoon.

"Yes," Betty said sullenly. She gave a little terrified glance at Laurence, then added: "He was all right."

"He was so *sensible*," Isabella explained. She put such meaning into this phrase that they all felt it directed against themselves, and Laurence felt it most of all.

"He has been so sensible that he is now confined to barracks," he said, in a moment of bitterness. Once it had been his object to raise his friend in Isabella's eyes:

202

now he wished to destroy him; he sensed, though she did not glance at him, Betty's gratitude.

"What has he done?" his mother asked, prepared to hear of some injustice.

"He has been where he shouldn't have been, with someone he shouldn't be with, and at a time when he ought to have been somewhere else."

"Otherwise all right?" said Vinny.

"How pompous you sound, Laurence!" Isabella said. "It is just for effect."

At his parties, when he was a little boy, she had often told him not to show-off and he had never forgiven her those humiliations. He had shown-off to hide self-consciousness and she had deepened it.

"And I am sure," she went on, "that whatever his boyish exuberance leads him into, he has his head screwed on all right."

"'Boyish exuberance' is an excuse you would never make for me."

"We will leave that until we see the exuberance," Isabella said lightly. "Emily dear, shall I have your cup?"

"It is filled," Emily said in a startled way.

"To overflowing," Laurence murmured, for now he *was* showing-off and he returned Isabella's hard glance with another of the same kind.

"What I feel about Len," she said, in a different, reasonable voice, "is that his kind are really the backbone of the country. In wars, and so on."

"He is the salt of the earth, too," Laurence said.

"He would not" (Isabella's voice rode above her son's mutterings and her face was flushed) "*ever* go to pieces in a crisis."

Vinny, who knew the truth of the occasion when

Laurence had gone to pieces, stood up quickly and handed round a plate of scones. Laurence, who saw that Vinny had remembered his own frank description of his father's death, reddened and then paled.

"Perhaps there won't be a war," Betty said, still dwelling on Len's qualities, and hoping to make her mark.

"Oh, you can't change human nature," Laurence said carelessly.

"If there isn't a war, I still see him seizing his chances, working hard—ambitious; thrifty; buying his own house . . ."

"I certainly can't see him buying one for anyone else."

" . . . never content to stay in a rut, not hoping to throw away his advantages, as you do, Laurence—education, background."

Betty blinked her eyes as she drank her tea.

"Len has no education," Laurence said, "and we all have background."

Isabella, having exposed them all to an agonising moment, now went smoothly on, to cover it, she thought. "You know Laurence's great ambition in life, Vinny? To be an agricultural-labourer."

"Oh, is it?" Vinny said with a relieved smile. "I believe he once mentioned it to me."

"His classical education will stand him in great stead."

"I always think it does that," Vinny said. "If it has been a pleasure, as it is a privilege, nothing can take the experience from him. Why should we want to make money from it as well? It should stand a farm-labourer in as good stead as anyone—and perhaps better than a lawyer, for instance, who must learn, I presume, to pronounce Latin afresh; or a psychologist, who has to put his Greek to some funny uses."

"It wasn't a pleasure," Laurence murmured.

"I never know what 'stead' means," said Emily.

"Five pounds a week is the summit of Laurence's ambition," Isabella continued, and her glance took in everyone but Betty, at whom the words were aimed.

"Six pounds," Laurence said.

"Six pounds then, darling," Isabella said with a broad, indulgent smile.

"It sounds a great deal," said Emily, whose natural extravagance had been in abeyance for years and who, even nowadays, rarely entered a shop; but Betty, Isabella noted, seemed not to agree. She was dreadfully at Isabella's mercy, they all saw. She accepted or refused what she was offered with a startled alacrity, and when Laurence asked her to accompany him to the place on the main road where he took up his position for begging a lift to Aldershot, she picked up the silk net gloves, on which Isabella's eyes had dwelt, and stood up at once.

When they had gone, Isabella went out to fetch drinks. By the time she returned, some arrangement seemed to have been reached by Emily and Vinny, for Emily at once excused herself.

"Must you go?" Isabella looked from one to the other, the decanter in her hand. She was unwilling, after her bad behaviour, to be left alone.

"I must help Rose," said Emily.

"She will soon have to manage on her own."

"We shall make some other plans for her," Emily said, "but we have not made them yet."

"Not even a quick drink?"

"Vinny will stay. He·is always ready for a drink."

"I can't let you walk home alone, if Vinny can," Isabella said. "Or I shall feel I am really out-of-step with the times. Laurence has astonished me enough for one day. He not only doesn't see the girl home, but makes her trudge along with him."

Vinny thought: 'It is the least she has suffered today.'

"Give him his drink, darling," Emily said, and she put her gloved hand in Isabella's and her cheek to Isabella's cheek. "It will keep him out of the kitchen while I am getting the supper."

"And we shall have a lifetime together," Vinny said, giving word to their happiness.

When Emily had gone, he said: "You were upset about the girl, Isabella."

"I hope I did not show it."

"Yes, you showed it."

"Then I wish I hadn't," she said, remembering the advice in the women's magazines, which she had only half-followed. "It was Laurence I was cross with, really."

"All that about his lack of ambition! You were trying to defeat her on two fronts—on the ground that he is too good for her because of his education, and also on the ground that he is not good enough for anyone because of his unpromising future."

"Both are true."

"You should have chosen one or the other, although a clever woman would have used neither. They are only children."

"But he has lied to me. If he had been frank about her in the first place, I could have advised him," she said, remembering the women's magazines again.

"Advised what?"

"That they should give the matter time . . . not see too much of one another . . . wait . . . and find other companions."

"That would have been meaningless advice. It is lucky you did not give it. And you jump to the conclusion that they are to be betrothed. Is every girl Laurence brings to the house to be his future wife?"

"He could have only one wife at a time," Isabella said, without looking at Vinny.

"What did you say, darling?"

"He could have only one wife at a time."

"Well, naturally."

"And he has never brought any girl here before."

"Nor will again, I imagine."

"Oh, you are very modern and broad-minded," she said quickly. "And no wonder, to be sure. How dare you criticise me! I have only behaved as it is natural for a mother to behave—however petty I was. Laurence is all I have left."

They were the words Laurence himself had always felt hanging in the air.

"Then you cannot risk him, as you risked him this afternoon."

"Suppose he should get the girl into trouble."

"I should suppose nothing of the kind. It would be intolerable to go about supposing such a thing of every young person one met. Is that behaving as it is natural for a mother to behave?"

"I think so."

"You can do nothing beyond indicating to him the lines on which he should behave with the other sex. And that should have been done before this."

207

"Oh, I suppose Harry did. But it was always difficult to talk to Laurence. It was years before he learnt the facts of life, because he never asked those questions which children are expected to ask from their natural curiosity. We had to broach the matter ourselves—or Harry did. Laurence hardly listened. At the end, he just said: 'Whatever next!' It is easy for you to laugh, Vinny. For all your experience, you have never had to bring up a son."

"I haven't had much experience either."

"Haven't you?"

"Isabella, why are you crying? It was all a strain for you and at the end there was nothing to cheer you up—nothing but my censure."

"It isn't that."

"That what?"

"I have to say something to you, Vinny."

He waited.

"I am so upset. It is about you and Emily. Your marriage. I don't know what to think, or how to find the courage to speak."

He was silent and, beyond her tears, she felt wariness steal over him.

"I have always been so fond of you," she said hesitantly. "And I can understand that you are often sorry for women and might let your sympathy run away with you, put you in a false position. In the end, only you can know what is right for you to do."

Vinny was appalled. 'She is in love with me herself,' he thought. 'And although we cannot often help loving, we can sometimes help being loved.' A great deal of her past behaviour seemed clear to him now, and his obtuseness filled him with remorse.

She raised her tear-stained face and he mistook anxiety for shame in her expression.

"I must say this thing," she said, "or it will be on my mind for ever. And no one else can say it for me. They must be my own words, and I have rehearsed them so often that I know them by heart. A word from you could put me at peace. An answer to my question."

Before she could abase herself further, as he thought she would, he went behind her and put a hand on her shoulder. "Darling, I will never ask you such a kindness again; but for both our sakes, forget the words. No good can come of them and speaking them will only give them more reality. Let us forget that they were ever thought. I shall forget. And no one else shall know. I have never wanted to do any harm; but only Emily herself, or death, shall stop me marrying her. It is the only strong thing in my life, the only time I have felt passion or jealousy or despair or any of those other emotions which other people seem to come by so easily. It is my Wuthering Heights," he said, with a wry smile which was wasted, as her back was to him.

"Your . . . concern . . . for me," he went on, choosing the words carefully, "must be a thing we shall both understand and never mention again. With that secret behind us, we could mean a great deal to one another . . . as dear friends," he added.

"It is your guilt," she said in an astonished voice. "*I* have done no wrong."

"I must ask your forgiveness."

"I could not forgive you," she said in alarm; for she thought that bigamy was more a matter for the Quarter Sessions. "We must hope that God will," she murmured, not liking to mention Judge or Jury.

"I hope you will pray for that," Vinny said coldly. "Now dry your eyes and have a drink, and we will never have this conversation again, or any part of it."

His intention had been to save her pride; but she thought that he was saving himself. Neither seemed as grateful as the other expected.

*　　　*　　　*

On the telephone, a little later, Isabella said to Evalie: "I tried to speak to you-know-whom?"

"What did he say?"

"He wouldn't let me put it into words, but he said that nothing would stop him, and he begged me to secrecy."

"Do you mean he is going ahead with the arrangements?"

"Yes."

"And has he no conscience?"

"None, it seems."

"I don't think you have managed very well."

"I did my best."

"Does Emily *know*?"

"He said that no one must ever know, but he and I."

"He cannot bind you to such a thing."

"He can. Especially when it is what I want to be bound to."

"I am shocked at you, Isabella."

"Yes, I suppose you must be."

"It is sure to come out. Those things always do."

"Sometimes after so long that it makes me think that often they never come out. If people can hide such a thing for ten or twenty years, as I have read of them doing, others are likely to hide it for thirty or forty

years, and die with it hidden, and then one never reads
of them at all."

"But it is a crime, and you are condoning it."

"It is better than committing it. But we shouldn't
talk of it any more on the telephone."

"I shall be round in the morning. Did you see that
Stream of Consciousness is running tomorrow at
Brighton?"

"No," Isabella sighed. "There has been too much
on my mind."

"We'll talk of it tomorrow."

"And not a word, to anyone, ever?"

"Of course not," Evalie said.

*   *   *

Betty and Laurence stood at the kerb watching the
cars flashing by. Every now and then Laurence jerked
his thumb in the direction he had to go.

"You'd stand more chance if I left you now," she
said. "They think we both need a lift."

"Well, go if you want to."

"There's no need to be bad-tempered with me. I
haven't done anythink, except listen."

"If you are to go so far in life as you indicate, you
must learn not to say 'anythink'," Laurence said, in
his most wounded and wounding voice.

"Don't you criticise me!"

"Before this evening, I shouldn't have thought of it.
But, then, I had no idea of your ambitions. Now I know it
is my duty to give you a leg-up if I can. What would have
seemed perfect to me—and did seem perfect—may not
do in an ambassador's wife. And it would be nice if someone could benefit from my education, as I have not."

"You don't know what poverty is like. Your mother is right. You would be wasting yourself."

"And wasting you? My mother is always right. All my friends think so. One glance at her puts me in the wrong immediately. And one glance at *them* makes her see how unsatisfactory *I* am."

Laurence was fighting desperately before he acquiesced, so that in his own mind he could look back and see that he had fought. Vinny alone had understood this, and he had meant to tell Isabella to let him have his rope; but Isabella had given another turn to the conversation and Laurence was forgotten.

It was very hot and the cars flashed by, their tyres licking the tarry road, gravel rattling under their mudguards. Laurence looked so fagged standing there at the kerb, so cruelly hot in his harsh khaki and great boots.

"It was only that you hadn't said anythink to me," she said gently. "Not beforehand."

"Anything."

"Anything."

He had not done so, because it was not a serious enough intention: only a dream, a half-desire, an escape. To make him defiant and tenacious of the idea was a disservice his mother had done him.

"You've always lived in luxury, so how can you imagine the other thing?"

"I hope a car soon comes to take me back to my luxury."

"You can bear anything if you've got a nice home to go back to, with a bathroom and so on."

"I can see myself wasting my life in some office so that I can occasionally take a bath. *My* life!" He suddenly laughed. "Who am I to call it that?"

This time, as he jerked his thumb, a car slowed down.

"Not a perfect choice, but it will do," he said, moving towards it.

He climbed into the back and turned to wave, as curtly as he could; but she had already begun to walk away.

Chapter 14

"WE shall be full of beans tomorrow," Benjy said.

"I am full of beans now," Constance said, standing up on the swing. "This is a dangerous thing to do, you know."

"You could break your neck if you fell," he agreed.

"No one can do such dangerous things as me. And they aren't funny either."

"Is there a swing at home?"

"You know there is. And a sandpit."

"There are some frogs in the sandpit. I shall see them tomorrow. I sometimes hit them with my spade."

"Then you are a cruel, wicked boy," Betty said, but without conviction or interest.

"I don't mind."

"It is a cowardly thing to do."

"No, it isn't, because I am not afraid."

"I don't know what your father would do. He would stand you in the corner," Betty said, supplying her own answer.

Emily and Philly came from the kitchen-garden with a basket of sweet-peas.

"What a heavenly perfume!" said Betty.

"Are you going to the Regatta?" Emily asked them.

"Madam said to take the children down after their rest."

"And there are fireworks tonight," Emily said in the voice—over-charged with anticipation—which she used with children who slightly alarmed her. Constance stared back, standing up very straight on the swing.

"Won't that be lovely?" Betty said.

Philly tugged pettishly at Emily's skirt, urging her on towards the house.

"I don't like that silly lady," Benjy said in a clear voice, as they walked away.

"How dare you talk like that!" Betty hissed. "I don't know what your mother would say, if she could hear you."

She spoke as if she could only see their behaviour through other people's eyes, and dismissed her own scandalised reactions as of no account.

"We don't give a damn," said Constance.

*   *   *

Rose was in her sitting-room, writing out the Tillotsons' account.

"That stupid Evalie Hobson telephoned," she said to Emily, "to ask me to help her with some fête or bazaar she is running. She knows that I never do such things. It was only to try to get into conversation with me about your wedding, which seemed to be food and drink to her. Mrs Siddons has arrived. I suppose I shall get used to the name."

Mrs Siddons was a clergyman's widow, obliged to find some light employment; and to look after Philly when Emily was married had seemed to her to be that.

"She can have this room," Rose said. "It has never seemed to be mine. If I have time to sit down, I can do so in the kitchen or my bedroom."

"In the winter, there is plenty of time."

Then Emily saw in her mind the house on a

215

December day drawing towards the dark, buffeted by the wind. Rose would be sitting in her bedroom, alone, staring out at the bare branches—never consenting to comfort, cosiness or intimacy.

"I feel such a sense of my own treachery," she said.

"Why? You have your own life to live."

Rose folded the account and put it in an envelope. "There! That is the very last one I shall write for them." She was a person made indifferent by defeat.

"Philly, will you fetch me a vase for the sweet-peas?" Emily said, speaking slowly and touching the flowers in explanation.

Rose's eyes followed the girl from the room. She said: "In the last few months she has changed so. She looks like a middle-aged woman—and uncouth and clumsy."

"Oh, darling!" Emily said, and turned quickly aside.

"I think she feels that something is wrong . . . I mean that something is different, or going to be. I wonder if Mrs Siddons will ever understand her. I hid nothing from her, about Philly. But she has hidden something from us. She is really very deaf, you know, and hoping we shall not discover it."

"How terribly sad! Thank you, Philly dear. Now can you fill it at the tap outside and bring it carefully to me? I wish you had done as Evalie Hobson suggested, Rose. It would have been a change for you and something to be an interest to you outside the house."

"I could never bother myself with women like that— she and that silly Isabella. They have never grown up."

"It was meant as a kindness."

"Yes, perhaps."

Mrs Siddons tapped on the door and came in. She was a small, elderly woman, with thin, short hair. A hand-knitted jumper was stretched tightly to her flat chest. She looked, Emily thought, like a rather studious little boy about nine years old. A tangle of veins on her cheeks gave her a rosy appearance, and her expression was that of a child—timid and eager to be loved. This eagerness, and her timidity from being alone in the world for the first time and unprotected, had given her movements an uncertainty, too faint to be called clumsiness, but still unnerving to other people.

"Oh, never knock," said Rose. "This is your room. I am moving out."

"Thank you, Philly," Emily said again, and she took the vase quickly before the water was spilt. She said: "I meant the flowers to be ready for you, as a welcome. There!" She put them in the middle of the table. "Philly, would you like to show Mrs Siddons your shells, or your cutting-out books? And perhaps she will help you to water the ferns."

"Luncheon in half-an-hour," said Rose as she went out.

"This is our special shell," Emily said. "But it was one we bought in a shop." Although talking to Mrs Siddons, she spoke so that Philly might understand. Mrs Siddons took the shell and held it to her ear, smiling at Philly as she did so. Her expression then was lovely and encouraging, and Emily guessed that, in her, self-confidence could only come from doing good.

*　　　*　　　*

Betty led the children past the pier, glancing at Isabella's house as she went by, but venetian blinds were drawn down as if against the Regatta. The esplanade was crowded. To add to the confusion, shops debouched over the pavements stalls of souvenirs; revolving-stands of picture-postcards; trusses of straw-hats and canvas shoes and paper parasols. The bay was full of little boats. The paddle-steamer was leaving the pier, water tumbling furiously beside it. As it backed out and turned, the wake smoothed and widened like a fan. On deck, men had already knotted handkerchiefs on their heads and were leaning against the rails in the sun.

"Why are there flags on the steamer?" Benjy asked.

"It is dressed over all for Regatta Day," Betty said.

"How do you know that that is what it is called?" asked Constance. "Over all, I mean."

"I happen to have a cousin in the Navy."

"You are always boasting. I think you are getting a bit too big for your boots."

"It is what Nannie said *you* were," her brother reminded her.

"I bet you wouldn't have the nerve to take us on a boat," Constance said, but casually and without optimism. Benjy looked quickly up at Betty's face, and then away again, seeing that the idea had not had her attention.

The glittering pavements were hot through their sandals, the soles of which seemed to be melting.

"What was that gun?" asked Benjy.

"It was the race starting."

The yachts spread across the bay, rocking on the water like wounded butterflies.

"I suppose your famous cousin told you that, too."

"No. My common-sense told me that."

Constance blushed.

"What is your cousin's name?" Benjy inquired.

"Roger."

"Roger," Constance repeated, smiling.

"Where are we walking to?" Benjy asked, beginning to lag behind.

"To see the decorations and the boats."

He looked out at the bay, then up at the strings of flags, at the baskets of pink geraniums swinging on lamp-posts.

"I would rather go in here," he said, stopping at the entrance to the fun-fair from which braying music and laughter and the clanging of slot-machines came forth.

"I don't think Nannie would like it," Betty said, pretending to a doubt she did not feel.

"She wouldn't know."

"What the eye doesn't see the heart cannot grieve over," Constance said, using some more of Nannie's words to suit her purpose.

Just inside the entrance was a wax image in a glass case. Shoddily draped, with jewelled *bandeau*, sickly-looking, this figure gazed down into a crystal. When Betty put her penny in the slot, a chipped, yellow hand was jerkily raised, then sank, and a card fell out of the machine. Suddenly popular, she read it out to the children. "You are the creative type and will make your mark as an artist or with your pen. Great changes and travel will be coming your way. Do not let your head rule your heart. Lucky colour: indigo."

"It is very true," said Constance, now amiable. "You are going all the way to London tomorrow: although travel doesn't come *your* way; you have to go *its*."

"What is indigo?" asked Benjy.

"A colour," Betty said.

"And you are not very artistic," Constance added.

"No, they are wrong there," Betty agreed. She took no offence, for she had never been in circles where this would be felt a disgrace.

"How can your head rule your heart?"

"She knows," said Laurence, standing behind them. The children swung round, a little frightened, and came closer to Betty, who was too confused to speak.

"I was looking for you everywhere," Laurence said. "Let us go and have a cup of tea."

"No, of course not. I should be in dreadful trouble if I did. We ought not to be in here even."

"Let me give them a shilling's-worth of coppers for the slot-machines while we go and have a chat."

Benjy turned hopeful eyes on him, but Constance knew more of the world.

"You can't be serious," said Betty. "They are never allowed to do such things."

"I used to, when I was a child."

"Not so young, I am sure," she said firmly.

"Oh, well! Now, George, would you like to put a penny in here and see a man hanged?"

"No," said Betty quickly.

Benjy who had looked round quickly for George, then decided that it was himself, took the penny and forced it in the slot. At once, the prison-gates clicked open.

"It isn't much," Constance said, when it was over. "It doesn't take long."

"No, I am sorry about that."

Betty caught a glimpse of herself in a distorting mirror—her apron hideously widened, her legs shortened—and stepped quickly aside. The children and Laurence stood hand-in-hand and laughed at this new vision of themselves, then moved on to the next

view of elongated bodies and domed heads. Benjy
began to caper about and blow out his cheeks.

"We have to go," Betty said. "We shall be late for
tea."

"Is this soldier your cousin, as well?" Benjy asked.

"No, not my cousin."

"What then?" Constance asked lightly, hoping to
confuse her into a reply.

"She may one day do me the honour of becoming my
wife," Laurence said. "Although I doubt it."

"I should think she would jump at it," Constance
said. "I should."

"I should, too," Benjy said.

"She won't do that. I shall have to work very hard
before I ask her, and earn a lot of money."

"What for?"

"To buy her as nice a home as she deserves."

"Would she leave us then?"

"Of course."

"You could come to live with us. We have a nice
home," Benjy offered.

Constance laughed. "I can see Nannie taking that
with a pinch of salt," she said.

They walked homewards. When the road began to
rise towards the cliff, and at the back of the cinema,
Betty stopped. "Don't come any farther. I'll have to
say goodbye now."

"Can't you come out tonight?"

"No. I have to help pack."

"Oh, damn!"

Betty glanced at Benjy; Benjy glanced at Constance.

"Then give me your address."

"Four Bretton Gardens," Benjy said.

"N.W.8," Constance added.

"Do you forgive me? About last Sunday?" he muttered, his glance away from the children, as he wished theirs was from him.

"Yes, I suppose so."

"Have you had a quarrel?" Constance asked. The more daring her questions this afternoon, the more they seemed to be answered; but this one was ignored.

Laurence and Betty looked at one another, trying to say what the children's presence forbade. Inside the cinema, muffled giant-voices echoed—sometimes a phrase distinguishable, a lugubrious American cliché, embittered, self-pitying. A leaden tongue seemed to be rolling the words round an ogre's mouth, launched them into the cinema. They sounded inhuman and meaningless. Coarse music engulfed them.

"It will just be a different place," Laurence said. She smiled brightly, but she could not help asking herself, as she took the children's hands and walked homewards, if she would ever see him again.

"You can rely on us," Constance said. "We shan't breathe a word."

"We shall say we just walked along by the sea," Benjy added, his face assuming a look of innocence in readiness.

"What a way to talk!" Betty said. "Whatever would your mother say?"

*   *   *

Before it was dark, the fireworks began. The children knelt in their beds and watched the lights arching up over the misty opal sea and sky—all one now. Rockets went looping up, hanging for a second in bursts of light; golden ostrich-feathers, vanishing.

Emily went out to the garden-seat where Philly was sitting with Mrs Siddons. The girl leaned forward eagerly, more childish than Constance and Benjy, who did not withhold criticism and sophistication. ("What a dud!" Benjy kept saying. "What is happening now?" Constance asked, as soon as there was the slightest pause.) They made room for Emily in the seat and, as she moved closer to her, Mrs Siddons took Philly's hand.

'We are soon replaced,' Emily thought: and yet, for years, she and Philly had been one another's lives.

Darkness grew. The crescent of lamps along the curving esplanade sprang into light. "Ah!" sighed the crowd, as each rocket shook down its brightness. 'Oh, Vinny!' Emily suddenly thought; for next week they were to be married. She felt a sadness for her past life which was not nostalgia and had little of haunting sweetness in it. She imagined, with great relief, their honeymoon—they would drive inland, farther and farther into the heart of England, away from the sea.

At last there was a great burst of clapping from below and a silence; and then the band began to play God Save the King. Unsteady, but really unmistakeable, the set-piece glowed on its framework—Their Majesties, in full regalia of dazzling light. "Splendid!" cried Mrs Siddons, and she clapped briskly: then, deaf as she was, catching the strains of the National Anthem from below, jumped to her feet and stood at attention. Philly, in admiration, and with a sideways glance, stood up beside her. Emily thought: 'If Mrs Siddons suddenly cast herself over the cliff, Philly would do the same.' Feeling immensely foolish, she was obliged to stand as well. 'Vinny would laugh!' she thought. She

223

was impatient to tell him, to run to him with each trivial happening, as if their married life had begun already, and in her mind, as she stood there, was heightening and embellishing the scene, for his amusement.

*　　　*　　　*

The next day, the Tillotsons went home. The children sat with Betty in the back of the Bentley behind their parents. Nannie and baby and the luggage followed more sedately with the chauffeur in the large Humber in which Lindsay drove to board-meetings.

Emily and Rose said goodbye to them outside the house.

"And next week you will be going, too," Rose said, as the first car drove away. They waved back to the children, who were letting ribbons of seaweed stream out behind them.

"I will go more unobtrusively."

Nannie held up baby, as if feeling sure they must want the last possible glimpse of him.

"We shall not talk of it, after all, as the summer that the Tillotsons came," Rose said. She watched them take the curve of the drive, her elbow crooked over her brow to shade her eyes.

"The wheel has turned full circle," she said, "as wheels so often do."

Chapter 15

ISABELLA had drawn the curtains, and the afternoon sunlight was held out, except a wavering thread or two across the carpet. The room had a sub-marine look, in the greenish dusk, so that the litter of crumpled newspapers on the floor might have been lying on the sea-bed. Isabella and Evalie were resting. Their arms trailed over the sides of the chairs. Their faces were caked with a white clay, which, drying, had drawn up their skin beneath so that they could hardly part their lips to speak; from this frightening pallor their discoloured eyes looked mournfully out. The wireless, not quite tuned in, gave forth some jarring woolly little tune which they did not hear. Isabella had switched it on as she always did, as a part of her settling down in a room. Its sound broke the silence of the house when she was alone, as she was nowadays so often alone.

They had run into an end-of-summer dullness. The St Leger was behind them; but the crisp exhilaration of Autumn not yet begun. They felt anticipatory; but nothing happened. Their desire for renewal, and also novelty, was unsettling. They longed to be creative and had nothing to create. The idea of autumn—a romantic season—stirred them with the sensations so mistakenly associated with Spring. But no miracle happened. The town emptied. They could walk briskly along the streets now, instead of merely joining the stream of loitering, shuffling holiday-makers. The shops, cleared of summer goods, looked larger; some closed, as the Fun-fair did, for the winter. The residents returned to their own life; met for morning-coffee again and even strolled along the pier. Evalie picked up the threads of charity left loose since Easter—her bazaars and sewing-parties. Isabella had cast on stitches to knit a bed-jacket, hoping to please, but unable to imagine doing so.

The knitting lay discarded among the newspapers on the floor. Even Evalie had put hers aside while magic —she hoped—was transforming her appearance. Both were confident that this time, under the stiff clay, new faces awaited them, rejuvenated, unbelievably braced and smoothed.

"I can never do this at home," Evalie said. "Someone always comes in and one feels a fool."

"Perhaps we should take it off now," Isabella said. "It hurts to talk."

"What was that noise I heard?"

"The postman, I daresay. Only bills come in the afternoon when I most long to have a letter. In the morning I seem not to need them so much. Mornings are more hopeful."

"But I thought I heard a door being shut."

Laurence and the postman had arrived together.

Seeing her son, standing there, holding out a little white box to her, Isabella quite ignored him—as if by not looking at him she could make him disappear. She began in desperation to gather up the newspapers on the floor. Evalie held up her knitting as a screen.

The vision of those two leprous faces in the greenish gloom, his mother's absurd confusion, Evalie's frenzied eyes rolling at him above a piece of red knitting, made Laurence feel the victim of a monstrous joke. He was so thrown-out by the scene that he could not think how he was expected to behave, and from awkwardness walked unsmilingly across the room, forced Isabella to take the little package and said in a cold and angry voice: "Some wedding-cake for you."

She looked at it in fearful incredulity and almost backed away as if it were a cruel joke; believing that Laurence had got married himself and was choosing this unpardonable way of telling her. It seemed to her the final betrayal of her life. Her face was from necessity expressionless, but every gesture showed him her fear and bewilderment. He supposed that even the cake from Vinny's wedding was abhorrent to her, bringing sad reminders: a cake she neither wanted to eat or have.

"We feel such fools," Evalie said.

Then Isabella's mind cleared. She dropped the racing-papers and took the little box with its silver lettering and opened it. Broken icing fell out and a card with a currant stuck to it.

"Oh, from *Vinny*!" she cried.

"Why do you look so awful?" Laurence asked.

"We didn't expect you. These are face-packs."

"What for?"

"We hardly like to say," said Evalie.

"Why are you here, Laurence?"

"I wanted some clothes. I am going to a dance in London."

"You aren't staying, then?"

"No, I'm afraid not."

"Oh, it doesn't matter." She tried to smile, but could not. His eyes were now on the newspapers and very slowly he bent down and picked one up.

227

"What would my father have said to this?" he asked.

"It happens to belong to me," said Evalie. "Or, rather, to the gardener."

"Then why, in mother's handwriting, do I see 'Two Pounds Each Way, Fishwife' written in the margin?" He put the paper down, strolled over to the window and drew back the curtains, then said with wonderful ease: "I think you know, don't you, mother, that my father despised all money not won by the sweat of the brow. That he would only have countenanced a little flutter for fun, on what you yourself described as the Big Races."

"Excitement makes one's brow sweat more than work," said Evalie.

He turned to face her, able to condescend because of her appearance.

"I meant *honest* sweat," he said briefly.

Confidence uplifted him. He felt, faced by these two silly women, as if he were more manly than he had had the audacity to be before: he seemed to draw level with his own father; but with the additional advantage of being alive. Isabella, by her frailty and frivolity, added to his stature; and, as she stood before him with her caked eyelashes downcast, the strange inversion took place, in which her child became her parent, hoisting himself up on her shrunk authority. Though she did not know, she was, as a mother, worth her weight in gold at that moment. Laurence knew. He saw all at once a way of behaving to her. Helped by the presence of Evalie and their ridiculous appearance, he had managed to speak of his father, and subtly, without disrespectful words, revenged himself of his death and all the punishment that had been dealt out in his dying;

self-reproach; the lesson of his successful life, with its high standards.

"What sort of example is this to me?" he asked. "Two pounds each way! Two *pounds*!"

"You must allow me to spend my money as I wish, Laurence. When you were at school, I had to economise. Now I shall please myself!"

"You don't mean that you lose into the bargain?"

"I try not to."

"It has been a great shock to me."

"He was teasing," Isabella said uncertainly when he had gone.

"All boys tease their mothers at that age. I think it's rather sweet," said Evalie. "It's only a phase. What a good thing . . ." She was half-way to saying: "What a good thing Harry can't know about this," but, altered it to: "What a good thing *I* have not been found out," which was not very much better.

"He is singing," Isabella said, listening. "How extraordinary!"

"So Vinny sent you some wedding-cake," Evalie said. This was true cattiness, wounding for the fun of it.

"I think it is Rose's writing."

"Yes, it is. I remember from her letter about the bazaar. Rather a masculine hand."

" *They* wouldn't have thought of wedding-cakes, I am sure. I can imagine Rose's efforts to make a proper wedding of it."

"It would take more than Rose to do that."

"She seems to have tried so hard to make it appear respectable."

"Which makes me wonder how much she knows. That is what fascinates me. She was so prim at the

229

committee-meeting. We mustn't do this and mustn't do that—and as she hasn't done a thing in the town since that drunken husband of hers killed himself, I felt it was a little uncalled-for to snub me about the raffle. 'Illegal,' she said, and she rolled her gloves into a ball and popped them into her handbag as if that were that. So old-maidish. I felt like saying: 'And what about your sister?' "

"Oh, but you wouldn't!" said Isabella.

"Of course not. Am I a person who *could* say: 'And what about' anything? Like those Labour people at election-meetings? All the same, I'd love to know. And one day we *shall* know. I believe that wrongdoing always comes to light."

"What we know about has come to light obviously."

"Now, mother!" said Laurence, opening the door. "I want to say something important and I want you to listen. If you are to be turf-mad, which a son hardly likes his mother to be, you must remember this, so do carefully attend. Seven furlongs—do you understand— *seven furlongs*—is the utmost distance for Fishwife— and the going firm. I tremble to think of my father's money being frittered away incompetently—money earned by striving to put forward the views of nonconformist, teetotal, non-racegoing Liberals. I have been sitting in my bedroom thinking of it."

"Have you, dear?" Isabella said complacently.

"It sounds as if you were thinking about horses," said Evalie.

"Let us wash our faces and make some tea," Isabella said.

*   *   *

Rose had rounded off the wedding with the little boxes of cake. She had tried to make a fuss and business

230

of it all, to help her over her aversion to the marriage itself. Their—Vinny's and Emily's—carelessness about all arrangements and ceremony had served only to bare their desire for one another. "Oh, *not* a wedding-cake!" Emily had protested. And Vinny had set himself against all invitations and announcements.

Rose had her ally in Mrs Tumulty, who was ready with her usual phrases—"a hole-and-corner affair", "only once in a life-time", "something to look back upon", "flouting public opinion". She was disappointed for herself, relishing all change and excitement. Her antagonism to Emily had receded since, through her, both change and excitement had come her way: a new status for her—"You won't find me the usual interfering mother-in-law"—a new flat near Whiteleys; a new home—theirs—for her to invade. "I told the workmen to change the paint. A hard gloss will wear much better," she had said after one of her visits, uninvited, to the little house in Chelsea. "But Emily chose the paint herself," said Vinny. "You must try very hard not to interfere." "That's one thing you can never accuse me of. I just happen to know from experience that a matt surface shows every mark."

Emily herself only smiled and agreed. This Rose noticed with revulsion. Her sister seemed lulled and sensuous; her unconcern both indecent and indiscreet. Rose had covered her own marriage with social observances, a flutter of arrangements, lists, patterns of material, fittings, house-furnishings. But Emily let her mother-in-law choose the paint for her bedroom. This negligence exposed her love, made all but their desire to live together, incidental.

231

"I had eight bridesmaids," Mrs Tumulty said. "All in white. I was glad to see the Princess do likewise."

It was difficult to imagine Mrs Tumulty as a bride, and in Rose's mind the eight white bridesmaids followed down the aisle a battered, flapping figure, raven-black.

"How many did *you* have?" she was asked.

"Only two—Emily and my cousin, Cynthia," she said humbly.

"But still—two are better than none," said Mrs Tumulty. "I had a three-tiered cake and I cut it with Digby's sword. We didn't have hotel weddings in those days. We had our own house and marquees in the garden and the bridesmaids staying overnight. A proper old rumpus. All the aunts and uncles." This long-ago wedding grew in all their minds as the days went by. It assumed a grandeur suggesting Tsarist Russia or the Hapsburgs. In the end, a photograph was brought out, showing a group of ill-favoured girls and absurd young men standing before a conservatory. The bride's mother sat wearily on a fancy chair; two young bridesmaids were arranged on a moth-eaten rug in front. The bride loomed authoritatively over her husband, who barely reached her shoulder and looked as if he thought it effrontery to do as much.

"Something to keep and look back on, you see," Mrs Tumulty said. "A day you never forget. Poor Lottie Bloxham, look at her swollen face. She had toothache all day long. Your godmother, Vincent."

"Yes, mother."

"Or *was*, I should say."

In her robust way she wanted the wedding with all its symbols of thrown rice and floating veil; but unlike

Rose, who wanted only the symbols, she felt a curiosity about the marriage itself; told Emily some nauseating details of her own honeymoon and would watch her figure with attention in the months to come.

It was not a successful wedding for anyone. Vinny and Emily only endured the attempts made to enhance it —the confetti Mrs Tumulty threw about so recklessly, the cake which Rose had ordered. They escaped impatiently—Rose put her cheek to Emily's, Mrs Tumulty stood out in the road like a policeman, signalling the car out.

They drove from London through suburbs where women were shopping, as if the day were no different from another; children ran home from school and traffic blocked the roads. In this banal scene, a sensation of the enormity of his behaviour, the step he had taken, swept over Vinny. With his beloved beside him, he began to suffer terror and loneliness, a feeling of being singled out, abnormal, monstrous.

At six o'clock, they stopped at a large roadhouse for a drink. Still shedding confetti, they stood in the empty bar, nervous and depressed by the day, what had been made of it. A curious malaise drifted over them. The stale air of the bar, the ticking clock, seemed to demand 'Now what?' Mrs Tumulty, with her blushful qualms, could scarcely have felt more apprehensive than they —left at last with the burden of one another's personalities; the terror of striking a false note; or none. With more drink, and darkness, and a loosening of the claims of the day, the mood dissolved. The world appeared less callous to them and once assured of this they could forget it, and begin their happiness.

*   *   *

Rose returned to Seething, having made what she could of the wedding. Mrs Siddons welcomed her with solicitude as if she were returning from a funeral: for travel seemed thought to be a serious illness. Rose, convalescent, drinking tea, felt the anti-climax of after-arrival. Going away had made the house seem shabbier and she noticed little faults about it, as if she were seeing them for the first time. Once, keeping it in good order had been part of her dedication to Emily; part of her scheme against Emily's nature. To enslave her with comfort, to lull her, imprison her, had been her absorbing intention and had kept her busy and inventive. But at the first touch of love, the inanimate things had lost all power: now they had lost their power for Rose, too. She looked upon the worn carpet, the chipped cup, with indifference. She had no motive now for furbishing, contriving; no purpose but to keep up a home for Philly, from whom instinct continually turned her thoughts away, though guilt turned them back. The girl's abnormality was too fitting a reminder of the terror of her birth, the humiliations of Rose's married-life. There were also temptations so taboo that they could enter her mind only by a sudden assault—thoughts of release, of deliverance; and, glancing across at Philly now, such a thought pierced her fatigue. 'People would say it was all for the best,' she told herself and stood up suddenly and went to the window. 'I am her mother,' she thought; and to Mrs Siddons' talk of household matters replied only vaguely. 'We must surely live for some other person,' she thought, 'even if it should be someone with whom all horror is related.' Mrs Siddons, who at this moment was cutting Philly's bread-and-butter into strips, seemed contented enough, could devote herself to the girl, without inhibitions, and with full play to her feelings of pity; might even feel genuine grief, a sense of loss if . . . whereas, her own mother . . .

"The michaelmas-daisies need staking," Rose said. "I must remember that in the morning."

It looked a sad, unwelcome garden with its yellowing leaves. Rotten fruit lay in the grass. A mist was breathed upwards from clumps of rusty leaves and the mauve flowers. Remote, pervasive, so Englishly moody, with its muted colours and still air and medlar-scent, it appeared expectant, ready to match itself to an intruder, to be in tune with the nostalgic or the romantic; with magic for lovers; and echoes for the forlorn. Rose had nothing: was nothing.

"And someone telephoned," said Mrs Siddons, "leaving no name; but saying something about serving on a committee."

It was years since Rose had served on any committee. Her self-immolation to Emily, her diligence, had left so little time: although she was a person who needed to use some authority; to make her mark; and the open respect of others, which she had not had because of scandal, could have closed some of the chasms in her private life.

She said: "I have no time."

"How the light fails," said Mrs Siddons. "We shall soon be putting the clocks back or forward."

It had seemed to Rose that the garden awaited someone, like a landscape which needed some figure to dramatise it. But at the end of the summer, and after tea, there was no one to come.

Then someone did. She was turning from the window

235

when she saw Evalie Hobson coming up the drive. She was swinging her gloves in her hand and smiling at the michaelmas-daisies. She walked with a consciously casual air, as if she had a legitimate purpose, something to divulge. Once she even bent to sniff at a late rose, as if she enjoyed being the object of conjecture and felt herself observed.

Chapter 16

IT was late Autumn when Vinny and Emily returned to Seething. They drove down for the weekend at Rose's request. Her letter had been curt, but veiled. "Perhaps Mrs Siddons is leaving," said Emily, who could think of nothing worse.

"Then why not say so?"

"It is Rose's way to like to be there when bad news is given out."

They arrived at tea-time. The house seemed to have pulled its thick ivy round it for the winter. "Oh, *God!*" Emily whispered, thinking of other winters. Vinny took her hand. They stood in the porch and waited, looking back across the lawns which were covered with yellow leaves.

Rose opened the door. Her look of composure unsettled them, for they felt that she would not need to look composed if nothing were wrong. Yet in the drawing-room Mrs Siddons sat happily with Philly, doing a jig-saw puzzle. She was managing the puzzle herself while Philly offered pieces which would not fit in, but which were politely considered and then put in a special heap. Philly looked up, but seemed in no mood to recognise Emily.

"It is our own drawing-room again," Rose said in her hostess voice. "All of our visitors have gone."

Around the room were signs of handwork—raffia baskets and pieces of coloured felt. "Mrs Siddons and I are busily working for a bazaar. Mrs Siddons had her training for it all through her married life. I am a beginner."

"What bazaar?" Emily could not hide her astonishment at the change which had taken place.

"The Moral Welfare," Mrs Siddons said quickly, as if she must answer for her own province.

"Evalie Hobson roped me in in the end," Rose said, as she poured out tea. "It is not my style—not what I have ever done before; but Mrs Siddons helps me. And it will pass the winter for us. I hate to be idle. You have cut off your hair, Emily."

"Your lovely hair," said Mrs Siddons.

"It was very wilful of her," Vinny said. "But at least before she did it, I had that lovely experience of seeing her let it all down, over her shoulders, coming down like a shawl. Nothing could be more romantic and exciting."

Rose handed his tea-cup without a glance at him. Mrs Siddons began hurriedly to pack up the puzzle. Emily had a slight smile on her lips and she lifted her cup to hide it.

"Bread-and-butter?" Rose said.

"No, thank you, darling."

"You are beautifully dressed."

"Very," said Mrs Siddons, as if she had already noted this.

"Oh, thank you."

After tea, when she and Vinny were alone for a moment, Emily said: "I have been lulled into a sense of false security. I shall go and unpack. At least it isn't Mrs Siddons."

As soon as she had gone, Rose came in. Her brisk manner of shutting the door behind her Vinny found alarming.

"If Emily comes down, I shall stop what I am going to say."

"She has gone to unpack."

"Then I will say it quickly."

"Yes."

"Vinny, I believe that you have married Emily when you had no right to do so."

"Why do you believe that?"

"I heard a rumour, and I did the only thing which I could do in the circumstances."

"What was that?"

"I made enquiries."

"But not of me. I think *that* was the only thing you could do in the circumstances."

"No. The hint was dropped by a foolish woman whom I do not trust. She said that it was her duty to tell me, but she is not the person to be swayed by her duty; only by pleasure, and it was her pleasure to tell me this. I had to find out more, before I insulted you by making such a suggestion to you."

"You are making it now?"

"Yes."

"May I smoke this pipe?"

Mrs Siddons put her head round the door and at once withdrew.

"How did you conduct your investigations?" Vinny asked, and settled back in his chair, as if he were greatly entertained.

"Evalie—it was she—told me that she had heard you were already married and thought that you could not be divorced. She imagined that this hint would be enough—although she did not say as much as that in the hint. She had had her pleasure, done her duty, and hoped to swear me again to secrecy, and say no more. But I will not be dealt with like that. I forced her to tell me all she knew. She said that you were married to a woman in Market Swanford, a dancing-teacher. It was easy enough to find her."

"Was it?" Vinny said, and put his hand over his eyes. "You went there?"

"Last week. I saw her and I made her talk to me as I made Evalie Hobson. I was desperate for Emily's sake."

"For Emily's sake?" he repeated, as if he could not understand this. "And what did she—this woman—say?"

"She denied it."

There was a long silence, and then Vinny said: "Of course!" and leaned farther back in his chair. "You were right to go. It was the next best thing to coming to me."

"But I did not believe her," Rose said smoothly. "I know a liar when I meet one. She told me that you had once pretended you were married—years ago, when she was expecting your child." Her neck reddened, and for the first time she seemed confused and disgusted. "She explained that she had had a miscarriage and that some time after that she married for the first time —an officer in the Royal Air Force."

"But you could not believe this?"

"I have told you why. She was not a woman who could tell the truth. As the story came to her more fluently, I could see relief and even gratitude in her eyes. She began to warm to it and was loth to come to the end."

"So what did you do?"

"I came home."

"And now you want a story from me, too? I must be careful not to warm to it myself."

"The next day," Rose continued, as if he had not spoken, "I went to Somerset House to see the marriage-certificate."

"You could have done so in the first place." He passed his hand over his face wearily, pressing it hard against his trembling mouth. Then he said: "I am sorry to have put you to this trouble and expense."

"And grief and anxiety. I am not just a busy-body like Evalie Hobson or Isabella. I was not enjoying the task."

"Isabella?"

"It all came from her in the first place, you see."

"Yes, I wondered how, but did not like to ask. That hurts me very much," he said; for suddenly all sweetness went from the world, kindness soured into treachery; there was no trust.

"I am sorry you were worried, then; and grieved and anxious. Now I am the same. What is the use of a friend who, under some hallucination, builds up a story to destroy me? You do know, do you, that a divorce would not appear in the marriage-licence? You agree to that? I wonder it did not enter your head."

"It has only just entered yours. You are warming to it, I can see."

"It entered my head long ago," he said quietly. "What have you against the divorce? I can see you have something."

"If you had been divorced from that woman, she could have said so, but she did not even think of it. She has some reason for denying the marriage, as you most certainly have. I don't pretend to understand what it is."

"She doesn't want a scandal. She has told her friends —her 'set', I think she calls them—that she was married to a fighter-pilot who was killed in the war. She has built herself up as a plucky little widow. If the past cast its cold light upon her, from any aspect, she would appear the liar you saw her to be."

"Then you admit it all?"

"What are you going to do?"

"Tell Emily."

"May I do that?"

"You should have done so at the beginning. Oh, why did you not? You see where your kindness and sympathy and interfering has brought us all?"

"It is just Emily's happiness that weighs with you?"

"And what is right. Although I know you think that I ignore other people's opinions of me, I am weary of tongues wagging. All through my married-life they did that. My husband was always drunk; he behaved badly; people said that he was drunk when the accident happened. I did not know how to hold up my head." As she spoke, she held it very high, her usual posture.

Mrs Siddons opened the door again and this time apologised. "Oh, may I just . . .?" She indicated her raffia-work and scuttled across the room to fetch it from the sofa.

"What would *she* say?" Rose asked, when she had gone. "You might have to go to prison."

"I have faced much worse: I might have lost Emily."

"You could have waited for a divorce."

"She would not divorce me."

"You could have divorced her."

"I had no grounds."

Rose, angrily upset, turned aside. "I think you had,"

242

she said. "A man came there while I was with her that day. He let himself into the flat. She was dreadfully agitated. Of course they were lovers. I always know those things—perhaps because I so badly don't want to know."

She spoke in a muffled voice, her handkerchief to her face. 'She can say anything else,' he thought; 'only mention of sex throws her out, however remote; the idea only.' He said: "And I did not know—and perhaps it was because I too badly wanted to."

"You should have waited," she repeated.

"I could not, for fear of losing her. People who are wakened from a long sleep are exposed to many dangers. The prince in the fairy-tale knew that, when he wakened the Sleeping Beauty: and he married her the very same day. The difficulties began—they did not end—with his kiss. I am no prince, as you are, very reasonably, waiting to say; but I am not above learning from a fairy-tale. When I first met Emily, she was dead to the world; shut up in this house; thinking herself unlovely; believing that no one could desire her, because one man had rejected her; uncertain even of her own identity or how she should behave—since she could not seem to behave in her old way."

"So she has told you of that old way?" Rose said.

"There was no need to tell. It was in the photograph you showed me, and was only lightly buried in spite of all her endeavours. It came more and more to the surface. But bringing it to the surface had its responsibility. That, I thought, was marriage."

"Bigamy. You faced many things in your mind. Did you face that word?"

"Yes."

"And faced involving her in it?"

"I faced it alone. I had hoped—I hope—always to do so. Only the slightest chance led you to this. It will teach me not to look out of windows. I remember that unlucky day so well, but I thought that no harm would come of it—that perhaps Isabella would think it just some squalid entanglement—as it was. It is hard to believe that she—that Isabella—could work so busily against me . . . You have all worked busily behind my back, while I was happy with Emily."

"It would have come out another way if not that way."

"I thought not. That woman, as you and I call her, had reasons for hiding it, and so had I. No one else knew, who is still alive. Even my mother did not."

"Yes, your mother," Rose said quickly. "I have thought of her, too. To have this happen at her age!"

"'This' can only happen, as I see it, if you wish it to."

"How could *I* wish it? It is my only desire that it should not."

"Then there are three of us hoping the same thing."

"But crime should not go unpunished."

"You cannot have it both ways."

"Now that I have most cause of all to hate you . . . I do so less."

"It is because I am in your power."

"Oh, I expect so. I am coming to have a low estimate of everyone—even myself. Until now, I thought that it was almost a different race of people who had their names in the papers—not anyone I knew."

"I have had my name in the papers rather less than other people . . . for instance, I never have my marriages announced."

"It is a poor joke, for it involves Emily's disgrace. And you have said you loved her."

"It is the love you mention which explains and dignifies the situation."

"Dignifies! There is not even an element of tragedy to do that, only shame and absurdity. You would appear a figure of fun."

"I have sometimes been that lately. I am not what I was. And step by step, I have gone over it all—how could you think I had not? Yet it has always seemed to me that I was making plans for something which would never happen, like my own death . . . those practical plans, about money; and legal ones . . . to have Emily safe from blame."

"And now plans for throwing dust in Evalie's eyes . . . what am I to tell her, for her to tell Isabella?"

"That I was married and am divorced. You might say that I was trapped into a youthful marriage by a woman pretending pregnancy, and that when the marriage was dissolved, so, it was supposed, was everyone's interest in it. You will be clever enough to dispose of their objections as they put them forward. You will not make the mistake of warming to your theme. And the story is partly true."

"What part is not?"

"The dissolution, and the emphasis on youth."

"She pretended . . . that she was pregnant?"

"Yes, that part is true."

"How evil women can be!" Rose said quietly. "I almost pity you."

"I shall be glad of your pity," he said, knowing that only with that would her support be given.

"And you will tell Emily?"

"I think now that I must. I do not quite know how—although I have given hours of thought to the subject.
. . . There is no way of doing it, but just by saying it, I suppose. I know how you feel, Rose, about crime meeting its reward. It is good of you to waive that." Then he looked up quickly. "You *are* going to waive it?"

"You have met your reward," she said sententiously. "The longer you live without your punishment, the more it will be with you."

"There is the danger that I might grow accustomed to it."

"To what?" asked Emily, as she opened the door.

"To what I have to confess to you," Vinny said.

"And so you really do all these good works?" Emily said, picking up a half-finished tea-cosy. "A new life has opened for us both."

"You see, the sooner I tell her the better," Vinny said to Rose, who stood up and went quickly from the room. Emily glanced at her in surprise, and then at Vinny's white face.

*   *   *

"So we have only been through what newspapers call 'a form of marriage'," Emily said, drying her first tears. "I have sometimes read those reports. They call the women by their surnames. Why must they do that? How can it help matters to be so rude? I should seem a different person to myself for ever afterwards if I heard them referring to me in that way—without a 'Mrs'. Or 'Miss'," she added, beginning to weep again.

"You will not be referred to at all, my darling angel. And the occasion shall never arise when you are in danger of it."

"This makes a mockery of the law—when you and I

are so happy and harming no one, yet in such a situation."

"We cannot blame the law. There has to be some order, some protection."

"You have too much respect for rules and regulations. It has brought us to this pretty pass. And I thought that married people shouldn't have secrets."

"This secret went with the marriage."

"Oh, love me, hold me! Why need we have married in the first place? You are always so prim and proper and now it has made you break the law. It will be forever like living at the edge of a volcano."

"Our lives are that nowadays, no matter how we behave."

"Oh, bombs!" she said in a contemptuous voice. "They are hardly to the point. Don't drag bombs in to try to make this seem any better. There may never be another war; or it may be years ahead: but this trouble is with us now; this absurd, indecent word is with us." He kissed her, silent. Then she said, turning her head from him: "How can you trust her . . . your wife?"

"I forbid you to give her that name. She has never been given it by me. Rose and I call her 'that woman', and I should do the same, if I were you. How can I trust her? Oh, I think with the best and safest trust—an enemy's. I have been a victim of the other kind, and it seems to be a victim itself; of the first lonely moment; the slightest temptation to talk in confidence. This trust is more wholesome, I believe. There are no illusions and no obligations. Just the advantage of us both. No harm can come to you, you know; but it is very important that we never speak of it, or use those tiresome words— which you so rightly call indecent."

"You have had to lie beside me at night thinking of these things."

"No, I have thought of other things."

"I can bear anything, but not your being taken from me, being sent to . . . being sent away. I could not imagine such a thing happening. You are not cut out for it."

"That is the very worst, and will not happen. If we face it now, for a moment, we will never face it again. I should not be there so very long—in the place where I shall never have to go—a few months, perhaps."

"Yes, we will face it. It would be an experience," she said, wiping her tears away roughly, "which, as you say, may never come to you."

"I once heard . . . years ago, before it had any application to myself . . . that men who commit . . . who make this sort of mistake, are the worst treated by the other . . . by men who have made different mistakes. They are said to resent the tendency in their colleagues and look down on them."

"You mean, in this place it would be such an experience to go to?"

"Yes."

"I wonder why?"

"It is a thing above others that they moralise about."

"How very strange! There might be bullying, then?"

"I saw my way through that at school. And this could not be as bad, because not for so long. And might only be ostracism; easily borne."

"And perhaps may never happen."

"It is too remote to contemplate, in a world where one expects much worse."

"Yes, there is that comfort. And if it did happen, could you write to me?"

"I suppose my weekly letter. As at school."

"And would it be censored?"

"Yes, it would be on a printed form and read and signed by someone else."

"You know a great deal about the whole subject."

"It has interested me for some time."

"We will have a secret code for our loving messages —though what is the use of love on paper? I shall send you presents."

"And books."

"The books would be presents. I am beginning to choose them already in my mind. You will lie and think of me in your . . . little bedroom? Oh, my darling, it could not be true!" She pressed her cheek to his and closed her eyes. He stroked her throat, which tightened again in her struggle not to weep.

"And I should mark off the hours until the holidays," he said. "Do not cry inwardly, my love. Your tears are my worst punishment, and Rose would think it wrong for me to escape them."

Hearing footsteps, she went over to the window and stood with her back to the darkening room, hoping to hide her tears.

"Oh, excuse me!" Mrs Siddons said. "My handbag! Philly and I are going for a little stroll to give her an appetite. Thank-you so much." She ducked under Vinny's arm before he could properly open the door for her.

"What would *she* think of all this?" Emily asked. "Don't put on the light yet. Oh, there they go, down the drive. I might have grown like Mrs Siddons in the end. Those little strolls, as she calls them. At this time of the year, I remember them especially—so sad, sad—smelling of bonfires."

She watched the two figures in their dark coats going down the drive. Pale leaves drifted from the branches above them. Philly's walk was uncertain. She collided with Mrs Siddons, then, trying to straighten her course, tripped at the grass-verge. Mrs Siddons took her arm. They disappeared behind the trees.

"There is so much to be sad about," Emily said. "We should be selfish to think of ourselves." But she went on doing so; and then said: "It is wrong of me, but I begin to admire you more. I didn't know you had this in you. And I admire myself more; for bringing it out."

She leant against him, smiling at last. It was some time before they spoke, and then Vinny said: "Rose is the one I am worried about. Our love has harmed no one but her and now she is alone. We must do something for her."

Sympathy expanded in him. Pity stirred his old longing to console. Emily, seeming to sense this, drew his arm round her again, claiming all consolation for herself.

"Yes, we must," she agreed.

THE END

250